P9-CQM-639

cupcake

Also by Rachel Cohn
Gingerbread
Shrimp
Pop Princess
You Know Where to Find Me

For younger readers:
The Steps
Two Steps Forward

cupcake

Rachel Cohn

Simon Pulse

New York • London • Toronto • Sydney

If you purchased this book without a cover, you should be aware that this book is stolen property.
It was reported as "unsold and destroyed" to the publisher, and neither the author nor the publisher
has received any payment for this "stripped book."

This book is a work of fiction. Any references to historical events, real people, or real locales are used fictitiously.
Other names, characters, places, and incidents are the product of the author's imagination,
and any resemblance to actual events or locales or persons, living or dead, is entirely coincidental.

SIMON PULSE

An imprint of Simon & Schuster Children's Publishing Division

1230 Avenue of the Americas, New York, NY 10020

Copyright © 2007 by Rachel Cohn

All rights reserved, including the right of reproduction in whole or in part in any form.

SIMON PULSE and colophon are registered trademarks of Simon & Schuster, Inc.

Also available in a Simon & Schuster Books for Young Readers hardcover edition.

Design, illustrations, and hand-lettering by Cara E. Petrus

The text of this book was set in Adobe Garamond.

Manufactured in the United States of America

First Simon Pulse edition July 2008

2 4 6 8 10 9 7 5 3 1

The Library of Congress has cataloged the hardcover edition as follows:

Cohn, Rachel.

Cupcake / Rachel Cohn.—1st ed.

p. cm.

Summary: Former "bad girl" Cyd Charisse moves to New York City

to live with her half brother Danny while exploring career options and various relationships,

including the one with Shrimp, who is surfing in New Zealand.

ISBN-13: 978-1-4169-1217-0 (hc)

ISBN-10: 1-4169-1217-7 (hc)

[1. Interpersonal relations—Fiction. 2. Stepfamilies—Fiction. 3. New York (N.Y.)—Fiction.] I. Title.

PZ7.C6665Cu 2007

[Fic]—dc22

2005035934

ISBN-13: 978-1-4169-1219-4 (pbk)

ISBN-10: 1-4169-1219-3 (pbk)

To Real Danny
&
Anna
(who's really a cupcake)

acknowledgments

With deep, deep thanks to: Patricia McCormick (this book's fairy godmother and this author's cherished friend); Señora Sandi Merrill (gracias for the español); Sharon Brown at Oren's Daily Roast on Waverly (who doses the love into the caffeine); David Levithan (way more a Jimmy Stewart than a Thelma Ritter); Cecil Castellucci (the Queen of Cool, and of Los Feliz); the many fine and dedicated folk at S&S and WMA who have made these books possible—in particular David Gale, Alexandra Cooper, Jennifer Rudolph Walsh, and Alicia Gordon; my friends and family (for the ongoing love and support); and last but certainly not least, all the lovely readers who wrote asking for more, more, more.

One

A cappuccino cost me my life.

I have only myself to blame, thinking myself even capable of starting a new life.

Also, I blame my mother. She lured me to my doom.

"Cyd Charisse, how many times do I have to ask you?" my mother had said into my cell phone as I traipsed down the stairs of my new apartment building in my new life in New York City. "Have you registered for a culinary school class yet or not?" Just like my mother, to send me off into the world on my own and then let barely a week pass before attempting to micromanage my every move from a coast away in San Francisco.

"Soon, my little pretty," I promised. "I have more important business to take care of first." Like, go out for a coffee—then figure out how to execute the Plan for my new life. No civilized person should be expected to go about the routine of their daily lives until they are properly caffeinated in the morning. It should be written into the Bill of Rights.

Proving miracles do indeed happen, I'd passed through the first stage of the Plan for the new life by graduating high school. (Pause for moment of shock and a giant sigh of relief from my parents.) That mission accomplished, my Plan laid out that I would then celebrate liberation from my parents' college dreams for me by (1) moving into the empty bedroom in my half brother Danny's apartment in Greenwich Village (done); (2) possibly enrolling in some culinary school classes (working up to it), where I'd definitely win all the important awards like Student with Most Potential to Perfect the Art of the Peanut Butter Cookie, or the coveted So Culinarily (shut up, it is too a word) Blessed She Can Jump Right into Building Her Own Sweets Empire After Only One Class; and (3) the linchpin of the whole Plan—I would not obsess over turning down the marriage proposal from Shrimp, the love of my former high school life, so he could move to New Zealand like he wanted and I could move to Manhattan like I wanted (not there yet with achieving the non-obsession part of the goal). Of course, let's not forget (4)—find the perfect cappuccino in my new city (I was on my way).

And besides, why would I—hello again, (3)—bother mourning the end of my relationship with my beauty surfer boy when I'd be too busy scamming all the hot guys in NYC, right? The Plan had wiggle room to allow for the probability that almost immediately upon embarking on my new Manhattan existence, I would jump into some sexual experimentation, not with the usual same-sex relationship or the even more unusual longing for androids, but like experiment-fling with a really old and sophisticated guy, like maybe thirty years old. He'd own some anti-hip music club, not one of those chic clubs with VIP rooms for supermodels and underfed movie starlets, but like some raging punk thrasher club. The club would probably be called something like Che or Trotsky, and it would be the choice dive venue, where starving artist musicians wailed from grimy floors and a snarly ambience of hot punk guys with crazy hair and tattoos lit the room and wait a minute, why am I going for the older owner guy when all these gorgeous young indie boys with spiked hair and fully kissable lips on stubble mouths are right in front of me?

SHRIMP!!!!!!!!!!!! WHY DID I LET YOU GO?!?!?!?

"CC," my mother stated, for a refreshing change acknowledging my preferred letter name over that movie star name she'd stuck me with, "Are you still there? I said which class are you planning to take first? I looked through the catalog, and it looks to me like if you intend to pursue the pastry rather than the cooking curriculum, you need to start with Introduction to Baking Techniques and Ingredients. And have you looked through the home decorating catalog I sent you? I flagged the pages with window treatments I thought you'd like in your new bedroom."

"Caffeine," I muttered into the phone. I needed caffeine before I could think about following through with the culinary school part of the Plan. I'd need a whole new identity before I'd let my mother choose bedroom window treatments for my new room.

The caffeine quest beckoned me out of doors. I craved a reminder taste of Shrimp and our espresso-and-fog-hued old life together in San Francisco. So I wanted to cheat a little on the Plan. What choice did I have? My new bedroom in my new life in New York City lacked the vibe only Shrimp would have brought it—his paintings on the walls, his surfboard parked at the door, his weird art of smashed pieces from cell phones and pagers melded into crucifix sculptures, his rap songs whispered into my ear as I fell asleep spooned inside his body. No catalog could deliver me Shrimp's fundamental *Him*.

Damn. Shoulda been part of the Plan—Shrimp. Me and my ignorant aspirations for self-actualization. What drug had I been on? I had to be so mature about letting Shrimp go. Big mistake number one.

I tuned my mother out and repeated a mantra inside my head—*stupid CC, stupid CC, stupid CC*—as I banged down the stairwell of my new apartment building. Five freakin' flights down, five freakin' flights to ponder the Shrimpless fate and the questionable java awaiting me once I reached ground level and flung myself out onto the streets of New York City.

The strange, unspoken truth about Manhattan: It is very hard to get a good coffee here. Believe it. Here in one of the most bohemian neighborhoods in the world, finding a quality espresso is about as easy as finding an available straight man at the Whole Foods store in Chelsea. No, it doesn't make sense.

I'd already spent my first week here hunting through the Village in search of that perfect espresso shot: dark, thick, and rich, a tan layer of crema on top, at just the right temperature, in just the right properly warmed espresso cup, as Shrimp taught me to appreciate. A dozen different cafés, and zero luck. It's not that the espressos I consumed on my quest were terrible. They were worse. They were mediocre. Flat and too watery, made with beans ground too coarsely, using machines clearly not maintained with the proper measure of reverence and affection, brewed without love or any discernible sense of quality control. Don't get me started on the cappuccinos I sampled. Foaming milk is an art form, but no place I went seemed to care. The baristas were all about moving the customers through the line and shouting back "TALL SKIM VANILLA SOY LATTE" orders like they were working the drive-through window at Burger King. Posers.

I had expected more from New York.

I had expected the top-secret alternate Plan to have kicked in and for Shrimp to have voluntarily given up on New Zealand and found me here by now.

At least I could count on my brother Danny to get me through, no matter what the Plan. He'd sent me bounding out of our apartment with tales of a place on a Village alleyway somewhere near Gay Street (bless him), where some man-god barista called Dante made the perfect espresso shot. Dante was a true coffee legacy, descended from a long line of Corsican baristas, according to Danny. The trick with Dante was you had to catch him. He'd be there for days or weeks, and word would spread of his greatness, and soon the café would be packed with the obsessive espresso lovers who could find their way to the secret alleyway. Then Dante would disappear for months or years, with no warning.

That very morning Danny had told me the neighborhood was rife with rumor that Dante was serving up again in the West Village. I had decided to believe my concierge, I mean my brother. Big mistake number two. I had dared to answer my mother's telephone call as I walked down the stairs in pursuit of that Dante cappuccino. Big mistake number three.

My mother said, "You don't mind if we give your bedroom to Ashley, do you? Your little sister is taking your leaving San Francisco very hard, and she's been begging to sleep in your room, and with the new baby coming, we could really use the space."

I replied as any sane just-moved-out daughter would to such a query—I hung up on my mother. As I did so, I tripped and fell down the flight of stairs between floors two and three of the apartment building.

Fractured my leg in three places.

All for a cappuccino.

NOT PART OF THE PLAN!!!!!!!!!!!

The upside was the gorgeous EMT worker who helped lift the stretcher down the stairs and into the ambulance. His name is George, he's training to be a firefighter, and he's a burly guy with curly brown hair, smiling brown eyes, and a pudgy-muscley Guinness Man body. I would bet that if George puts in quality gym time, he will one day look fightin' fine as Mr. August in the firefighter calendar. As George left me in the ER at Saint Vincent's, I was very brave and did not scream my digits, even though I wanted to when he asked for my number. I whispered the phone number very politely, and I hope the reason he hasn't called me yet isn't because when the nurse touched my leg and asked "Is this where it hurts, honey?" I replied "YES, THAT'S WHERE IT FUCKING HURTS!" even though it wasn't personal against the nurse.

I just missed my mommy.

You think it will be so great to turn eighteen and move out on your own, but then you have it, and you hardly know anybody in the giantropolis of a gazillion people swishing right past you, and your new bedroom is too small and the stairwell in your apartment building is dark and creepy and taunts you to fall down it. You think it will be so great to be liberated from your parents and their home and their rules. You think it will be so great to have almost-firefighters flirting with you in your moment of dire pain. But once you have it, you think: Eh, maybe it's not so great.

It's lonely here. Different cool, and different scary.

The pint-size surfer-artist love of my life is somewhere on the flip side of the universe with apparently no thought to tracking me down in Manhattan and begging my forgiveness for his having chosen the sea over the CC. My mother was practically to blame for my accident (in my opinion), yet she and my father abandoned me after it. "Broken leg? Oh, that's too bad, dear. Keep the leg elevated and get lots of rest!" My parents are too consumed with the household I left back in San Francisco to worry over the tragedy that has befallen their eldest child. My father told me, "I know you're not ready to give up on Manhattan so soon, when you've only just gotten there. Right, Cupcake?" I said, "Right," even though I meant, *Wrong!* I mean, I may technically be Sid-dad's stepdaughter, but I am his Cupcake, his pet, and how he figured I would prefer the delivery of a lavish bouquet of Get Well Soon roses to a chartered plane to deliver me home to recuperate, I have no idea. I don't know my own family anymore.

Now the giantropolis is closed off to me. When you have a broken leg with a cast and crutches, you do not want to climb five flights of stairs every day.

I am stuck in my new room but in what is not my new life—
it's no life. All I do is watch movies, sleep, eat, and wait around for
something—*anything*—interesting to happen. My favorite inspira-
tional movie to watch is *Rear Window,* because that's the other thing
I do in my new not-life. Alllll . . . dayyyy . . . looooooong I conva-
lesce on a long chaise, looking out my bedroom rear window and
sweating in the glare of the afternoon summer sun, cursing the Plan.

When I fall asleep into a painkiller-induced commune coma
of me and a rear window, I dream of Shrimp. Our reunion opens
like the first love scene in *Rear Window,* where Grace Kelly greets
James Stewart. I'm asleep in my chair at the rear window at dusk,
the binoculars on my lap, my leg propped up, with a cast that reads,
*Here lie the broken bones of Cyd Charisse. She prefers to be called
"CC" now.* A shadow falls over my face, and even though I am half-
asleep, I sense movement—someone is near. The soundtrack of
some mournful-sexy jazz music coming from God only knows
where syncopates my racing heartbeat. I glimpse him through the
fogged-in lens of my slowly opening eyes. As my eyelids raise, I see
Shrimp in colors: the platinum patch of light blond hair spiked over
a head of dirty blond hair, the cherry red of his lips, the deep ocean
blue of his eyes. I almost want to stay in my half-awake Crayola
Shrimp dream state, to hold on to the anticipation of his nearness.
Then I feel his tight little body leaning over to kiss me, and my eyes
spring wide open. He's here, finally, and I must touch him. Shrimp

is dressed like the King of Hearts, surfer version, in a black wet suit with red hearts emblazoned on the left side of his chest, and a white string necklace with heart-shaped puka shells. As my lips turn up into a lazy smile, Shrimp closes in for our close-up kiss. Like Grace Kelly, he can make even a closed-mouth kiss sexy. But when I try to part his mouth with my own, smother him in kisses, he is gone, because I am awake for real. Shrimp is on the other side of the world and I let him go, and I'm left here in the most exciting city in the world with nothing to do except long for him.

More than I want a good coffee, I'd like a new Plan, one that assures me that by the time I am liberated outside of this apartment again, the Dante barista-man of the perfect cappuccino will not already be back in Corsica, and my Shrimp-man of the dreamy kisses will not be in love with some g'day-sayin' surfer bitch in New Zealand. I still want the new-life-in-New-York part of the old Plan, but I wouldn't mind it revised to include some of my former life in San Francisco, where it's never warm but it's always safe, and I had a true love supposedly for forever.

TWO

True love. I'm starting to suspect the concept is pure illusion, an insipid brand name manufactured by Hallmark and Disney.

"There, there, Ceece," Danny soothed. "So young to be so jaded. If true love is pure illusion, then what is this the two of us have here?" He sat on the toilet next to the bathtub, a dark shower curtain allowing him to see just his sister's face and her garbage-bag-wrapped-cast leg propped up on the bathtub ledge, rather than a full-on vision of her nakedness. From his side of the curtain he handed me a pitcher of water to rinse out the conditioner in my hair.

"This is just weird, bordering on platonic incest, if such a concept is also available for branding," I answered. I poured the water over my head, then dipped my head under the bathwater for an extra rinse.

Branding is what Danny oughta do for the cupcake business he started after the café he owned with his former boyfriend went under. This city has gone crazy for cupcakes. They're sold everywhere: in cafés, in bakeries, even in street corner bodegas. The heavenly creations Danny sells to these establishments go way beyond the simple devil's food cake with buttercream frosting formula to include Oreo, Reese's, and Snickers concoctions; genius with marshmallow fluff; and pastel-hued fondant layers with Matisse-like confectionary portraits on top. And while I would very much like not to be seduced by anything so fashionable, I can't help myself either. When I came up from under the bathwater, I told the cupcake mastermind, "And I'm gonna be really happy if you tell me you baked the chocolate cupcakes with your signature cappuccino-flavor frosting as a reward later tonight for me making it through this bath experience."

Even if I hadn't known my biological half brother my whole life, I still couldn't think of a single other person now whom I'd want sitting alongside me in the bathroom as I attempted the annoying and painful task of not only stepping into the tub, but also bathing with a cast on my leg that wasn't supposed to get wet. I'd only met my brother baker man for the first time the summer before last, because of that small complication of my conception being the result of my mother's twenty-year-old girl dancer-model affair with Frank, the big boss at the advertising firm, who already had a wife and children, namely Danny and our other sister, lisBETH. Yet for all that I've only known Danny for a small fraction of my life, from the instant we met I felt this instant *ka-pow!* connection with him. Maybe a shrink would say the *ka-pow!* was really *ka-phony!,* but that assessment would be wrong, because mostly what I've felt with Frank and lisBETH since getting to know them has been, *We share nothing besides some random DNA, and it's gonna be a long time before—and if—we ever truly bond.*

"Then be happy, Dollface," Danny said. "I made you a special cappuccino cupcake batch this very afternoon." He placed a bottle of bubble bath on the ledge, and I couldn't help but pause and (non-incestuously—seriously) admire his nice face before turning my body slightly to run fresh warm water into the bath. Sometimes when I look at Danny's happy face with kind brown eyes shaped and colored as perfect as espresso beans, framed in bushy brown eyebrows and a mop of messy black hair, a chronic grin charming his lips, I think, *How did I get so lucky to discover you?*

"Oh, be Thelma Ritter, would you?" I asked him. She's the wisecracking, all-knowing insurance nurse who tends to James Stewart in *Rear Window.* She's kinda my hero.

"You start," Danny said.

Yes!

I mimicked clipped consonant Grace Kelly-speak. "Did you bring me dinner from 21, darling?"

Danny rolled his eyes like Thelma Ritter and imitated her exasperated, seen-it-all, middle-aged lady nasal tone. "Didn't you hear, Dollface? 21 went out of fashion years ago."

"Darling," I repeated, trying hard at Grace Kelly's cool sophistication, but succeeding mostly with CC's spazification, "are you aware that the swank new restaurant where Aaron took the chef job does home delivery? I bet if we called him now, he'd deliver dinner to us himself!"

Bye-bye, Thelma. It was fun while it lasted. Danny returned to normal voice. "Nope, I'm not playing. I know you love Aaron—we all love Aaron—but if you don't give up the campaign to reunite him and me, I'm going to fess up and tell you that my 'hopeless optimism,' as you call it, is indeed just that. I'm going to tell you that there is no such thing as true love. Also, Santa Claus and the Easter Bunny? Total fabrications."

I pouted. Danny laughed. Then he announced, "Your punishment!" He ran out of the bathroom long enough to queue up the old stereo turntable in the hallway. He stepped back inside the bathroom to flash me an album cover picturing a fifties-looking, chirpy-happy lady with a bouffant hairdo. "Nanette Fabray!" he said.

Besides cupcakes, my other Danny treat to placate my suffering is the collection of one-dollar old records he buys me from the guy by the West Fourth Street subway stop, who hawks ancient record and book memorabilia laid out on a sidewalk sheet. Danny has made it his personal mission to enrich my convalescent time beyond movie-watching and boredom-whining by introducing me to music that does not involve my preferred brand of musical entertainment, which would be beautiful punk emo boys screaming about "The world's ending, but I love you so fucking much!", or any song from *The Sound of Music* soundtrack. So far I admit I indeed have new appreciation for the musical stylings of the Electric Light Orchestra, Minnie Pearl, Liberace, and the Big Bopper. I especially love Danny's selections of wailing blues ladies from the scratchy old turntable days, and in particular I can never hear enough of the Esther Phillips dirty dentist song where she sings about "How you thrill me when you drill me," except the song also makes me homesick because my dentist in SF is so hot and I will never find another dentist like him and why did I have to move to NYC, anyway?

FACT: I miss home *mucho,* and being laid up in a cast completely sucks. But, FACT: It is very enlightening being housebound in the heart of one of the gayest neighborhoods in the universe. I mean, I need not worry that I chose not to go to college.

I am getting such a better education from my brother Danny.

THREE

The highlight of being laid up with a cast is all the people who feel sorry for you. They bring treats. Me hate cast, but me like treats.

Autumn led the procession. She arrived bearing a bag of mini Nestlé Crunch bars, and a postcard from Shrimp.

I wanted to sulk that Shrimp had written to her and not me, but in all fairness, the last negotiated point before he and I went our separate ways was the one called our "clean break." We thought we were so cool—we'd never be like those pathetic former star-crossed lovers who torture each other with clinging cards, letters, phone calls, and whatnot. We were going to start our independent new lives properly. Independently.

Stupidly.

Would Shrimp be tortured to know my new life involved a broken leg that had resulted in my lying on my bed for days on end, entertaining truly naughty sex fantasies about him? I mean, places we'd never gone before. Higher ground, so to speak.

As Autumn handed me Shrimp's postcard, I couldn't help but breathe out a small sigh of relief. The postcard was of the generic tourist variety, picturing a pretty New Zealand beach, and was not a postcard Shrimp had drawn himself, like he used to send to me. Shrimp and Autumn had been longtime friends before their almost-fling back when he and I were broken up the first time. Luckily, their almost-fling resulted in her deciding she was gay and his being totally weirded out to be the guy to have made her realize that, so happy ending all around for the Autumn-Shrimp-CC triangle.

Autumn said, "I find it interesting that our Shrimp, who couldn't be bothered to finish high school, should write haikus so nicely yet, perhaps not so surprisingly, he can't spell for shit."

I turned over the postcard to see what he'd written on it, resisting the urge to pass the postcard quickly under my nose in case I could still pick up any of Shrimp's boy scent, even after the postcard's across-the-equator travel. At least I got to see Shrimp's graffiti-squiggle handwriting, and in haiku, no less!

New zeelind surf calm
sea sieghs on empty canviss
pig Appel bites girls?

"He's miserable without you!" Autumn said. "How great is that? And he's using me to get to you."

"How do you figure?" I bit into the bite-size Nestlé Crunch bar. Newly discovered understanding about starting a new life: You need old friends along to ease the process. College girl Autumn might be all fancy freshperson at Columbia University uptown, but how lucky for me that she could work a MetroCard downtown to deliver her San Francisco friend's favorite old candy bar treat. It never tasted so good.

Autumn flopped on my bed and picked up Gingerbread. I laughed at the image, my old childhood rag doll being held by the girl literally wearing a rag around her head: doll meets doll. Gingerbread's rag style is timeless and unchanged, but Autumn has adopted the arty-sapphic-chic look since moving to NYC. Along with her baggy white carpenter's pants, black leather belt framing her bare waist, and pink gingham cutoff blouse, she wore a white rag wrapped around her head and tied at the front, Rosie the Riveter style, allowing premium view of her melting pot of a Vietnamese-African-Russian-Irish-American model-pretty face.

Autumn held up Gingerbread and spoke to her in teacher voice. "You see, my little one, it's like this. I've known Shrimp since kindergarten, and he's never once in all the years I've known him sent me a postcard. If we want to decode this haiku of a postcard,

I'd guess he's bored and restless in New Zealand, the art isn't happening for him, and while he makes inquiries as to how the recently transplanted New York contingent of our former Ocean Beach girl crowd is, his use of the plural form 'girls' really refers to one certain girl. And not the one he sent the postcard to."

Gingerbread glanced in my direction, as if to affirm, *Autumn's right, right?*

I wasn't having it. I said, "Or it could just mean New Zealand is like this Zen surfer bliss for him and he hopes you're scoring lots of babes in your new life at Columbia."

"Sure, that's what it means. Because Shrimp's so crude like that. Stop projecting." Autumn tossed Gingerbread to me. Gingerbread didn't mind. She's retired now, but she likes the exercise. Gingerbread also wouldn't have minded for Autumn to continue the Shrimp speculation conversation in painstaking detail, but a VROOM VROOM SCREECH CRAAAAAAAASH boom boom boom series of noises cost Shrimp his focus in our conversation. "What the hell was that?" Autumn asked.

"My favorite part of the day! Mystery man is out to play!" I hobbled over to the window next to Autumn and pointed to the courtyard garden below us. Window-gazing has become my favorite form of solitary leg cast entertainment when not watching movies or imagining me and Shrimp trying out the Kama Sutra poses from the book I found hidden at the back of my bedroom closet when I first moved in. "Could you hand me my binoculars over there on the desk, please?"

My convalescent time has not been completely without educational value about life in New York. What I've learned: Those privileged enough to be able to walk down a residential street in the Village may see townhouse buildings next to old carriage houses next to tall prewar old buildings alongside short modern apartment buildings, but to look down these streets from the front views, you'd have no idea about the whole other worlds that exist on the other side. From my window view facing the backs of the buildings on the next street, I see the usual brick architecture and wrought iron of fire escape landings, window grills, and balconies, but I also observe wild kingdoms back there: gardens everywhere—on rooftops, on outdoor terraces, in courtyard patios—and animal life too: There's the lady with the ferrets, the couple with the snake collection, and the freak with a livestock of homing pigeons. Oh yes, freaks! They're the highlight of my new rear window life. You see plenty o' freaks when walking the streets of the Village, but the rear window view takes their entertainment value to the next level. These neighbor freaks are often (a) naked, (b) half-naked, or (c) trying to get naked with someone (or some *thing*—yikes!) else.

My favorite freak is the mystery man who occupies the ground floor garden apartment opposite my building. Although mystery man is very ancient, like probably around fifty or sixty, and some-

rachel cohn

what scary-looking, owing to a perpetual case of creased eyebrows and a downturned-lips frown, I am positive he's not the psycho killer of my backyard view, like the Raymond Burr character in *Rear Window*. Mystery man practically lives in his garden, reclining hour after hour on a hot-pink-painted wooden lounge chair under an upright lamp with a blood-red Chinese lantern lamp shade. He is partial to iced tea, which he brews on his outdoor table in the sun, with fresh lemons floating at the top of the pitcher, and he eats random food throughout the day, like cucumber slices, beef jerky, beets from a can, Sour Patch Kids, and lox chips, but never whole meals. Most times he hangs out with headphones on his ears, composing music on a laptop, but sometimes he forgets to plug in the headphones and I can hear the music on his computer. A sampling of what I've heard wafting up to my window from the laptop's portable speakers (with little pride flags affixed to them like talismans) would be: monkey wails, piano bang noises, bird chirps, ambulance sirens, a playground full of kids squealing, a harsh old-man-voice bellowing "Get outta there," *meow meow,* and one time Christopher Plummer singing poetic about edelweiss—and right then I suspected I adored mystery man.

No one ever calls to him from inside his apartment.

I feel a connection to mystery man, because I think his garden is to him what my old bedroom in San Francisco, with a Pacific Heights view overlooking the Bay and Alcatraz, was once to me, during those grounded sentences of my wild child past: prison. I know he's waiting to be rescued, like I used to wait for Shrimp to rescue me.

The not-mystery man who'd arrived at my bedroom door rescued the spy mission from where it would likely have led next—to the binoculars turning north, up to the porno couple in the penthouse apartment above mystery man's garden. "That's it, young lady," Aaron said. "I have found you in that position one too many times. I hereby revoke your binoculars privileges. C'mon, hand 'em over."

I turned to look at my brother's ex, who still had the keys to my apartment—what used to be his and Danny's apartment. While their ten-year relationship was not yet a year over, their "just friends" status now had not required the revocation of key privileges. Not like I was complaining. Aaron's key privilege has been working nicely in my favor, as I could see it was now, given the stack of movie rentals he held in one hand for me, and the box of Italian cookies from Mulberry Street in the other hand, also for me.

I smiled and dropped the binoculars, but tucked them under my pillow rather than delivering them to Aaron. He's one of those people you almost can't help but be happy to see, even when they threaten to cut off your peeping privileges. Aaron himself seems to genuinely have no idea how great he is, which maybe is the key to his greatness. Aaron's heart is as big as the vintage Heart band logo on his wrinkled T-shirt, worn completely sincerely and without sarcasm. When I've asked him why he hasn't started dating again (the sooner that happens, the sooner Danny can jump on the I'm an Idiot, How Did I Ever Let Aaron Go jealousy bandwagon), Aaron answers that he's a chunky awkward dork whose one relationship started in high school and lasted ten years—he doesn't know how to date. Aaron doesn't see the hotness in his husky tallness, in his shoulder-length thinning strawberry blond hair that he sheepishly tucks behind his ears, or in the grease spot on his Heart T-shirt. It's like he's so uncool as to positively burn up with cool. The kind kind of cool.

Autumn appraised the treats in Aaron's hands and wagged her index finger at me. "For a person who can't go anywhere, you really know how to work the system," she said.

Aaron said, "For your viewing pleasure today, m'lady CC: *Twin Peaks: Fire Walk with Me* and the Andy Hardy collection. If David Lynch coupled with Mickey Rooney's scariest film character doesn't break your spirit out of rear window spy mode, I don't know what hope there is for you."

Hope! That came from the doorbell, ringing in the arrival of the last treat.

My month-long stay trapped in my new apartment has not only been of educational value, it's also been a meet-and-greet period. Despite going outside only for doctor visits in the last month, I have personally cultivated relationships with some of the most important people in New York, namely the food delivery guys who make sure I never go hungry. There's Pedro from the (truly original) Ray's Pizza, who seemed somewhat pissed the first time he had to haul ass up five flights of stairs just to deliver me a small pizza, but who quickly forgot his pain when he saw my long black hair and how short I wear my skirts (and, sorry to brag, but may I say, even with a cast, my long legs still got it). Phuoc from the Vietnamese restaurant is only a year here but already more fluent in English than Pedro, who's lived here for a decade. Phuoc is a real sport about occasionally stopping at Duane Reade for Nestlé Crunch bars for me, since he's on his way over with my rice noodles anyway. Unfortunately, I had to let loose one of my best discoveries, Stavros from Athens, who's working at his cousin's burger joint for a year and would like a date with me as much as he'd like a green card wife prospect. When Stavros started delivering me cheeseburgers when I hadn't even placed an order, I knew I would no longer be turning to him for late night carnivorous solace.

Aaron ushered Phuoc into my room. "Hey, CC," Phuoc said, holding up a plastic bag filled with food containers. "How's the leg coming along? You want me to set up the noodles on the tray for you like last time?"

I had a better idea. I said, "There's four of us here now. How about we start a bridge game?"

"You play bridge?" Aaron asked.

"No," I said. But learning the game could keep my treat-bearing friends here for days—maybe even until the cast came off. "We could try, though, don't you think? Then we all could become bridge buddies, where we meet every week to play cards and drink tea and eat cookies and like gossip about lots of different stuff."

Autumn said, "So basically you want us to expend our valued time by role-playing like we're sixty-year-old about-to-be retirees who just sent their kids off to college and have nothing else to do?"

I swear, Columbia University really did the right thing accepting that smart lass into its lair. "Exactly!" I said. "Don't you agree it'd be fun?"

Autumn, Aaron, and Phuoc answered as a collective: "NO!"

And then they left me to my treats, all alone again. I don't even like tea.

All my cultivation appears to be harvesting a new me. From weeks lying around in stasis with a steady stream of food delivery treats, a new CC has sprouted. Good-bye mutant tall flat-chested scrawny girl with the bottomless metabolism, hello mutant tall woman with the new bottomful bottom, who needs jeans two sizes bigger than her old ones, which isn't so terrible when you consider the upper end of her filling out. For the first time in my life I appear to have boobs! Real ones! Like, truly cup-able. Maybe this convalescence wasn't such a tragedy after all.

Against Gingerbread's advice I placed Shrimp's postcard—

addressed to Autumn, not to me—inside my desk drawer, out of our sight. No need to obsess over the meaning of poorly spelled haikus from Down Under, what with a bed heaped with mini-Nestlé Crunches, Italian cookies, some Vietnamese noodle containers, and a stack of movies waiting to be watched.

Anyway, I think I might be ready for a different kind of treat.

I want to do something with these new curves.

FOUR

I had no idea my cabin fever burned so high. One simple excur-sion outside the apartment, and my loins were on fire. Even with all the damn ants trying to crawl up my cast. But so many cute boys on display to admire my form when I bent over in my foldout lawn chair to flick the ants from my foot!

"I recall . . . ," Autumn sang out.

"Central Park in fall," I finished. I sighed. Central Park in full green, red, yellow, and gold autumn glory, with kids playing, sports games going, people hanging out, had to be the greatest leg cast almost-begone destination ever. I could probably be content to sit out a lifetime at this one perch, never mind going to culinary school and finding a job, hunting for a new true love, getting a life, whatever.

Autumn passed my lemon ice back over. "I can't remember the next line. Do you?"

We both paused to watch the girl on the pitcher mound, whom Autumn thought was hot, do the windup pitch to the hitter guy standing at the diamond mound, whom I thought was hot. And it's saying something that a corporatemeister dude with preppy hair, wearing perfectly unscuffed white sneakers with white tube socks and a Merrill Lynch-logo'd baseball shirt that looked like it had been ironed, would appear attractive to me. In fact, after six weeks cooped up inside my apartment, with only a few days left to go before the cast officially came off, it was possible *every* guy in Central Park on this perfect, balmy-brisk autumn afternoon looked hot to me. Even the crazy guy with Charles Manson hair sitting on the ground by the ice cream vendor, trying to eat dirt.

I said to Autumn, "Something about 'I tore your dress, I confess'?" Wow, even pitcher girl with the muscle legs, bending over for one more pitch but stopping long enough to psych out the hitter with a booty-shakin' glare from under her baseball hat, looked appealing in her tight black biker shorts.

Autumn said, "Gross, sounds too potential for sexual misdemeanor. Next line, please."

Stee-rike three, hitter was out. I smiled at Merrill Lynch boy as his shoulders slumped and he returned to his team's bench. Autumn

rachel cohn

gave the thumbs-up to the pitcher girl, baseball shirt courtesy of Manny's Hardware.

Autumn sang out, *"Danke schön,* darlin'.*"* I joined her on the second, *"Danke schön"* as a shirtless Frisbee guy with killer abs jumped for a catch in the near distance. If only I'd thought to bring my binoculars here. The view! The view! Full frontal *and* rear fine.

"Whoever invented Central Park ought to have won the Nobel Prize or something," I told Autumn at the end of our song.

"I love New York, but this city kinda overwhelms me," Autumn confessed. "Except for Central Park. Like it's not hard enough to adapt to dorm life, work-study job, a thousand pages a week of reading material, and being surrounded by strange, new people, this city lives up to its reputation as a place that never stops going, going, going. That's why I like to take sanctuary in Central Park. To stop. It's like Golden Gate Park, but without the fog, and a million times more interesting."

"Is that why you dragged me down five flights of stairs to come here today? To remind me that we're not in San Francisco anymore, Friend of Dorothy?"

"No, smart ass. And I think it's the bois who are Dorothy's friends, not the femmes, so get your stereotypes correct if you're going to drop them. Anyway, I wanted to come here today because it's the only place in this city that I can *afford* to be. Costs nothing to sit here and admire the view. Also, CC?"

"Yeah?"

"Do you not remember calling me at three in the morning? Singing a song to me about 'Shrimp dumpling tra-la-la/Shrimp dumpling tra-la-la'?"

"No memory of it whatsoever."

Autumn reached into my handbag and took out the prescription bottle. "These are going down the toilet. No more pain medication for CC. I can't bust you out of that cast, but clearly it was time to bust you out of that apartment."

Two gawky high school age boys who'd been loitering by a nearby tree, earbuds dangling from their heads like jewels, approached us, probably drawn over by my new bust.

"Let's have fun with them," I whispered to Autumn. "Hold hands and make eyes at each other and totally play the girl action provocation card."

"Let's not and never say we did," Autumn whispered back. "Lame." Then, "Hi!" she said as they stood in front of us. "Did you know my friend here thinks there is no good cappuccino to be found in this whole city?"

"Dude," manchild number one said, "that's so wrong. You're working from bad information. There's gnarly caffeine to be found at this place not far from here, Seventy-third and Madison. If you don't mind the whole Madison Avenue whacked-out chi-chi vibe."

rachel cohn

"Dude," manchild number two said, "chi-chi Nazis charge like five bucks per drink. Outrageous!"

So many views had been offered up to me on this afternoon, I figured now was the time to offer one back up to the universe. I performed the arms-behind-my-head, I-love-Central-Park-in-fall, boobs-out, happy-stretch-yawn for the fellas. Premium view. Then I said, "Go get me one? I'll be here when you get back." I pulled the bag of mini-Nestlé Crunch bars from my purse. "With treats."

I didn't know boys that skinny could sprint so fast.

Autumn advised, "I see you talk the talk." She held up my crutches. "But next time, when a real live manbait approaches, I expect you to walk the walk."

I pointed at the pitcher girl. "Ditto," I told Autumn.

Five

For a corporate executive chick with an undoubtedly bad throwing arm, my sister lisBETH had some curve balls to pitch me on my first public outing free of the leg cast. As we sat side by side in the nail shop getting pedicures together, lisBETH laid out her customized Plan for my new life. She could barely acknowledge me when I first arrived in town two summers ago, yet now it would seem lisBETH had upgraded me from Farm Team Illegitimate Begrudging Biological Connection to Major League Sister Project.

Uh-oh. Beware the thirtysomething Wall Street managing director with too much time on her hands during a bear market.

First, lisBETH announced she had bought me a gym membership to help ease me off Danny's cupcakes and the extra poundage caused by the leg cast inertia. Second, no sister of hers should lounge around the apartment all day without a Meaningful Future.

Hence (she actually used this word), lisBETH had taken the liberty of enrolling me in the Introduction to Baking Techniques and Ingredients class at the culinary school in Chelsea. Talk about a mixed message.

I'd like to know what is the big deal expectation that when a person finishes high school, they should automatically further their education in some purpose-driven academic type of way? I know I said I was moving to New York to *possibly* explore the idea of one day going to culinary school here, but what's the rush? Note the word "possibly." There's a massive city out there waiting to be explored. Why would I want to be confined inside the sterile walls of a classroom when I'd only just broken free of twelve years of such torture?

LisBETH thumbed through the school catalog while her feet were pumiced. She said, "The introductory course doesn't just cover baking basics. You'll also learn cost analysis, weights and measures, culinary math, food safety, sanitation, and equipment identification."

"I'm bored already." Somehow the fact that I got kicked out of boarding school and only made it out of the follow-up alternate school by way of a stellar record of mediocre grades does not seem to impede the adults in my life from holding out hope that I will survive yet another exercise in learning boredom. But it must have been the toxic nail shop fumes breaking my spirit, because I told lisBETH, "Okay, I'll give the class a try." I did not add, *Thank you, sir, may I have another!* She can forget about the gym part.

LisBETH had further educatin' to do me. "My dear, a word of unsolicited advice. You want to be in school if you hope to find an acceptable mate. You realize there are very few single straight men left in this city, don't you? You've got to find yours before they're all taken, and school is just the right environment for that. Trust me on this one."

Thanks, lisBETH, thanks a lot. And that was more than a word of unsolicited advice—it was a disaster stream. I mean, I was finally able to go out and about, start my new life, and this was the sisterly wisdom she chose to spring on me?

I looked up from the alternate toe blue-green-blue-green polish coats being applied to my toenails, searching for the closest EXIT sign. If lisBETH followed up our talk by directing me to the nearest sex toy pleasure shop for sad-sack single females, sister bonding time would be so over, even if that meant ruining the fresh polish by not letting it dry long enough.

No. I was just not hearing it.

I told lisBETH, "Wrong. You obviously need to spend more time scamming the baseball fields and basketball courts in Central Park. And remember about George, the hot ambulance driver? He finally called me and asked me out. We made plans to get together once my cast came off. And lookee here . . ." I swung my healed castless leg in the air, the one with the set of toes not currently being polished. "Me all fixed up and ready for a fix-up."

Before lisBETH's proclamation, I'd considered canceling the date with George. He happened to call when I was coming down off the last painkiller left in my dresser drawer after Autumn tossed my stash. In that moment I was so groggy and happy I would have accepted a date with Oscar the Grouch—and planned to do some serious feeling up on the green furry beast too. Yeah, stooping to pharmaceutical-inspired sex fantasies about garbage-can Sesame Street characters—that had to be the best Just Say No drug lecture a girl in a leg cast could ever receive to make her go cold turkey off the meds.

The sober truth is, I may have new curves to flaunt, and hormones yearning for action, but in outright defiance of my Plan, my heart is not over Shrimp. Autumn's right. I talk a big talk, but I am not ready to walk the walk. I don't know if I ever will be. Ready. Or over Shrimp.

That didn't stop me from refuting lisBETH. I'd only spent years developing this skill with my mother. It's like a sport, one of the few I excel at. I said, "George and I made plans to go see some apocalyptic action movie—his choice not mine, by the way—not some sensitive art-house flick about a complicated trio of sexually confused Brazilian petty thief street urchins. So not only am I confident George has the all clear on the heterosexual radar, but further, he might think he's getting death and destruction in stereo surround sound on this date, but what he'll really be getting is a seat at the top corner of the theater and acts two and three drowned out by some serious making out. Count on it."

The nail shop girl paused from applying the blue coat on my pinky toe to smile up at me. "That's what I'm talkin' about," she said.

My new best friend. "What's your name?" I asked her. I wanted to kidnap her to the nearest coffee shop and tell her all about Shrimp, and my big mistake in letting my true love get away, like over one mega-whopper-mocha oozing with whipped cream. Hopefully nail shop girl would have a similar tale of woe to share that would convert us into instant compadres without us ever having to bother with the getting-to-know-you grace period for new friendships.

"Constanza Guadalupe Lourdes Maria," she said. Constanza Guadalupe Lourdes Maria had long black hair like mine, but way curlier and separated into two ponytail bunches tied at the nape of her neck. Her beautiful collection of names was highlighted by her lovely olive-of-indiscriminate-extraction skin tone—she could easily have passed for Hispanic, Middle Eastern, or South Asian, although her tight-white belly T-shirt announced DR: DAMN RIGHT I'M FROM DOMINICAN REPUBLIC! over a picture of the red, white, and blue DR flag. She added, "But you can call me Chucky. Everyone does."

"Why's that?"

She shrugged. "A couple bad hair days in fourth grade and some mean mofo kids on the playground, and here I am. Chucky, like the crazy doll. Gotta tell you, though. I feel more like a Chucky than a Constanza."

"Good enough for me, Chucky," I said. I understand about spiritual affiliations with dolls. "You have a boyfriend?"

"Yup." She took a laminated photograph out of her rear jeans pocket. "That's Tyrell." Despite the true love sigh that escaped her mouth as she handed over the picture, I felt sure Chucky had a past littered with boy heartache, so I could forgive her the Tyrell happiness.

Not only was Tyrell a stone-faced, crew-cut babe of a Marine, he also looked large enough to beautifully serve my just-now-thought-up master plan. I asked Chucky, "You two want to meet up with me and George after the movie next week? Maybe go to some diner and save me from having to break it to George that making out in the theater is as much as he's getting on the first date?"

"We're there for you," Chucky said. "Give me your cell and we'll text up later about when and where to meet up."

LisBETH groaned. She leaned down, placing her head of frizzy-wild-beautiful black tresses prematurely streaked with gray onto her lap, as if to wonder, *What just happened here? And how exactly did my Meaningful Future talk get so far out of my reach?* From underneath all that hair my sister grumbled, "George better pay for your movie ticket. If he's a gentleman."

I don't want a gentleman. I want a cute guy to kiss. I can pay my own damn way.

"By the way," Chucky interjected. She motioned her head backward, in the direction of the row of manicure tables at the opposite end of the shop. "That bald dude getting the manly manicure at the center table?" LisBETH leaned back up. Chucky looked directly at lisBETH. "Notice how he always comes here the same time as you, noon on Saturdays, after the gym? Let me be the first to break it to you, *chica.* There are plenty of straight men left in this city, and that one, he's got an eye on you."

I almost jumped out of the chair to get a look at the guy, but all I could see was the back of a bald head, and some unfortunate neck hair poking through his shirt. I couldn't see his face, but his hunter green polo-shirt was totally uptight Ivy League, which was a promising sign, especially since Alexei the Horrible, my polo shirt-wearing Ivy League friend from back home, whom I had all cued up to matchmake into lisBETH's prospective boy toy, had decided to transfer to Stanford and thereby become a geographic undesirable.

Make that Uh-oh an Uh-huh: possibility for lisBETH.

As we tried to catch a better glimpse of him, baldy's head suddenly dropped down to his chest, relaxed into a catnap by the massage on his hands. His very loud snore could be heard at our end of the shop, even over the sound of the Lite-FM radio station attacking our eardrums with some lame Nashville-country-queen-gone-pop-star power ballad crap.

Reality check: When I am sad from missing Shrimp and cursing myself for letting him go so I could start up this new life in New York City, I kind of like that power ballad crap, but I will die a thousand deaths by octopus-handed Muppet tickle monsters before admitting that out loud and not-proud. When Danny finds me alone in my room staring out the rear window and he asks me what I'm listening to on my headphones, I will name some obscure alt-country-soul band, but what I am really listening to is a crap UK dance remix of a pop princess ballad or some American Idol's pukey winning song.

A girl's gotta do what a girl's gotta do to work her way through the heartbreak. Forgive me.

Six

In my commune land of make-out make-believe, I am not walking through Washington Square Park with freshly painted blue-green toes and ginormous headphones over my ears to drown out the singing street performers, the chattering students on study and smoke breaks, the bike messenger snarling "Welcome to New York, bitch," as he almost mows down a photo-taking tourist.

In my resurrected commune world I am with Shrimp at foggy Ocean Beach in San Francisco. We are sitting on the cold concrete ledge at dusk, watching a speck of orange pink sun muted by gray fog as it sets over the Pacific. Our legs intertwine and our feet rock against the ledge in time to the crash of the ocean. Here nature requires no headphones, and the chill ocean breeze rules out exposed feet. We are silent *sympatico*.

The News are all Olds. I've given up New York, and Shrimp has forsaken New Zealand, never having bothered to find out what the Old Zealand may have been about, although the name alone is pretty compelling, and maybe for our next new commune that's where we'll go, Old Zealand. We'll make it up as we make out in our make-believe. Except it will be real. We will New the Old, as if time never went by with us apart.

Shrimp's shivering in his damp black wet suit, but I warm him right up. I am an Ava Gardner hot tamale, rubbing against his side. We turn to each other so our lips can meet all over again, and he tastes like home, like espresso and sea air and true love. His kiss is nothing like Old York, where I might have had to kiss strangers whose espresso taste would be second-rate, and where the air smells like taxi and bus fumes and hella toxic house wine spilling outta street corner restaurant Dumpsters.

Shrimp pauses the melding of our mouths long enough to lean up and mumble his old standard into my ear, "Burr-ito."

The whispering of this sweet nothing except it's really something makes us hungry, and we look longingly behind the concrete ledge, where my real family is throwing us a vegetarian barbecue in the parking lot. A power ballad wails from the boom box on the red-checkered picnic blanket, something about "I can't live without you lighting up my life forever and ever baby, baby, baby," while Sid-dad stands at the grill, flipping a Velveeta cheese sandwich without once winking at me in irony. I am his Cupcake, and we don't need secret signals to have that father-daughter understanding. My mom is flipping out, trying to contain the squeals of Ash and Josh—"Kids, they can hear you two all the way up in Marin County. Pipe down!"—while she flips through the Neiman Marcus catalog with one hand and pats her pregnant belly with the other. She's an excellent multitasker. Her normally pale-pink manicured fingernails are painted goth black, in my honor, with ghetto fabulous little orange pink rhinestones shaped like shrimps on the tips, in honor of he whom she used to grudgingly refer to as "That Boy."

We've all evolved.

Danny has come along to the New-Old commune too. He's wandering the beach alone, forlorn, thinking very hard about what a big mistake he made letting Aaron go, and planning grandiose schemes involving mountains of cupcakes to win Aaron back. Once he accomplishes that, all will be right with the world and with true love again.

My Greenwich Village existence will not be wiped from memory, but it will be wiped out of the time-space continuum that finds me walking down Bleecker Street past a diner offering a stoner food menu of sushi, sundaes, and syrup-covered pancakes, a dive that just begs for CC and her imaginary new friends George, Chucky, and Tyrell to hang out there after a movie. In the New-Old commune back at Ocean Beach, there will not be a tantalizing flyer advertising Hot Nude Yoga taped to that same Manhattan diner's door, literally calling to me to snatch it off the door and investigate the prospect. The city that never sleeps will have decided to take a nap long enough for me to return to my regularly scheduled boyfriend in my predictably foggy broody city, where people leave their hearts and their wallets, and sometimes their minds if they spend too much time on Haight Street.

In the land of make-out make-believe I will not have to possibly deal with the *possibility* that Shrimp and I are truly over. It's my land. I make the rules.

SEVEN

I have walked the walk. Straight into the bathroom at the Starbucks across the street from the restaurant where I was having dinner with George.

I do not drink Starbucks. Please. But I could only applaud and thank Starbucks for the spacious and relatively clean lavatory into which I'd snuck away—it was the perfect venue for an emergency cell-phone-tarot-card-reading with my major-arcana life advisor back in San Francisco.

"Please don't make me go back to that date," I pleaded to Sugar Pie. I was only an hour into my date with George, we'd barely been served our main course, and already I knew he and I were a no-go. But how to extract myself from the rest of the evening? No way would I make it through dessert *and* the movie we were supposed to see next—and on our own, too, since Chucky had text messaged that she and Tyrell couldn't meet us, on account of a late evening nap situation from which they could not extract themselves (totally understand: envy).

"Guess what card I just turned over for you?" Sugar Pie asked. "The Five of Cups. That card whips you every time."

Maybe my big mistake in moving to New York was not in breaking up with Shrimp but in not demanding that Sugar Pie accompany me on the journey. I have Danny here, I have Autumn here, but in the soul connection sweepstakes, Sugar Pie wins hands down, despite the May to December gap in our friendship. But considering that Sugar is a first-time bride at age seventysomething (courtesy of my genius fix-up skills), sharing true love with Fernando, Sid-dad's right-hand man, and given her recent reverse retirement move from an assisted living facility to Fernando's apartment at the side of my family's house in San Francisco, I guess I could understand if now wouldn't be the time for her to take on Manhattan with me. I'd have to settle for a cell phone Sugar-cup.

I said, "Five of Cups haunts me! What do you think it means this time?"

"False starts. Choices that have left you with a bereft feeling. But the Five of Cups tells you to be thankful for what those choices have left you with. Don't worry about what cannot be changed. Turn what you think holds you back into a step forward instead."

"You're saying I have to step back into that restaurant with George? Because you don't understand. For all that he is a very, very cute guy, we have nothing to talk about! And he was trying to play footsie with me under the table! I hardly know him!" George's footsie game was not only highly unwelcome, it also derailed any flirtation I might have thrown back his way. Too bad George lacked X-ray vision, because if he had been bestowed with that superpower, he might have seen inside my shoe to know that his foot action had knocked against the kiwi ring I wear on my toe, the customized CC ring that Shrimp designed and carved himself. Shrimp gave it to me when he proposed. Each time George grazed that ring, he unwittingly pinged my heart, and grazed farther away from any interest I might have developed in him. Also, George might want to invest in some breath mints.

Sugar Pie asked, "How do you know you have nothing to talk about? Did you really give this George a fair chance?"

"I know all I need to know already. When George came to the apartment to pick me up, I asked what he was listening to on his headphones? He was listening to a mix of jam bands like the Grateful Dead and Phish. Gross! We're musically incompatible. There's no hope left once that's been established. George and me: DOA."

"You don't think you're being too hasty in your judgment?"

"Absolutely not. Right now we're—well, he is—eating at this

British restaurant that he chose. It looks like the living room set on one of those BBC America shows, with ugly wallpaper and ceramic figurines, and the restaurant's tables are like two inches apart. So not only am I bored to death listening to George talk about his summer vacation with his buddies trekking to concerts of THE WORST BANDS EVER, but we're seated way close on either side by British expats who sound really smart and are having way more interesting conversations than ours."

"In other words," Sugar Pie said, "George is no Shrimp."

There it was. "Exactly. He's cute. He's nice. Don't want to kiss him. No chemistry."

If I were sharing this night with Shrimp, first of all we wouldn't call it a "date," we'd call it "hanging out" (obviously) followed by "fooling around" (implied). We probably would have passed the afternoon in Colma, where Shrimp likes to sketch the graveyards of San Francisco's "dead city" to the south, then maybe we'd trek a little farther down Highway 1 and stop at the cliff-top perch over Maverick's, to watch the pro surfers in all their glory ride the gigantic-dangerous-awesome waves at their sacred spot near Half Moon Bay. Shrimp and I wouldn't close out the not-date by going to some trendspot for dinner either; we'd share a vegetarian burrito from a taco stand somewhere along the highway and consume many espressos, because that's what true loves do. We'd end the night at any random vista point overlooking the ocean, in the backseat of

Shrimp's Pinto, TCOB after our TCBY froze yogurt stop. "Burr-ito," Shrimp would whisper in my ear, after, as he held me tight to keep me warm in the Pacific fog chill.

"Won't George be wondering where you are?" Sugar Pie asked.

"No. I told him to be patient cuz my stomach was having issues from the Welsh rarebit I ate, which is a very fancy way of describing bread with melted cheese, tomato, and mustard, by the way. And did I mention how George chose the British restaurant because he said it had the best mac and cheese in the city? As anyone in their right mind knows, there is no macaroni and cheese better than the Kraft kind from the box, and if you're going to a restaurant specifically for its Britishness, why wouldn't you try bangers and mash—"

"Cyd Charisse?"

"Yes?"

"Your last card. Ah, I like what I see now. The High Priestess. Her power is hidden in mystery. She is the path to realms that we may never fully comprehend or master."

"I love her," I sighed. I had no idea whatsoever what Sugar Pie meant, but I could get on board with having my fate guided by a higher being shrouded in mystery. That'd be fuckin' awesome.

"The High Priestess seems to me to represent a sign of the hidden side of your personality that no one sees, and that you yourself could be unaware of. She's opening your powers to you. The

Priestess here could indicate passivity in a situation, hanging on to the veiled mystery. Like she's telling you, it's not always necessary to act. Sometimes goals can be realized through inaction."

"So I can bail on this date?"

"Personally, I don't advise it. Poor George deserves better than that. The cards, however, seem to be giving you the green light."

One more phone call and I had the green light I needed.

Danny arrived at the restaurant within minutes of my return to it. "Thank God you told me where you were having dinner, CC," he said, breathless from the sprint over from our apartment nearby. "I've got an emergency. The super at the kitchen space I rent for the cupcake business just called to tell me there was a major water main break in the building. I have to get over there right away to salvage the baking equipment and I really need a second person to help. You understand if I frisk her away, right, George?"

And before George could tell me, "Cheerio, you won't-be-my-mate," Danny and I were outta there.

"Thank you *so* much," I told Danny. I leaned my head into his shoulder as he wrapped his arm around me.

"You get one Get Out of Jail Free card from me," he said. "Now you've used it, and now you're gonna have to make it through the tragedy of future dates with hot guys on your own. But for now . . . there's this joint down the street that makes great steak-cut fries, and they show episodes of *The Simpsons* on the bar TV, but dubbed in foreign languages like Hindi and Finnish. It's even funnier than watching the show in English."

"Brilliant, mate!"

We stopped at a crosswalk—red light—but we both took one look at traffic and dodged across the street anyway. As Danny has informed me, I am a New Yorker now, and jaywalking is not only my right, but my responsibility.

And I will totally walk the line for Danny.

EighT

I met Sugar Pie because of a court-ordered community service stint following a little shoplifting problem back in the day. But she and I got on so well, I kept visiting her even when I was no longer legally obligated to do so. We became family.

The lisBETH and Frank ends of my bio-family here, I've decided, are my new community service project. Visiting with them can certainly feel like a chore.

At least with lisBETH the time is not a complete waste. Manicures and pedicures are important community service projects in the public interest of not having ugly hands and feet. But with Frank there's no getting around the fact that the time with him serves no purpose other than . . . passing time.

Frank has weird rules about his apartment. He'll sometimes but not always ask guests to remove their shoes upon entering the front hallway, since in his advertising-man-CEO heyday he took many business trips to Asia and decided he liked their footwear policies as much as he disliked their undervalued currencies. Last year when I visited Frank, shoes were acceptable. Now, no. Frank's never been one for consistency, according to my mother. He is consistent in requesting that guests who join him for lunch at his place arrive promptly by 11:45, because he is deep into punctuality, and into leaving enough time between shoe removal and the basic exchange of "How ya doin'?" pleasantries to allow for sitting down to lunch at noon exactly.

Despite his worldliness, Frank doesn't seem to know the one basic rule of welcoming his illegitimate eighteen-year-old bio-daughter who's only recently moved to his city and possibly into his life: She might not welcome an invitation to lunch at his stuffy Upper East Side apartment. I mean, Frank, dude, take me somewhere good! We could as easily have taken our shoes off at a swank sushi restaurant, where we could sit on pillows on the floor, get ripped on sake, and try to determine the ranks of the Japanese businessmen in relation to one another by the depth of their bows, as Sid-dad once taught me to do to keep my attention deficit problem in check while awaiting the arrival of appetizers at a fancy restaurant.

I hardly know Frank, but I understood him enough to know better than to expect him capable of such an experience with me— um, like an interesting experience. When I'd been cooped up for six weeks with a leg cast, Frank didn't visit me once, didn't perch himself next to my bedside and offer to play board games with bored me like Sid-dad used to when I was little and sick in bed with the chicken pox. I don't take Frank's lack of face time personally. Frank moved into the city after his wife died a few years ago, but Danny told me Frank hasn't visited Danny's apartment in years because of the five flights of stairs, so given Frank's advancing age and senior moments, I shouldn't have expected lunch on pillows or sake shots. Lunch at his apartment did spare me having to watch his womanizer self checking out the hostess ladies in geisha costumes. Ew, just the thought of.

Frank *is* learning consistency with the phone calls. He didn't stay in touch much from that first time I came to visit him in New York up until I graduated high school and moved here. However, now that he's discovered the modern wonder called the cell phone, he can't ring-a-ling-ling me—and lisBETH and Danny—enough. I also don't take these calls personally, as Danny says Frank's cell phone habit has nothing to do with Frank mastering the new technology so he can keep in touch with his kids. It has everything to do with his utter boredom since being forced into retirement.

With Frank, you take what you can get.

Frank called regularly during my leg cast experience, matching his consistency in calling with his consistency in having very little to say to me.

Frank: "How are you feeling, kiddo?"

Me: "Fine." *Do you not recall I don't like being called "kiddo"?*

Frank: "Do you need anything?"

Me: "No." *I'm bored! I need to be entertained while Danny is out during the day! And I know you're bored too! Do you not sense the solution to our two problems here?*

Frank: "You don't need money?"

Me: "I'm sitting around with my leg propped up on a pillow all day watching movies. What would I need money for?" *Because we all know asking me if I need money is really your way of saying "Here's a check with some zeroes at the end. The fact of your ol' bio-dad ignoring your existence for the first sixteen years of your life feels better now, doesn't it?"*

Nothing felt good in Frank's apartment, except for the quiet hum of the A/C. It's not the type of place where a new daughter would feel comfortable reclining on a leather sofa, for instance, or throwing water balloons down to the street from the balcony. In Frank's world the furniture and surroundings looked corporate and stiff—except for the high-rise view overlooking Central Park, which was totally ace.

Lunches of New York deli sandwiches, I guess, were what Frank had to offer at this point in our relationship. Having spent a career mastering the art of the business lunch, well, lunch is what Frank knows. And frankly, Frank probably doesn't know what else to do with me. Again, I choose not to take it personally. I don't know what to do with him.

"Why are your fingernails green and blue?" Frank asked me as he poured tea for us following our pretty much silent lunch experience, catered courtesy of Frank's morning walk across the park to Zabar's.

"'Why are yours not?' is the better question, I would say," I answered.

Frank shook his head in confusion. A guy in his late sixties really should have the dignity to be balding and graying, or at least to not have that aging debonair movie star look about him. It's freaky for me how, along with my movie star name to go with his movie star looks, I look so much more like him than like my mother. I doubt there's anything about Frank I would hope to emulate.

"Would you like to make a regular date of us having lunch together?" Frank asked.

Because this silent experience had been so much fun!

I said, "I believe in randomness over regularity. Let's play it by ear?" I wiggled my outstretched green-blue pinky and thumb fingers in the *Call me!* gesture.

"Huh?" Frank said.

"Never mind," I said.

The Rule of CC: Frank will have to learn to take what he can get from me, too.

NiNe

There's a big city out there waiting to be explored, sure—but Autumn and I prefer our Central Park hideaway. We're California spawn. We need to be outside while we can, before that fearful experience called winter sets in. Even if meeting that need means ditching school.

The stone ledge bench outside the top level at Belvedere Castle, a small building built in the style of a medieval castle, could possibly become permanently engraved with our butt imprints, based on how many hours we've whiled away here. Our post at the top of the moat-encircled castle offered a dazzling display of hazy dusk sky flirting over the grand apartment buildings along Central Park West, as the sun prepared to set over that unknown westerly wilderness called New Jersey. What better way to pay tribute to the sun and the choicest spot in all of Manhattan than by neglecting our new lives to idle our afternoon there?

Adapting to New York turns out to be not so hard. So the buildings are tall and there are lots of people. The noise never stops, and the energy is unrelenting. Breathe. Then buy yourself a MetroCard, get some exploring going on, just try not to walk down dark alleys alone at night. Go with the flow. Because the hard part isn't the intimidating masses of strangers, skyscrapers, and energy. The hard part is that which you can't see—it's adapting to the expectation that you're supposed to *Do Something* with your new life.

Autumn said, "I don't quite understand how I was ranked fifth in my senior class, practically killed myself through four years of high school taking honors and AP everything, and now that I am Ivy League Girl—you know, the whole goal of all that ass-kicking study regimen—I am barely passing Lit Hum because I couldn't give less of a shit about so many dead white guy philosophers. And it's likely I will outright fail astronomy. Not to mention how broke I am. I ran through my summer savings in the first month here! I can't concentrate on schoolwork because I can't stop concentrating on all the debt I am accumulating to be here—and the fact that my meal plan only covers so much, and if I eat one more slice of Koronet Pizza to get me through the day, I might get turned off pizza entirely for the rest of my lifetime. Which would be very, very wrong. And for the record, you were right. The tamales and burritos in this city suck."

"I love being right," I said, "although it pains me to be right on that count. And you can come to Danny's and my apartment anytime and we will feed you for free. I can't study for you, but we'd love to cook for you!" As proof, I opened the lunch box of cupcakes Danny had prepared for my first day of culinary school. Much as I loved the lunch box effort, his attempts at brotherly kindness are kindly starting to suffocate me. I can figure out lunch on my own!

"Says the girl who made it through one day of culinary school," Autumn said, biting into the peanut butter cupcake.

"Shh," I said. "That will just be our little secret."

If I wanted to spill the real secret, I would confess I never intended to follow through with the culinary school part of the Manhattan adult girl life. One day of class fully fulfilled my expectations of the suckiness I'd encounter should I return for a second day. The gadgets and equipment and ovens and mixers were intriguing, I guess, but it was just way too much . . . stuff. The other students, who all appeared at least five or ten years older than me, looked all confident and happy to be there, sure the class was the first step on a path to a dream career. I couldn't take my eyes off the rear window view: escape. I ditched the class during the break, called Autumn, who couldn't wait to escape her afternoon classes, and hello, Central Park—love ya.

Here's what I'm going to do, until I figure out a better Plan. I'm going to let my family believe I am going to culinary school, but I am going to Do Something . . . Else with that time instead. Possibly I will play Job for a Day, Manhattan-style. One day I will hand out the free daily newspaper outside the subway stops and I will be sure to offer that "Have a nice day!" California platitude ray of sunshine to all the scowly-faced straphangers who haven't had their coffee yet. The next day I will hang out at Strawberry Fields in Central Park and pretend to be a tour guide and I will give totally false information out to the tourists, like "John Lennon originally planned to pursue a career as a Scotland Yard bank robber investigator before his dreams were sidetracked by all that damn songwriting ability," or "If you come to this spot at two a.m. and point your binoculars toward The Dakota apartment building, you may glimpse Yoko Ono in a tawdry moonlit make-out scene with the graveyard shift doorman in that window there." The other days I will probably hang out on my bed, listen to music, and stare out that ol' rear window, pondering the injustice of the world that Dante, the legendary cappuccino man, apparently returned to Corsica during my leg cast convalescence and is personally responsible for my inability to find proper caffeination in this city. Jerk. When Danny comes home from work and asks, "How was your day, dear?" I will make up stuff about culinary school using an outstanding system of subterfuge wherein I tell him details about the fictional other students while never being held accountable for information about what I may have learned in class: "Brenda from Flushing—you know the girl with the big hair and fake boobs that I told you about who doesn't know the difference between a Le Creuset loaf pan and a regular aluminum one—well I'm fairly sure she is doling out sexual favors to the instructor in the closet of the cookbook library during the breaks, and I will be so pissed if she gets a better grade than me," or "Should I be worried that I ate the Linzer tarts we made in class today even though Nikolai from Latvia sliced his thumb in the mixer while we were making the dough and had to go to the hospital for stitches?"

If I spent half as much time *going* to school as I did thinking about what I'll do while *dodging* school, I would probably be master chef by, like, tomorrow.

"Helen got it right," I announced to Autumn. Our other close girlfriend from San Francisco had been headed to UC Santa Cruz after high school graduation—until she wound up pregnant this past summer. And proving Helen was the only true punk of our group, she decided to keep the baby—and get married!

"How do you figure?" Autumn asked. "I mean, I'm glad Helen's happy with the choice she made, but how weird is it that she's giving up on her dreams of art school?"

"I don't think she's giving up dreams. Her dreams just changed. And now her choice means she'll have to adapt to the circumstances.

Rise to the challenge. No possibility of falling into slackerdom."

"Slackerdom really does not get its fair due in our wealth-driven society. You know?"

The sun had set over the horizon, chilling the air. "Do you miss San Francisco?" I asked Autumn.

"Yeah," Autumn sighed. "Do you miss Shrimp?"

"I can barely figure out how to get through the day without missing Shrimp."

"You going to do anything about that?"

"If you mean am I going to break the 'no contact' agreement with Shrimp, the answer is no. I haven't broken down that far yet. But I'm reserving the right."

I want Shrimp to break the agreement. And since he apparently is not psychic, or he has other ways to spend his time (don't think about that, CC, don't even consider the possibility that Shrimp has happily adapted to NZ), I want to figure out how to get this new body of mine some attention that does not involve "dating." I want that connection to be hassle-free, safe, and easy. I want an orgasm that's not a gift from my own hands.

It's like my leg is healed but my heart refuses, and until it does, I don't know how to get out of the rear window mentality.

rachel cohn

Ten

Houston, I have a problem. I seem to have lost contact with the heterosexual world.

Dallas, if you're listening, the scarier part is that lisBETH may have been right about the men in this city—at least from my current view of it.

And yo, Austin, if you're out there—could you lend our party one of those twangy alt-country singers who croak out brilliant tumbleweed lyrics?

Danny decided to throw me a "coming out" slash belated eighteenth birthday party to celebrate my reintroduction into society as a newly minted adult with a newly minted castless leg. But at this rooftop Halloween party in Greenwich Village, Danny's society was made up mostly of alterna-crap indie-band-type gay boys with super-cute faces and superbad haircuts. The few females in attendance were of the Ani variety, whom I have mad respect for, but those chicks don't tend to gravitate toward ones like me. I am Chaka Khan meets The Clash in the land of full-on boy-girl lust-o-rama. I had no place at my own party.

Even my Halloween costume alter ego, Mrs. VonHuffing-Uptight—the Chanel suit–wearing society bitch who is so desperate for male attention she would shoot up Botox-crack cocktails if she thought it would make her look more attractive to men—was feeling the confusion. It's not that she/I wanted to experiment on the other side. It's more like we weren't so sure anymore that pure straight folk still roamed the earth.

I may have been dressed like the fabulous socialite Mrs. VonHuffingUptight, but she and I suffered a big case of wallflower-itis. I could not be bothered to work this rooftop, despite the chatter and good times being enjoyed all around, particularly on the dance floor. From my wallflower observation point the dancing area highlights included: some dude dressed and coiffed like Morrissey grooving with one of those French Louis kings, an Ani girl who was lip/hand/hip-locked with a black leather-clad dominatrix-headmistress, and, awwww, Holly Hobbie (him version) and a gender-ambiguous Cabbage Patch Kid definitely teaching each other the meaning of dirty dancing.

While partygoers laughed and danced, I took position next to the food table, mute, watching, and wondering if anybody was keeping count of how many of Danny's cupcakes I'd eaten while standing there all by myself. As I munched cupcake number four (really number five, if you count the devil dog cupcake I spit into the trash because it gave me some kinda Cujo flashback moment), the thought occurred: Where did I belong in this blacktop swirl of strangers, most of them at least a decade older than me, college grads with cool jobs and interesting lives? As if to point out how much I didn't belong at my own party, Autumn and Chucky had declined the party invite, because they were reveling Halloween elsewhere, within their own age and geographic vicinities.

This guy who I think was supposed to be Jerry Lewis came up to me and said, "Great coming out party. You're Danny's sister CC, right?" He held out a coin donation can in my direction. "Got anything to spare for Jerry's kids?"

"Sorry, pal," I mumbled. "I got nothin'." Which was true. Danny went to all the trouble to throw me this party here in the heart of all that is Halloween glory, with a view from the rooftop down to the Village parade of Halloween costume fabulousness marching up Sixth Avenue, and all I could think was: *I'm kinda lost and out of my depth. Also, I want my fucking boyfriend back. What part of the "No" that I said to Shrimp's marriage proposal because we wanted different things from life, wanted to experience different places, did Shrimp misinterpret as sincerity? I want a Do Over in place of a*

Do Something! And in the absence of that, I want a straight boy at this party!

New existence, I defy you. I shun you.

I squirmed in my Halloween costume. Mrs. VonHuffing-Uptight's couture suit—conveniently swiped from my mom's closet last spring—was loose on me when I visited New York last Easter, when I was only dabbling with the idea of living here but had yet to make the full commitment because I had a true love Shrimp waiting for me back home, and we were going to start our new lives together. Now look at us, on opposite ends of the earth, no longer in contact with each other. Now I have to take deep breaths because the zipper is about to bust open from my new ass trying to break free from the fabric.

By the way, I totally get the control top panty hose thing now.

Jerry gave up on mute me, lured to the dance floor by a Dino. I looked toward the stairwell door, but Danny intercepted my attempt at exit. "SULKING MUCH?" he yelled over the Pet Shop Boys song coming from the DJ booth.

It was hard to answer Danny seriously. He wore a very tight white polyester disco suit with a chest stick-on badge that said HELLO. MY NAME IS DENNY TERRIO. Danny/Denny's bush of black hair was whisked and feathered so high and with so much mousse that it was almost like a disco hair jello mold, not to mention a stunning display of hair product prowess.

"I'm not sulking," I answered. "This Chanel suit is so tight on me it renders facial expression impossible." I resisted his arm swinging around me, trying to trap me into a dance, into a good time.

"Aaron looks great, don't you think?" Danny dance-gestured in the direction of Aaron, but I knew Danny was really asking about the cute guy dancing with Aaron, not about Aaron, who did indeed appear to be having a great time. I'd been surprised that Aaron had accepted the invitation to this party (who'd want to go to a party thrown by your ex and watch that ex flirt with budding prospects?); surprised, that is, until Aaron showed up in the newfound glory-confidence that must have come along with working past his self-esteem dating trauma. Not only did Aaron arrive with a new guy to flaunt, but the new guy was *finger snap* *gor-geous* and also the head pastry chef at some hot new restaurant in Chelsea, a combination designed, of course, to make Danny rage with jealousy. Kudos, Aaron! Danny was the one, after all, who'd left him.

Yet Danny had the gall to not appear jealous of Aaron's presence here tonight, dangling some serious arm candy. Instead he smiled and waved at Aaron, who was also wearing a white disco suit with flipped-out hair. Danny said, "How weird that we both ended up in disco Halloween outfits without even consulting each other in advance first. Do you like Aaron's Andy Gibb Solid Gold-era thing, CC?"

Men. I give up on them.

If it were Shrimp over there dancing with a new love, I would absolutely have the decency to rage with jealousy for his benefit. So much for the stereotype that gay men are more highly evolved beings. I put Danny on too high a pedestal. I should have known he's a boy just like the rest of them. Clueless. I mean, how could you look at Denny Terrio staring at Andy Gibb on a moonlit Manhattan rooftop and *not* know they are like true loves predetermined by fate to walk through life together?

Luckily, two most excellent specimens of manhood emerged through the stairwell door and into our party, in the form of two NYPD cops. They approached me first. "This your party?"

I hoped this was some type of sick striptease belated eighteenth birthday present for me from Danny. I was all, "No way, officer," feeling the night's first promise of a smile on my face, but Danny's concerned expression let me know the cops were the real deal. Damn.

"I'm throwing the party," Danny said. "Is there a problem?"

At least if they weren't strippers the cops did have a quality good cop–bad cop routine. Good cop said, "Folks, we got a complaint about noise from one of your neighbors."

"Max!" Danny exclaimed.

Bad cop threw in, "Turn the fuckin' music down."

"Max?" I asked.

Danny said, "You know, Ceece, your favorite rear window binoculars victim during your leg cast imprisonment? The tyrant with the garden apartment in the building opposite ours, the most hated neighbor within our courtyard radius? Noise complaints are his specialty."

Mystery man! Who spends all his courtyard garden time making noise on a laptop, yet who complains about neighbors' noise!

Bad cop added, "It's Halloween, and we've got better things to do than respond to ridiculous noise complaints. Keep the noise level down or we cite you for improper congregation without a permit."

Danny made the throat slash sign toward the DJ, who turned the volume down and changed the groove, totally going Enya on us. Mean!

I handed good and bad cop a cupcake each for their service. They accepted the peace offering and left. From the rear view of their asses, I'd say if the cops lessened their doughnut consumption by about ten percent, they could have a definite future in stripping.

I was finally ready for some socializing. I grabbed a tray of party cupcakes and followed the cops marching down the stairs.

"Where are you going?" Danny called after me. "This is your party!"

"I have a date with destiny," I shouted up through the stairs.

This Max guy called the cops on a party in the *Village*. On freakin' *Halloween*.

That is SO punk.

I gotta meet this mystery man finally.

Shrimp is not coming to rescue me. Not now. Not ever.

New existence, let's get this party started.

ELEVEN

Buzz.

Nothin'.

Buzz.

Nothin'.

Buzz.

"Who the hell is buzzing?"

Contact!

"Avon calling," I said into mystery man's apartment building intercom speaker. I felt confident the Nixon administration–era intercom would work similarly to the one in Danny's and my apartment building, and that what mystery man would hear would not be "Avon calling!" but "Azhghrt kwz ing!"

The lobby door buzzed open. Gibberish, successful. Access, granted.

Hey now, I'm a sorceress in VonHuffingUptight threads.

Mystery man opened his apartment door only a crack, but I could see across the chain lock that he wore his trusty lavender silk smoking robe. He had one of those old-fashioned gentleman's pipes dangling in his mouth, yet he managed to bark out, "What the hell do you want?" without the pipe falling out. Impressive.

I lifted the tray of cupcakes for his view. "Noisy neighbor with cupcake peace offering? Sorry about the music!" I chirped. *Cuz I'm a gonna ferret you out and learn the secrets to yo' universe, sucka.*

Now, in no city, but especially not in New York City, would a person seriously consider opening the door to a cupcake-bearing stranger. But then, not every cupcake-bearing stranger arrived in a Mrs. VonHuffingUptight costume, looking like her mother, tall and ironed-straight hair and Chanel-elegant—like, totally-reliable-not-gonna-go-psycho-on-your-ass.

Mystery man opened the door a tiny crack more. "Chocolate?" he asked.

"Red velvet with cream cheese frosting, powdered cocoa and maraschino cherry on top. House specialty."

Door opened all the way.

Somethin'.

After the many weeks' binoculars observation of mystery man, it was strange indeed to see him in live 3-D form in front of me, wearing that lavender silk smoking robe over black silk pajamas with smart black loafer slippers. He was a short, stumpy guy with brown middle-aged-man comb-over hair and serious coffee breath, which would have been rank except for the *sympatico* potential it exhaled.

"That your party on the rooftop across the courtyard?" he bellowed. "Who raised you people to think it's acceptable to play music that loud, for the whole neighborhood to hear? And it's almost midnight. If I can hear your music inside the cavern of my soundproofed bedroom walls, you're violating city-mandated noise levels." Still, he peered down at the cupcake tray and took one into his hands. Taking the pipe from his mouth, he licked the frosting from the side. Then he said, "Delicious. I appreciate the peace offering. I never would have suspected anyone under the age of forty, and particularly anyone in this city's vicious yuppie climate, to have the decency to apologize to their neighbors for their bad manners. Thank you, young lady."

See? So not a tyrant. His behavior was directly at odds with the binoculars impression one might have of him, said binoculars having observed courtyard neighbors going back and forth between each other's fenced gardens, gossiping and sharing gardening tools and the occasional joint, but going nowhere near his. In fact, you'd think he had prison barbed wire lining his garden for all that the neighbors interact with him—or, rather, don't.

The sugar distraction going on inside his mouth allowed me a moment to inspect the interior of his apartment. On the basis of the silver framed black-and-white photographs sitting on top of his piano, showing a younger, lighter version of himself, sitting at that same piano alongside an attractive Bobby Darin–type lounge singer holding a microphone, I doubted mystery man had a murdered secret wife buried underneath the potted plants in his garden. And on the basis of mystery man's crankiness and the memorial candle that flickered next to a head-shot photo of the lounge singer lover-man, framed along with a death notice, a pride flag, and an AIDS awareness label, I further suspected that no true love had ever come to replace the one who'd been lost.

If I were a girl spy commentating about Max's apartment on one of those interior decorating home improvement TV shows, I would not start by describing his living room as waiting for a shabby chic makeover. Because it was a junk palace whose only hope of renovation was a plough ramming through and clearing all the waist-high stacks of newspapers, magazines, sheet music, and correspondence. Also, if I were design-commentating on TV, I would be sure to find some clever but polite way to point out that the most noticeable aspect of the apartment's interior was invisible—the aroma. The junk palace smelled like decades of accumulated pipe and cigarette smoke, cat, moldy newspapers, coffee grounds, candy wrappers, and . . . sniff . . . ramen noodles? My investigation of the artwork lining what appeared to be every available inch of wall space—photographs of musicians from long-ago eras, when the men wore tuxes and the lady singers had beautiful hairstyles and secret heroin addictions; the movie musical posters; and dozens of old *Life* and *Photoplay* magazine covers picturing old movie stars like Judy Garland, Lana Turner, and Joan Crawford—made for an easy deduction as to the key to unlock mystery man's heart.

Anyone who'd dare label me as a culinary school dropout with no Real Plan currently in operation could now reconsider me as Cyd Charisse, girl slacker sleuth. Big career potential. Step aside, Nancy Drew and Trixie Belden.

"I heard your name is Max," I said. "Wanna know my name?"

"Not particularly," he said, grabbing for a second cupcake. "But I have a feeling you're going to tell me anyway. Could you make it quick, because I'm ready to go to sleep."

"Mister," I said, "with the amount of sugar you're just now consuming and the amount of coffee I suspect you've already consumed tonight, you ain't gettin' to sleep anytime soon. And why would you want to, anyway, when your new friend named Cyd Charisse is calling on you?"

Until this point in my life, sharing a famous person's name has felt like a burden, keeping me from—or throwing me into, depending on your perspective—my own identity. Suddenly the name was my trump card.

"That's not your real name," he huffed.

"It so is too."

I took my Cali driver's license out of Mrs. VonHuffing-Uptight's chain strap Chanel shoulder bag, another item from my mother's closet. When I was younger, her fashion taste seemed horrendous. Now it still seems horrendous, but also kitschy and cool—and finger lickin' swipeworthy.

Max inspected my ID, then, satisfied with my name claim, said, "Go figure. A real live Cyd Charisse in my own apartment. I never thought I'd see the day. Do you have a dance to share along with the cupcakes?" He placed his pipe back in his mouth and lit up.

I said, "I'm not the dancer type of Cyd Charisse. But would you mind not smoking, because what if I did want to break out into a dance number but all that secondhand smoke of yours impaired my ability to perform?"

Max continued to puff away. "My apartment," he said. "My rules." I hope Danny never adopts this man's methodology. "I'm not entirely sure this isn't a dream, you know. Girl named Cyd Charisse appears at my apartment door, loaded with cupcakes? Why don't you have a seat and prove yourself. At least tell me about why you can't keep the noise down up there tonight."

I cleared about a year's worth of *New York Times* Sunday Arts & Leisure sections from his sofa and took a seat, crossing my legs like a proper VonHuffingUptight.

"First I gotta question for you," I said. "Are you 'Max' like Maxwell the singer or 'Maxim' like de Winter as in—"

"As in *Rebecca*!" Max said, sounding impressed—and pleased. Maybe all my *Rear Window* movie-watching time was not a complete waste of time. "Who's Maxwell the singer?"

"You know, neo-soul guy, really hot body in the practically naked videos on the Smooth R & B music choice channel?" To Max's confused look, I added, "Catchy groove tunes that sound great at first then just become kinda grating, at least when you're stuck in your bedroom flicking channels while waiting for a broken leg to heal?" Max's face downgraded from confused to bordering on bored. I can intuit people with short attention spans like me, so I figured I'd better change the subject. "Maxwell was so last millennium, never mind. So speaking of music . . . I realize you *think* our party was making too much noise, but are you aware that it's a Saturday night? And that tonight is Halloween?"

"Ah," Max said. He sat down on his piano bench. "That explains a lot about the noise coming from everywhere. The Village at Halloween. Nightmare."

"You must not get out much," I said.

"I try not to," he said, proud.

"Are you the neighborhood pariah?" I asked him, hopeful.

He chuckled. "That's got to be the first time anybody has ever said that to my face. Why yes, I believe I am. At least when it comes to noise complaints." Hard, loud footsteps thumped from the ceiling. Max reached for a long broom standing against the wall. He stood up on the piano bench and banged the top of the broomstick several times against the ceiling. Then he shouted up at his upstairs neighbors, "KEEP THAT RACKET DOWN!"

Keep that racket down? I had figured Max for being about fiftysomething years old, but sleuth girl with the old movie database in her head now had to judge that based on the ceiling-swatting broom and the dime-store dialogue of a grouchy-old-man-ruining-everyone's-good-time-in-a-Mickey-Rooney-movie, Max could possibly be closer to a thousand years old.

In response to the racket the upstairs neighbor thumped several times more on the floor. Then, from the neighbor's courtyard window, we heard "FUCK YOU, MAX!"

Max smiled, refuting my binoculars impression of him as the mystery man with the permanent frown. While live and in person Max's smile appeared much in need of teeth whitener, or possibly dentures would be the better way to go, it nonetheless reflected him as an old soul who clearly would be this lost soul Cyd Charisse's first new companion in her new life. "New York," Max said. "I love it!"

TweLVE

The name flashing on my cell phone reminded me that I haven't
picked up a book in a very long time.

Luis.

The name, not a book. Luis whose aunt knows my bio-dad,
Luis who drove me around the first summer I spent in New York
when I was sixteen. And, sorry to be a shallow girl here, but Luis of
the gorgeous athlete body, the wavy-slick black hair, the honey eyes
and cinnamon skin, and 'scuse me, lisBETH, the total heterosexual
swagger. Luis who, while no Shrimp, was also no George. Luis was
familiar. Familiarly enticing. (See: Earlier desire for uncomplicated
hook-up.)

"Are you going to answer that or not?" Max said, his hostile
expression indicating disapproval of ring tones belching out the

South Park song "Uncle Fucka" (Best song ever not involving KC and the Sunshine Band).

I sat outside in Max's garden (access! mission accomplished!), reclining on the hammock situated directly underneath a clothes-line that had country flags hanging from clothespins, instead of wet socks and reminder notes to water the plants. As I swayed on the hammock, Bolivia flew proudly over my face, with Namibia blowing a gentle breeze on my ankles. So much better than a Halloween coming-out party with Danny-boy strangers.

Even the phone's vibration felt good in my hand.

Loo-eese. Luis who's only a few years older than me but for whom I was still jailbait the summer I was sixteen, despite our one hot and heavy make-out session that was, 'scuse me again, cut short by the swagger of lisBETH's unexpected arrival into our scene that night.

"I gotta take this one," I told Max. *You have no idea.*

Luis is like a chapter from a book I put on hold and now I'm ready to take out.

"Rude ring tone," Max muttered, glaring at my cell. "Cole Porter it's not."

Max got up from his hot-pink-painted chair under the hammer-and-sickle flag lamp shade, where he'd been hanging with me for the last hour, eating cupcakes and smoking his pipe. The detective in me was sorry for the abrupt end to the getting-to-know-Max-time, but she could fill out her report later, after investigating the Luis interruption.

The report would detail these Max-facts:

(1) Mystery man is no mystery—Max will tell you anything, just ask;

(2) He earns his living as a composer, creating song jingles for commercials, TV shows, and movies;

(3) His true love, Tony, died from AIDS before I was even born, in the time before medications could contain the disease. And while Max shares my desire to experience true love again, meeting a new guy is hard, given Max's agoraphobic tendencies, which only further endears him to me, because how amazing are cranky people on a quest for true love, anyway—it's so cute and unrealistic;

(4) Max eats random food like beets from a can and lox chips, etc., because he is very into consumption of small food items but not so into real meals, for no other reason than "just because," and if Max were three generations younger, I would suggest Just Because as the name for his queercore swing band, because the name completely explains Max; and

(5) While Max does know many secrets of the universe (Laurence Olivier and Danny Kaye had a thing going on!—

rachel cohn

my supposedly fine-tuned gaydar would never have deduced this based on their performances in either *Rebecca* or *White Christmas,* respectively), Max knows nothing about Hot Nude Yoga, though he agrees the flyer, retrieved from Mrs. VonHuffingUptight's handbag for Max's inspection, is enticing indeed. Like most things in this city, I'll have to find out about it myself.

As Max stepped back inside his apartment for a bathroom break, I answered the call of the Luis. "Hey there," I murmured, in some previously unknown voice, as though Max's pipe smoke had wafted straight down my throat and was just waiting for Luis to check in so the voice could go all husky. And maybe get its owner lucky.

Luis did that New York thing I love of skipping over pleasantries. He jumped right in like the center hoops-player he is. "Rumor has it you moved to New York instead of Berkeley with your boyfriend like you were threatening to do last spring when we ran into each other and exchanged digits. Rumor also has it the boyfriend *es historia* and that you've been doing the Ma'hattan thing going on three months already and haven't rung my cell once to let me know. 'Sup with that?" That deep voice, holding out the promise of sculpted biceps and ripple-tight abs. That Nuyorican accent, hard and street-smart fast with soft Spanish echoes. Sigh.

I couldn't resist busting his chops, a short little detour on what would surely be my opportunity to bust out. I teased, "What makes you think it's appropriate to call a girl so late? Are you aware that it's around midnight?" I could hear the Halloween parade revelry going by in the background of Luis's phone. He idled within my vicinity. Rumor must have told him that the Village Halloween parade vicinity was also within the new neighborhood realm of Cyd Charisse.

Luis said, "Are you aware that I don't care? And if you're so concerned about the late night hour, why's your phone turned on, anyway?"

I took my shot to get right down to business—I could never play hoops guard, because I am totally forward material. "Are you aware of the rumor that I turned eighteen not too long ago?" Jailbait no longer, but totally willing to temporarily be taken captive.

Luis laughed. "Rumor might have heard that. So what's taking you so long? I'm right now in front of the Village b-ball court where I ran into you last time, right by your brother's apartment. You know the Mick D's round the corner from the court? How about I wait for your vanilla shake self outside the front, say—half an hour from now?"

"Rumor has it that vanilla shakes like some hot fries with extra salt to go along with," I said, jumping up from the hammock. "Rumor expects you to be prepared when she arrives."

I love rumors, at least now that I am freed from the boarding school drama that was my high school past and the rumors aren't vicious (if true) ones about me. They're delicious ones bringing Loo-eeses to me.

There's the key difference between me and those Nancy and Trixie sleuth girls. They never get to grow up and get theirs.

I do.

ThiRTeeN

Picture this.

You are striding through the Village in the middle of the night on Halloween, on your way to answer a booty call. You have permanently retired that VonHuffingUptight Halloween costume and changed into a comfortable and casual, old-school hip-hop look, with green Adidas track pants slung low on the hips, and a short, tight white Grandmaster Flash T-shirt. Your long black licorice hair is tied in a bunch behind your head, to allow maximum attention on your bare vanilla shake midriff. You've got new curves to strut, and you know it.

You do not answer a phone call from your mother on the way to this booty call.

YOU DO NOT!

Unless you are a glutton for punishment, as I apparently am.

"Cyd Charisse, why can I hear so much noise? Where are you?"

"Walking around the Village. I'm allowed."

"It's one in the morning there!"

"Which means it's ten in San Francisco. Shouldn't you be in bed by now, Mom?"

"I'm in the last trimester of my fourth pregnancy. I have two children running me ragged." (False. She has a nanny and a housekeeper whom my younger siblings run ragged.) "I do not sleep." (Translation: The doctor cut off her Ambien supply until the baby's born.) "I try to keep Ash and Josh from killing each other, I worry about you flung out in New York City, and I go to the bathroom regularly." (Fair enough.) "But I do not sleep." (Clearly.)

Silent pause followed by an audible sigh. On my part, not hers—though I'd just pulled off her signature move—the "Nancy Classic," as I call it. I swear, I am becoming her. It's scary. However, I further swear I won't end up like her, a fresh young thing who left home at eighteen to start a new life in Manhattan and wound up knocked up by a married man.

"Mom, why are you calling me?" *Don't ask me about the Plan, don't ask me about the Plan.*

"I wanted to hear how Danny's party for you went."

Phew. I could be honest about that one. "I don't know. I left it."

"You what? Isn't that a little rude?" A lot rude, probably. I had other things on my mind. Like that I was within a block of the Luis meeting point, and I didn't need my mother ruining my mood. "CC, are you still there? I don't like the sound of this. You're not getting into trouble again, are you? I thought we were through with that. I thought—"

Done. Click. Phone turned off. The CC signature move.

Everybody's good at something. Danny bakes. Shrimp paints. Max composes. I . . . don't know my own special skill yet, but if I had to nominate one it would probably be my ability to wear skirts that barely fall below my ass and yet somehow not come off looking like a skanky ho either. (I think.)

My mother? Her special skill is never letting me forget that once upon a time I was a so-called bad girl, a little princess who was pregnant on her sixteenth birthday. Expelled from posh boarding school soon after the pregnancy was terminated—and all because of a bad ex-boyfriend, who not only didn't help out with the clinic visit, but was also dealing drugs out of his dorm room (with me in it). All the trouble that came before I went home to San Francisco, grew up a little, fished out a Shrimp, and then bravely threw him back into the sea.

I'm on my own now. I don't have to answer to my mother. I made my sacrifice.

As I approached the meeting spot, I noticed Luis's center court height first. I loved my pint-size surfer boy Shrimp, but there's something intoxicating about a guy taller than me. For one thing, at my height there aren't that many of them dudes. For another thing, those extra inches towering over me somehow feel protective, and safe, and sexy—at least on the right guy. After Luis's height, my eyes honed in on the gold cross chain dangling over the black hair on his tank-top-attired chest's luscious cinnamon skin. The shine of the gold cross chain felt like a divine signal calling out to me, *Hail Mary, how've ya been? Is this center court body the answer to your prayers, or what?*

"Damn," Luis said. His hands mimicked the outline of a curvy female silhouette. "You look good." I believed his sincerity. He looked like he was about to salivate, and not on account of the milk shake in his hands. "Different. All grown up and filled out. You sure ain't no scrawny Lolita girl anymore. You still carry that old rag doll?"

"Gingerbread retired," I told Luis. "She came along for the ride to Manhattan, but she mostly just hangs out in my bed in my new apartment now. She's not into traveling in my handbag all the time anymore. She's got, you know, canasta games with the various bedroom tchotchkes to figure out. Better ways to spend her time than looking after me."

"Does she now?" FUCK! That Luis smile. He handed me a bag of piping hot fries. I could taste the extra salt.

Two summers ago when Gingerbread wandered this city with me, lodged inside my handbag, she shared my crush on Luis. She also shared a certain psychic vibe with me, and I could feel it returning full force now, wafting over from her current doll emeritus state of retirement in my bedroom. I knew she would not only authorize, she would also absolve me for the sins I knew I was about to commit.

FOURTEEN

So this was what the Walk of Shame looked like.

I stumbled past the white hallway walls leading from my bedroom, but the walls had turned psychedelic, swirls of sherbet pinks, reds, and oranges dizzying me. The hallway's round ceiling light appeared to hang extra low, hovering like a UFO, attempting to grab my throbbing head and twist it, throttle it, destroy it. Although the distance to my destination was only several feet, each step forward felt like two steps back, as if I were attempting to cross an infinite, barren dessert, parched, instead of simply trying to find my way to the bathroom, to puke.

I don't know how long my bathroom prison sentence, prostrate before the porcelain goddess, lasted. I could have been there for five minutes or an hour. The time-space continuum blanked out.

Danny stood leaning against the hallway wall when I finally emerged—or was it crawled? (felt like it)—from the bathroom. That hallway wall definitely played favorites, because it did not appear to sprout monster-goblin hands trying to envelop Danny, to harsh him.

My arms reached for a table to steady myself, but my shaking hands found no such support. My blurry vision tried to make out the time on the wall clock behind Danny. It may have read noon, or it may have flashed a rainbow-sherbet-colored neon sign: *Care to puke again? Care to puke again?*

Danny said, "Luis left about an hour ago, if that's who you're looking for."

Luis? Who's Luis?

Want to be magically transported back to bedroom without any physical effort on my part. Want peace, not *Loo-eese.*

Head. Pound. Head. Pound.

In response to my silence Danny continued, "Think you can make it to the living room for a little talk?"

From the tone of his voice, no way was the Talk going to be "little."

"No," I muttered. "Back to bed."

I staggered past Danny. I could barely find my way, for all the unkempt strings of hair falling in front of my face, but as I returned to my bedroom, I could see through the hair enough to spot a tiny Dixie cup on my nightstand, with what appeared to be green Jell-O inside it. As I collapsed onto my bed, an unopened condom wrapper fell to the floor from underneath the pillow at the far side of the bed.

Oh, that Luis.

Oh, shouldn't that wrapper be open—and discarded in the trash, after its contents had been properly used?

Vague memories crept into the available 1 percent of my conscious waking state. Something about Jell-O shots at a salsa club where Luis's friend worked and wouldn't card me. Salsa dancing with Luis even though I don't know how to salsa dance. Yes, yes, it was coming back, 28 percent and getting stronger, now I saw it: Two bodies jiggling, pressing together, the cinnamon boy can really dance and the vanilla girl really can't, but it doesn't matter, there they are, grooving and laughing, gulping *agua* with Jell-O chasers. Catch up with them now, *Ay ay ay,* they're making out in the bathroom (oh, so sweet), and hello, they're racing back to vanilla's apartment, toting along some extra Jell-O for the ride. Folks, they're too smashed and turned on to bother using the condom.

Amnesia, come back and stay awhile, why don't you? At least lodge long enough to drown the feeling of PANIC PANIC PANIC shoving its way into my hellacious hangover. Please?

Kids, do not try this at home.

I went off birth control when Shrimp left for New Zealand.

The pill made me feel bloated and crazy, which, because irony loves making a fool of me, was the same feeling I had today. Only now I had a 100 percent better chance of trouble like I had before, at least based on the red dot calendar calculations shooting poison darts into my throbbing head.

Kids. No.

Danny followed me into my room. "Sleep it off," he said. "Because when you wake up, we're having a serious talk."

Who did he think he was anyway, my father?

Danny slammed my bedroom door behind him as he stepped out. HARD.

Alas, he thought he was my mother.

I stared up at the ceiling from my bed. How did Gingerbread get into a sitting position up on the ceiling fan?

Right. Luis = tall. Luis = frisky.

"I'll get you down when I wake up," I promised Gingerbread. "Hang in there. And sorry 'bout the pun."

No worries, she intuited back. *From up here I can enjoy the view out your bedroom rear window. Notice the row of empty Dixie cups lined up along the windowsill? You don't even like Jell-O, you poser with the sweet tooth. Yessiree, it's a fine view up here. Much better than the one you left me with last night, that beautiful Luis writhing around on this bed with you, and you—*

"Shut up," I said, and fell into the sleep of the dead.

"Cupcake?" Danny asked zombie CC several hours later, dusk time, vampire time, HAMMER TIME, after I'd awoken and pulled off the miraculous feat of a return lap across the Walk of Shame, this time to the living room. Danny held out a tray of the previous night's party cupcakes to me. He must truly hate me.

Stomach. Lurch.

My love affair with cupcakes: Officially. On. Hiatus.

I fell onto the sofa and placed a throw pillow over my eyes. "Be gentle, Danny," I murmured. "Please?"

"Gentle?" Danny asked. I felt him plop down onto the end of the sofa. He placed my bare feet on his lap. "Gentle to the same girl who ditched the party that was being thrown in her honor last night? Gentle to she who disappeared for hours with no explanation?"

"I tried to tell you," I whispered. "I went back up to the party after hanging out with Max. I was going to tell you I was meeting up with Luis. But you didn't see me. You were making out with Jerry Lewis. You were—"

"I'm not finished," Danny interrupted. "Be quiet because I have a lot to say, and I don't want to hear your sorry defenses."

Ah, here was the harsh. Brother, that is.

FifTeen

Rules.

In my mind I'm eighteen years old, independent. In Danny's mind we may not have grown up in the same household, but I'm still his little sister, and he's "responsible" for me.

And so he decreed: If I'm going to stay out all night, I have to check in to let Danny know where I am. I shall never be thrown a party again, or invited to one he's going to, if I'm just going to ignore everyone, and then bail. The broken leg drama is over, done, *finito,* and given that I'm enrolled for only one culinary class (um, right), I'd better get myself a damn job to get some structure for the rest of my time, or I should think about moving back home to San Francisco until I'm grown up enough to accept the responsibilities that come with sharing this apartment with him. And by the way,

CC, you're not independent if your parents are paying your rent and you're not being held accountable for your actions.

Also, drunken hook-ups are not cool when brought back to an apartment shared with a roommate—especially a roommate who's a brother. Don't do it. He wouldn't do it to me, so I shouldn't do that to him—that is, leave Danny in awkward morning-after conversation with the object of my previous night's affection, or leave him to answer phone calls on the house line from my mother wanting to know if I made it home safely, and at what time.

Lastly, said Danny, "When I first met you, I thought the 'Little Hellion' label pinned on you by your family back in San Francisco was perhaps a bit unfair. Now I get it."

Ah, the return of the Little Hellion. Cheap shot. Maybe I deserved it? Last night I was a pretty cheap date. All it took was a bag of salty fries to make me go rated X. I mean, the sex part, at least what I remember of it, was quite nice. But was getting trashed so necessary to get me there? The problem with "quite nice" was that, despite keeping a Just in Case condom available in my purse, the not bothering to actually use said condom when the case called for it could bring about quite a few unpleasant consequences. Not such nice ones. And one in particular that I fully remember.

Don't anybody dare sing "Oops! . . . I Did It Again" at me.

So. My whole life I waited to live on my own in Manhattan,

and this was the person I had strived to become? Chick-flick-lit girl moves to Gotham, meets charming rake, charms rake with her spunk and quirky sense of style. Wacky hijinks involving sea green cocktails and spicy stud-boys ensue.

Bleh.

This transition to living in Manhattan was supposed to be easier. On TV it always is. When the spunky gal takes on the big city, she encounters certain obstacles but always survives through a combination of wit, fabulous shoes, secondary character friends who are far more interesting than she is but whose looks don't meet the network's beauty standard, and that grit and determination thing. Where was the dialogue for the strung out still-teenage girl getting chewed out by her brother—and he didn't even know the worst of her offenses from last night?

"Any questions?" Danny asked, his list of decrees finished.

Yeah. Where's the closest Planned Parenthood office?

"No," I mumbled. I pressed my face into the couch, so it would look like I wanted to rest, but really what I wanted was for Danny not to see my tears. I cried because I saw myself reflected back in Danny's eyes, full of disappointment. The hangover in my heart felt worse than the one in my head.

Guess what, Danny? My real mistake was so way bigger than ditching our party, or pursuing the desire for casual, uncomplicated sex that seems to make a brother-roommate so uncomfortable. That's what!

The real mistake was the drunken lack of inhibition, when Jell-O prohibition—or at least moderation—could just as easily have led to "quite nice," only without the complicated variants of an "uh-oh" hangover. But after hearing Danny's tirade of rules, I couldn't confide in him about the real mistake. Or wouldn't. Not after he'd thrown the Little Hellion label in my face.

But if the Little Hellion had been ready to go hog wild with the big fessing up, she might have found the not-chick-flick-lit girl dialogue to silence her Gotham roommate's tirade. *Danny, I assume you think you're being all Protective Big Brother, setting down the law about responsibility, but I know plenty on that subject already, I assure you. I just fuck up sometimes. Don't you? And if you had any idea what it feels like to sit in a clinic, alone, chewing on fingernails while your heart palpitates and your soul disintegrates, waiting for a nurse to call you inside the saddest of procedure rooms, to then wait for a doctor whom you don't even know to undo your body's accountability to your irresponsibility, you would back off. Except you're a boy with no ovaries to worry about, and maybe you think you could imagine it, but really you couldn't. I've been there—I don't have to imagine it.*

Danny stood up from the sofa. He placed a blanket over my body, and a quick kiss on the back of my sobbing/throbbing head.

I cried because I had wanted so much to live here with my

hero new-older brother Danny, but despite our *ka-pow!* soul connection, we had not yet experienced the investment of time and trust that might have clued him in that the real reason for my tears had nothing to do with my hangover and his disappointment in me, but with a New-Old frustration with myself.

SixTeen

Turns out there is decent coffee to be found in this city. I just didn't look hard enough. The perfection was right under my nose—literally.

The perfection could be found thanks to a voice mail left on my cell phone in the middle of the night by my friend Helen back in San Francisco. *"CC, oops you did it again is right! But don't panic. Pharmaceutical conglomerates more likely interested in positive profit margins rather than in selflessly serving women's health crises have devised a solution to your negative situation. It's called the morning-after pill. Ask for it at Planned Parenthood ASAP, and have a nice, relieved day. Call me after. Dumbfuck."*

My heart and head eased by Helen's message, I stumbled out of bed at noon on The Day After, only to be urgently informed by my stomach that the last step on my hangover recovery program would require a pizza slice. Although the corner pizza place was not the best place to grabba slice in the neighborhood (the best place would be Pedro's place of employ), it was the nearest, as hangover head demanded a slice within a one-block walking radius of the apartment (catch up with you later, Pedro). So imagine my shock when I took on the hardship of this half-block walk to the pizza place, only to see a sign taped in the window: CLOSED TODAY DUE TO ELECTRICAL FIRE. Horror.

And yet, my nose was not entirely displeased. Because from where I stood, at this corner block that usually smelled of cheese, tomato sauce, and beer, my nose picked up instead the scent of rich, pungent, heart-rate-racing coffee. What the Kona? Perhaps the upside of the posthangover haze was a heightened sense of smell, but . . . holy cowabunga caffeination!

I eyed the neighboring shops, trying to home in on the heavenly scent's beacon. My eyes spied a faded sign with missing letters at the shop next door to the pizza place.

L U _ C H _ O N E _ T E

Really?

Somehow in all my time either visiting with Danny or living with him on this block, I'd never taken particular notice of this rundown lunch shop; it flew completely off the radar of this San

Francisco coffee snob. If it's true that people judge books by their covers, then I had judged the luncheonette by its exterior window, which offered a view inside of a long old-fashioned Formica counter, Dairy Queen–type booths against the side walls, and fold-up bridge tables and chairs randomly strewn around the rest of the available space. The place was peopled by a smattering of old folks playing chess or cards, and blue-collar worker types, the work-boot-wearin', regular coffee drinkin' folk who definitely do not flock to the decaf skim vanilla soy latte establishments of the laptop/cell-phone-using student or yuppie set. It was the kind of ancient, real-deal cool mom-and-pop place you just knew was on its way out—soon to be replaced by yet another Gap or Starbucks, once the lease ran out and the building owners jacked up the rent in order to get the old tenants out. Why go in and get attached only to get your heart broken when the L U _ C H _ O N E _ T E sign got replaced by one that would drop no letters to spell out: L-I-Q-U-I-D-A-T-I-O-N.

But that smell. I had to take the risk.

I barged inside and walked up to the counter. A young goth-punk of unknown age—hard to tell specifically, what with his shaved head, goateed chin, tunneled ears, nose and lip rings, fully tattooed arms, and heavy black eyeliner—stood at the cash register, playing on a Game Boy.

"May I have a cappuccino, please?" I asked. I wanted straight-up capp simplicity. No flavored shots, no particular milk requests, no demands for diorama latte art formed in the coffee/foam mixture. Etc. My heart beat extra fast in anticipation. I knew I'd found the promised land. While my actions are often questionable, my instincts are impeccable.

"Nope," young punk said, not looking up from his Game Boy.

"Excuse me?" I said.

Still not looking up, as if I should have known better, he said, "Rita. She quit last week. She was the only person who knew how to work the espresso machine." He tilted his head over his shoulder, indicating the cooking area behind him. "Fresh brewed pot of coffee over there on the regular coffeemaker. Help yourself."

I did. I stepped behind the counter, grabbed the towel from the rack underneath the coffeemaker, wiped down the counter, which seriously hadn't been given any attention in like a decade, found the mugs in like an insta-second, and poured myself a fresh one. An immediate and happy sense of déjà vu, normalcy by way of working a coffee establishment countertop, eroded the last vestiges of hangover.

The coffee taste banished the Jell-O aftertaste. Judging by my whizzed-up heartbeat: Perfection. Even without the foamed milk. I knew it. Kona. My nose does not lie. Someone here had a good connection to an excellent wholesale coffee distributor, as well as a good sense for how to grind and brew java.

Still, I wanted what I wanted. "Do you mind if I make myself a capp, buddy?" I asked Game Boy. Perched like a grande dame on the counter, next to the coffeemaker, was a true vision of beauty: a La Marzocco espresso machine—only like the Cadillac of professional machines!

Now he looked up from the Game Boy. "You know how to work the machine?"

I did.

My delivery of a cappuccino work of art to his cash register stand got him to finally put aside the Game Boy. He took a sip. He did not smile, although a perfect peak of foamed milk resting on one of his lip rings warmed his face. He said, "Rita worked the afternoon shifts. You can have her shift if you want. Or just show up whenever you feel like it; I don't particularly care. But you should know, Rita quit cuz she wasn't making enough in tips. As you can see, this place doesn't have many customers. Rita was all uptight about money, man. She was like—"

"I'll take it," I said. Who cared about Rita? No job interview, no forms to fill out? I'm there. I pointed to his ratty T-shirt, which had a photo of a band performing on a ship plank with a masthead emblazoned with the words, "HMS Sucks-A-Four." I asked, "What does the shirt mean?"

"HMS Sucks-A-Four. My old band. Four guys. Punk covers of Gilbert and Sullivan opera shit. Sucky band, but good times, man. That's what it's all about, you know? Now I'm in a new band. We're called Mold. Much better than the old band. No more Gilbert and Sullivan, though. Bummer." He swilled another coffee sip. "Damn, that's one fine brew. You really know how to get a foam head on the steamed milk. So, you in school or whatever?"

"Nope. Just basic slackness."

"Cool. So you wanna start today or, like, some other day?"

"Today is good."

Game Boy–boy retrieved an apron from underneath the counter. When I put it on, a band sticker across the chest area read MOLD. Such an inviting advertisement in a food establishment.

"You have a name, Mold?" I asked him.

"Johnny," he said.

"Like as in Cash or as in Rotten?"

"Like as in Quest. Or, like as in my granddad. Old Man Johnny the First owns this place. Wants us to keep it open till he kicks it. Sentimental attachment and all. You got one of those name things?"

"Cyd Charisse. As in dancer. But my friends and family call me CC. As in myself."

"Okay. I'll just call you Myself."

"Good enough, Mold."

My lily-white hand met the Mikado/Penzance pirate emperor tattoo of his handshake. Here's to a beautiful L U _ C H _ O N E _ T E friendship, Myself and Mold.

Now all I had to do was take care of the little Planned Parenthood piece of business, and I could be truly ready to rock this new New York life—sober, contraceptively covered to allow for more Luis time, and with a master espresso machine to master and a Johnny Mold boss to usher in my next quest.

When caffeination calls, sometimes it pays to look a little harder.

SeVENTeeN

My New-Olds haunt me in Washington Square Park.

My old friend Helen must have wanted *everyone* in Greenwich Village to know the whereabouts I haunted. She yelled so loud, I swear she could be heard all the way from San Francisco through my cell phone in New York, broadcast for everyone to hear within the entire expanse of the park, where I sat on a bench awaiting the arrival of my new friend Chucky.

"NOW THAT I'VE GOT YOU LIVE ON THE PHONE INSTEAD OF VOICE MAIL, LET ME BE CLEAR: DON'T YOU DARE EVER SAY 'OOPS' WHEN I ASK YOU HOW YOU GOT YOURSELF INTO THIS SITUATION . . . A SECOND TIME!" Helen screamed at me, then a phlegm gobbet mercifully caught in her throat, and her voice toned down after she cleared it up. "If you didn't learn from your own previous experience, didn't you at least learn from mine? Once again, let's review. CC, WHAT WERE YOU THINKING?"

"I wasn't thinking," I said. "I was wasted."

"Yeah, so was I. Now I'm four months pregnant. And married. When you left San Francisco, I was supposedly on my way to college. But 'Oops' had other plans in mind for me. Can you believe I'm living at home and working in my mom's restaurant—like, the life I swore I would never have? 'Oops' is a crafty little fucker, don't you think?" Helen's words spouted disappointment in her unexpected circumstances, yet her laughing tone indicated otherwise. The camera phone picture she had flashed me, her dumpling cheeks puffed in a broad grin, her hands placed on her bulging belly, certainly proved it: Helen was not only knocked up, but happy about it—at least now that the initial shock (and morning sickness) had gone away. Marrying her true love, Eamon, and having a baby by the time she turned nineteen wasn't something she'd expected or wanted, but having gotten that lot in life, it turned out to fit her nicely. "Did you take the EC at the clinic?" she asked me.

"I did. Thanks for the information." The emergency contraception made me feel a little nauseous, and I'd probably beg Chucky for us to rethink our Tasti D-Lite plans, but at least I'd visited the clinic within seventy-two hours of the Luis experience. Thanks to Helen's emergency voice mail advice, I'd gotten the EC in time, along with a renewed prescription for birth control, my New choice.

Oh, and one more thing, Luis? Let's definitely continue with the body-melding friendship, but in the future: no glove, no love. New-Old double-packed protection action. I'd like more "quite nice," just without the panic hangover, please.

Helen said, "You oughta prostrate yourself with thankful kisses on that nasty New York ground right now, sister. With this baby starting to kick inside my tummy, I can't imagine how different my life would be today if I'd known last summer that there even was a morning-after pill. But by the time the denial went away and I went to the doctor, it was too late. Already pregnant. Damn Guinness and damn irresistible Eamon." She sighed the true love classic. Damn jealousy.

"But you're happy with your decision," I said. Because even if she hadn't known about the EC at the time of the damn Guinness hangover, Helen still could have made the Old choice I'd once made, back in my boarding school days. How relieved was I to not have to make that choice again? Thank you, pharmaceutical conglomerates.

"I am," she said, content. Helen would march on Sacramento and Washington a million times over to support a woman's right to choose—but it wasn't a choice she could make for herself. Which I totally respect. "Were there any crazy protesters outside the clinic office?"

"Not as many as the last time, back when I was at boarding school, but yeah, there were a couple."

"Didja give 'em the finger like I asked you to, from me?"

"Check out the picture I flashed ya."

"Good job." Pause. Then: "OHMYGOD, CC, what did you do to your hair?"

This was the same question Chucky had for me when she arrived at our park bench meeting spot. I didn't bother explaining about the New-Old rite of passage de-stress/de-tress hair change. I just tugged a strand of my new New Wave, Astor Place hair—totally a geometry-equation-equaling-chaos cut, with uneven bangs and the left side of my head clipped in an asymmetrical design so that strands fell in long-short random patterns, and the right side chopped to shoulder length and streaked indigo, like as in mood— and said, "I wanted to not worry about bad hair days for a long while. Now every day will be a bad hair day."

"Excellent logic," Chucky said. "Sorta like being a couch potato, avoiding the Advil, and eating plenty of junk food when you're PMS'ing, to ensure you feel max crazy."

"Exactly," I stated. I looked up into the twilight clouds, awaiting the dark starry night sky, whose astral projections would surely confirm that Chucky and I were going to be cosmic-kismet friends.

Our park bench conversation definitely promised such a possibility. Chucky didn't mind sticking around in the park rather than grabbing a bite, so we sat cross-legged opposite each other on the bench, watching the crowds and talking, munching street vendor honey-roasted cashews (Chucky), and very bravely turning down the weed offered us at a steep discount by a very cute traveling white-boy-Rasta-salesman (me). We talked about our dreams, which turned out to be pretty similar. Chucky wants to marry her true love Marine-boy, Tyrell, and eventually get a small business loan so she can buy out Mrs. Kim's nail shop when Mrs. Kim retires. I want to find another true love, and eventually start my own business too, maybe a café like Danny and Aaron used to have. Like me, Chucky has no interest whatsoever in the college experience.

"So, are we like entrepreneurial wannabe soul sisters?" I asked Chucky after about the second hour of hanging and chatting, save for one coffee and bathroom run. I loved that as the night sky settled over the city, I could look up over the marble arch at the entrance of Washington Square Park to see the Empire State Building lit up in blue (in honor of my new hair, I'm sure), but despite the contemplative nature of the dark sky and the peaceful lit-up building beacon, the whole while we'd been talking, the park never ceased humming with action. It had its own pulse, like the city. A beautiful model-type lady walked by us, wearing a live snake wrapped around her waist like a belt, her bored model gaze indifferent to the fact that she had a live boa encircling her body instead of, you know, a non-organic feather boa left over from some pride parade. Kids played on the swings, and parents shared private-school-acceptance-rate tragedies. Park performers—jugglers, mimes, the guy painted silver who stood perfectly still, the blind banjo player and one-legged fiddler who played kick-ass hillbilly music with a hip-hop beat, the obligatory crazy people shouting for Jesus— all livened the hang-out groove, as did the chilly late fall air settling over our shivering shoulders.

Even if Danny and I are wading into a new avoidance stage of our roommate connection, I still can't believe how much I love this city and how glad I am to live here. I may eventually have to give up living with Danny if doing so means rules that I thought I out-grew when I moved out of my parents' house, but I couldn't give up on Manhattan. Not now when it's just getting good—and cold, like San Francisco.

I told Chucky about my new job, about the Kona and La Marzocco and Johnny Mold. She said, "How you gonna pay your rent at a job with no customers? My tips barely cover food, my MetroCard, and laundry money."

Without thinking I said, "My parents pay my rent and help out with expenses. I just have to earn my own spending money." So maybe the caffeine wasn't as potently dangerous as Jell-O, but too much coffee = too much information. I hadn't needed to announce my privileged status, especially to a new friend who'd just spent an hour telling me about her mother's boyfriend who kicked Chucky out of their apartment when she turned eighteen and left her to sleep on the couch at her cousin's place till she could afford her own place.

"Oh," Chucky said. "So that's how it is." I sensed it wasn't just the autumn night air suddenly changing our vibe to chill. "How lucky for you."

I decided to change the subject back to a safe one: cute boys. "The thing with the ambulance driver George guy never took off," I told Chucky.

"*¿Por que?*" she said, smiling and hopefully warming back up to me.

"Bad first date. Also, he pronounced 'library' as 'libe-ary.' I have a thing about that. Also with people who say 'nuke-ular' instead of 'nuke-lee-ar.' Turns me off."

"With standards like that, *mamacita,* don't be surprised if you're single just a little while longer," Chucky said, laughing. Phew.

I showed her a picture of Luis on my camera phone. "Not totally," I said. "I've got a Mister Right Now." I didn't want Chucky to think I would camera-phone-photo a guy whom I'd just picked up any ol' where, take cheesecake shots of his laughing eyes, bare chest, and a hand holding a Dixie cup, so I added, "Luis used to work for my bio-dad."

Chucky's face looked less than enthused as she looked upon the gorgeous cinnamon vision that is Loo-eese. She said, "Oh" again, followed by some muttering in Spanish that went way beyond my twenty-word *español* vocab, but from the expression on her face, I suspect it translated to something like: "At least I thought I liked you, before I knew you were chasing after a hired help boy in my shade. . . ."

I knew I wasn't paranoid when, just like that, Chucky stood up and said, "It's late and I should be going. I'll call you later."

By the look on her face, I'd say the friendship that rocketed off to such a great start was not going to progress any further.

She won't be calling.

In the responsibility column of my New life, I'd gotten a job and back on contraception. But in the "Oops" column of my Old habit of pushing too hard too fast, I suspected I could add Chucky to the Danny pile of not-*sympaticos*.

EighTeeN

I stood before La Marzocco for the come-to-Jesus talk that's necessary to bless a barista's new relationship with an espresso machine.

"Look," I told La Marzocco. "My track record for making new friends in this city is iffy right now, so I have to call it straight with you: You and I are gonna be friends—no ifs, ands, or buts about it. I realize you have been neglected and unappreciated in the past, but all that's about to change. So, I vow to you: I will keep you cleaned and maintained. I will let you take as long as you need to get primed before you're ready to serve up. All I ask from you in return is absolute loyalty and unconditional love. Do we understand one another, Holiness?"

La Marzocco churned out the perfect shot in agreement. Amen.

My new boss Johnny Mold sanctified my new job with his own

form of baptism. He chugged down the perfect latte I'd made for him, then pulled out a gift from his jeans pocket.

He said, "Here. This belonged to the person who had the job before you. I adjusted it for you." He handed me a nameplate. The piece had a new name scratched in blue ink onto a piece of paper that had been cut to fit and messily taped over the nameplate's old name. Good-bye, "Rita." Hello, "Myself."

I started to say "thank you?" but Johnny Mold wasn't interested in my tender appreciation of his artistry. Instead, he sermonized a new employee initiation speech. His Game Boy in one hand, he pointed around the room with his other hand. "Be careful sitting down in the chairs at that table by the window. Kinda wobbly. That table over there, it's kinda a lot wobbly, so be careful when you set drinks down on it. As you can see here, we don't really have a proper kitchen, just a grill for short orders. Don't stand too close on account of the occasional electrical fire. Oh, and the cook doesn't always show up for work, so sometimes we don't serve hot food, we just serve whatever's available in the case or in the fridge, and the usual drinks and stuff."

"Sounds like a great business plan, Mold."

It's funny, but as Johnny explained the surroundings, I didn't see dilapidated fixtures. I saw potential. A fixer-upper. And that's funny *and* totally scary . . . because that's how my mother would envision the place too.

Johnny said, "What's it matter? The business will die out once my old man passes on, so I'm just gonna keep it running as long as he holds out. If he doesn't mind a business that makes no money, why should I? But if you're looking for job stability or something, you're in the wrong place."

"Job stability," I said. "Yawn."

"I think you and me are going to get on just fine."

Since there were no customers around to serve, I sat down at the counter next to Johnny. I like getting to know a new person by starting out with the big questions.

"What are you gonna do with your life once you don't have this place to run?" I asked him.

"I don't know. I guess if I ever truly thought about it, I'd say I kinda wanna be an architect."

"Every boy at some point says he wants to be an architect. What's up with that?"

It's true. It's like some biological boy imperative. No matter what level of talent or intelligence or whatever he might possess, at some stage of his life, a boy dreams of becoming an architect.

Sigh. Missing the Ocean Beach castles-in-the-cold-sand that Shrimp used to build me on lame waves, wanna-be-architect days.

Johnny said, "The first major accomplishment of my life was building the entire Death Star out of LEGOs. I was seven. That shit affects you, dude. Inspires you to want to keep building, I guess."

"Clarify. Makes you want to keep building fortresses of doom, or keep building . . . buildings generally?"

"Either/or. So long as the building doesn't get in the way of band practice."

"Good luck with that."

I might not need good luck wishes with this new job. It feels blessed already.

NINETEEN

I finally had to come out of the closet to somebody in my family, so I chose my dad.

"It's like this," I told Sid-dad over the phone. "I feel like culinary school was everybody else's dream for me, but I don't want that kind of structure in my life right now. I'm not saying later I might not want to go, but right now? No. I lasted one class."

"Cupcake," he responded, "it's your life to live as you choose. You're right, I think culinary school would have provided a good structure for your transition to living on your own, but you're also right that if it's not what you want to do, you shouldn't be doing it. That does leave a remaining question, however: What *are* you doing?"

What I am doing, Dad, is wondering what Shrimp is doing this very second. Is he staring at the moon in the New Zealand sky, wondering if I am watching it too, even with the time difference and probably it's the wrong time of day here to find it in the same place in the sky, but whatever, you get the point. What I am doing is planning to distract myself with Luis for a while and hope that heals the hurt of letting Shrimp go. I know you and Mom thought I was too young to be in a committed relationship, and you know I am proud to be an independent female and all that, but I totally think I would be handling this giantropolis transition better if Shrimp and I were sharing this new New York life together.

"I got a barista-waitress job at a place down the street from our apartment," I told Sid-dad. "I hope you're not disappointed."

At the moment that the urgent need had come upon me to call my father and then tell his secretary to interrupt his business meeting because I couldn't wait another minute to talk with him, what I was doing was sitting on a bench in a small park in the West Village near the obnoxiously popular cupcake bakery. Spying. The bakery is unfathomably one of the most fashionable places to see and be seen in the city—at least based on the line of customers out the door and down the street. The line confounded me because (1) the cupcakes from that place are not that tasty, and I should know, because I've tried them all, and (2) the attitude from the wait staff is ridiculous—you'd think they were selling Tiffany tiaras and Rolls-Royce cars and not tiny round pieces of cake with frosting gobbed on top. If I hadn't made it my new mission to avoid Danny and his rules, I would so take him up on the offer to go work with him part-time instead of taking on the L U _ C H _ O N E _ T E gig. Danny and I could expand his cupcake business beyond selling to small retail outlets and into our own empire.

"Why would I be disappointed?" Sid-dad asked.

"Because I'm not some go-getter who's all perky and like 'I'm going to get a job in the mail room at some superfantastic corporation and work my way up to the top, no matter how long it takes, gosh darnit!'"

He laughed. "I'm just happy you're working. And I think you might be more of a go-getter than you yourself realize. You just need to do it on your own timetable. Will this new job allow you the time off work to come home for Christmas? We've got the baby's room set up for its impending arrival in December, and Ash and Josh can't wait to see you . . ."

"I still haven't changed my mind that Ash can't have my bedroom." I have no intention of moving back home to San Francisco, but that doesn't mean I don't want the option to remain available to me. Just in case.

"Noted," Sid-dad said. "Just don't come home and expect to find your childhood Barbie collection in the pristine condition in which you left it in the box at the top of your closet. There may have been a massacre when Ash was denied the room change. Let's just say certain doll parts were roughed up, and clothes violated, and leave it at that."

Good ol' Ash. Bless her heart and her macabre Barbie fixation. I miss home.

When Autumn arrived for our regular park-sitting during her ditching of her Lit Hum class (and I still don't know what "Lit Hum" means, but I am imagining pornographic poses amongst philosophizing old white guys who like to hum together while they bang each other in that fine ancient Greek tradition), she asked, "Why are we here instead of Central Park?"

I pointed to the cupcake eaters on the bench opposite us. "I hate those people. They need to be destroyed."

"The cupcake eaters or the cupcake makers?"

"Makers. And also, I've decided Central Park is too far to go. Aaron said I would turn into one of those New Yorkers who does not like to go beyond a ten-block radius of my apartment, and it turns out he's right. Besides, don't you agree the rainbow mecca of Greenwich Village is way cooler than Central Park?"

"You're just being lazy and you know it. But I don't mind the travel because the farther away from that college campus I go, the happier I am. So listen. I have to come out to you about something."

"You're straight? Is it because you never got over when you

were in fourth grade and wanted to marry Justin Timberlake?"

Autumn shoved my side. "Get over yourself. I wanted to marry Kylie Minogue. No, what I have to come out about is that I made a big decision after midterms, but I've been holding off on telling you because I wanted the idea to settle and feel right. And now it does. I'm not coming back to New York after final exams."

"No way."

"Way. I talked it out with my dad, and he supports me. I'm going to go back home to San Francisco, work and take some courses at City College next semester, then hope to transfer to Berkeley in the fall. They accepted me last year, so hopefully they will again this year. Then I can stay living at home, but afford to go to college. And afford not to be so stressed all the time that I can't concentrate on school."

I let out a major Nancy-level sigh. But I placed my arm around Autumn's shoulder and pulled her tight. She rested her head on my shoulder. "You're not mad at me?" she asked.

"Of course I'm not mad at you. I'm bummed, but I'm not mad at you. I mean, look what happened to me just from your absence at Danny's Halloween party? Drunken escapade leading to pregnancy scare and a Frigidaire situation with my brother, soon followed by my first attempt at making a new girlfriend landing with a giant THUD. But I think you made the right decision for you, and I kinda admire you for having the guts to admit that the life you thought you wanted is in fact not how you want to be living, for cutting your losses to pick up and start all over again. I think Berkeley will be great for you. But how will I survive with your permanent absence?"

"Just fine," she said.

TWENTY

Luis and I had different ideas about where to drop some beat on a Saturday night. He wanted to go to his favorite hip-hop meets salsa club up in Harlem, and I wanted to go to an emo punk meets disco funk club in the East Village. We settled on driving to a park in Weehawken, New Jersey, just on the other side of the Lincoln Tunnel, where we made out in the backseat of the fancy sedan he drives for a local car service. The car window views facing the panoramic vista over the Hudson River, with the Manhattan skyline twinkling bright and spectacular in the night sky, had been inspiring before the languor of our kissing inspired the windows to go all steamy.

His long, hard body rested on top of mine—still fully clothed—but Luis broke our lip-locking interlude to come up for air. He informed me, "I hang out here sometimes while waiting to pick up fares from Newark Airport. Did you know this park was where Alexander Hamilton and Aaron Burr had their famous duel?" Ah, Luis was a great kisser, and a history buff, too. I love smart boys. Although, if Luis ever revealed himself to me as one of those Civil War reenactor history buffs, our lust situation would definitely dead-end.

"Did you know you've New Jersey devirginized me?" I asked Luis, pulling him back down to me. This night was not my first time with Luis, but it was this Golden State girl's first time on Garden State soil. Visiting it, that is.

I pressed my groin area against Luis, wanting to feel the weight and friction of him rubbed hard on my body. But he wouldn't have it. Instead he rolled off me again and sat up and away from me, resting his head against the window, smearing clear a fresh view of the Manhattan skyline. Hey now, lovely view indeed.

"What's the problem?" I asked.

Luis said, "If you really don't want this to go further now, then you've got to stop grinding against me like that. There. It gets me all bothered."

"You were the one who said you'd bring the condom."

"You were the one who said you were going back on the pill."

"I did. But I should give it time to kick in, just to be on the safe side. Like we weren't on Halloween, you know? Because I am not taking that risk again. The fun is not worth the hangover."

I sat up and snuggled up against him. Snuggling could work.

Luis pressed the button to open the window to allow some cold air inside the car. "Burr-ito," I said. Right phrase, wrong boy.

"It'll have to do in place of a cold shower."

I placed my hand on his inner thigh. "There are other ways . . ."

He placed my hand back on my own lap. "Nah, not like that, not here," Luis said. Then, "What are we, anyway? Are we gonna go out officially, or are we gonna be just friends?"

If you have to qualify your status as "just" friends, you are not *just* friends. Scientifically impossible.

"How about we're just friends with benefits who go out occasionally but not officially, as in bring each other home to meet the fam?"

"Why, you embarrassed of me?"

Was he kidding? Who would be embarrassed to be seen with him?

"No," I said. "I'm embarrassed of *them*." Embarrassed that Danny felt the need to text message my make-out session: *B home by midnite or b sure 2 call me.*

I might as well go back to San Francisco with Autumn for all that my new home life is starting to resemble my old Alcatraz one: hostile, and with curfew threats.

TWENTY-ONE

Shake it off.

This is what I try to do when Danny asks me, "Where are you going?" in the late mornings.

"Job hunting," I tell him. *And don't ask me one more time if I want to come to your rented kitchen space to bake stupid cupcakes with you. I don't. And I know you know I never followed through with culinary school, so why don't you yell at me about that, too, get it over with. Or maybe you'd like to impose some new rule, like Thou Shalt Not Covet Thy Brother's Baking Ability If Thou Is Not Willing to Put in the Time to Learn It Thyself? And by the way, Danny boy, I already have a job, but telling you about it would force me to engage you in conversation more than our fragile relationship can tolerate right now.*

"What time ya gonna be back?"

"I'll be sure to call you and let you know." Under my breath I mutter, "Commandant."

The Danny not-love is in full swing. *Shake shake shake, shake yo' hatin' booty.*

I don't care for this brother who abandons his perfectly wonderful true love then tries to tell his younger sister how to behave. I'm beginning to loathe this roommate who leaves his smelly socks on the bathroom floor, who watches old eighties soaps on the soap classics cable channel and cackles worse than that big-haired, big-shouldered lady from *Dynasty* at all the campy dialogue (which, admittedly, I enjoyed doing with him during the leg castage time, before the hating thing started), and who sings at the stove while he prepares his daily morning ritual soft-boiled egg—the mere smell of which can now turn me mental with irritation.

And I have serious issues with this hypocrite who somehow thinks it's okay for him to occasionally have casual fling-boy Jerry Lewis spend the night, even if Jerry works on Wall Street and is gone from the apartment long before I wake up so it's not like I have to interact with him; yet somehow it's not okay for me to have casual fling-boy Luis stay over at our apartment, allegedly because Danny is uncomfortable with the fact that Luis used to work for bio-dad Frank, but really because Danny doesn't want to fill in the blanks of my lies of omission in the telephone calls with Sid and Nancy. *Folks, CC's doing just great. Got it all under control here. The*

Little Hellion's fooling around with the dude that Frank hired to drive her around two summers ago, but she's back on the pill, and I saw the box of condoms under her bed, so no worries! Nah, I don't think this is a serious relationship. It's just sex and good times, which seems to be fine with both Luis and CC. You know kids today, don't like to be tied down, unless we're talking about those play handcuffs I found under her bed. Hah, hah, KIDDING! Don't you worry, I've got the Little Hellion contained with rules. Boundaries, just as you advised. What was that? Why, yes, Nancy, I'd love a copy of your grandmother's Minnesouda county fair award-winning maple walnut fudge recipe. Toodles!

Some mornings Danny offers me a hopeful smile and says, "I'll be at the kitchen space if you want to stop by and have lunch with me . . ." and I almost forgive him, because I know he thinks he means well, and he has almost the same face as me, only sweeter and like a boy and with more normal hair. Instead I head out the door and tell him, "Sorry. I've got plans. Thanks anyway. See you later."

I wait until I am outside the apartment to complete my super-secret identity transformation. Since I have posttraumatic leg-breaking issues with the stairwell between the second and third levels of our apartment building, I choose the basement laundry room to don my duds. I remove my long vintage trench coat and take off the faded jeans underneath my short Dickies Nurse Betty hot-pink dress. I chuck the Chucks off my feet and pull the replacement foot attire out of my backpack. Wearing combat boots with the short shift dress would be too grunge-expectational, so instead I go for grunge-couture, sliding on and zippering up Nancy's seriously overpriced but seriously hot Italian thigh-high stiletto boots, in the shade of suede *noir*. Nancy's too pregnant to wear the boots anytime soon, anyway. She won't miss them. I complete the last stage of my transformation by attaching the waitress nametag Johnny Mold had made for me, which announces to any customers looking up past my new boobs (love 'em, I swear!) that they are being served by "Myself."

Myself has transformed into a barista-waitress goddess, if she says so Herself.

While I may not be school smart, that doesn't mean I'm not competent. Throw me into daily shifts at L U _ C H _ O N E _ T E, and just watch me master the arts of keeping the counter area in tip-top shape, of remembering customers' orders and their names, and of filling in during the cook's smoke breaks and then making and delivering the grilled cheese and Coke that I was asked for (not Pepsi, not diet, and with a piece of lime and just a little bit of ice—s'my pleasure, Pete). Just watch me build up a caffeination following that has lines for espresso drinks snaking out the door in the afternoons—the time of day when Danny is far away in happy-boring cupcake-baking land and will never know the difference.

I mean, how many restaurant workers will happily take on every job there is—short-order cooking, waitressing, coffee-ing, cleaning, charming . . . ing? So long as customers don't order a soft-boiled egg, we're good. That's my one and only fiefdom rule. I don't like rules being forced on me, so I try not to force them on my customers. I'm generous that way.

Disguises work both ways—customers sometimes have them going on too. I didn't pay attention to the face underneath the sunglasses and baseball cap when the dude at table seven ordered an English muffin and a mocha. But when I returned to place the order on my favorite collapsible bridge table, which just last week I painted the number seven on top of, like as in *Sesame Street,* this table was brought to you today by the number seven and the letters *CC,* the customer had removed the hat and sunglasses to reveal himself as: Aaron.

Aaron said, "It's interesting. My new boyfriend came here last week and reported on a new barista-waitress girl bringing customers back into this old dump. I didn't think anything of it until he mentioned the girl's long legs, sexy boots, and her weird sorta blue hair, which sounded suspiciously like my former love's kid sister. And I couldn't think of any other waitress who'd willingly stand on her feet all day in stiletto boot heels. So of course I had to scope the situation out myself."

I've opted not to become acquainted with Aaron's new boyfriend (my choice—one issue on which I am strangely allied with lisBETH), but I didn't realize Blip, as lisBETH and I refer to him, as in the blip on the radar screen of Aaron and Danny's true love, was also such a busybody. I might hate Blip now, even if I barely know him—and it might be worth a phone call and a manicure at a new not-Chucky place with lisBETH to discuss, even if that call could mean coming out to her about my current new direction in life.

"Hmmph," I said. "You found me out. Employed."

"How embarrassing for you," Aaron said. "But probably a better way to spend your time than ditching culinary classes?" To my frown, Aaron added, "I *am* a chef, remember? I *did* graduate from that same school. LisBETH didn't find the school out of nowhere. Don't think I don't still know people there."

Fifty-buck bribes to staff members in culinary school administrative offices really don't go far in this city.

I sat down on the chair opposite Aaron. "Are you going to tell Danny?"

"No. But did no one ever tell you that having a job is nothing to be ashamed of? And that the best way for you and Danny to wade through your roommate and sibling relationship is to—call me crazy here—share your lives with each other? CC my darling, don't you think the silent treatment you've been giving Danny has lasted long enough?"

"How do you know about that?" I took a sip of his mocha. Excellent, as usual—just the right amount of whipped cream and a dash of cocoa. The secret to the perfect mocha is to foam real chocolate milk (Hershey's or Nesquick will do) rather than add chocolate to already-steamed regular milk. Some baristas will tell you this method clogs the machine and should be avoided, but some baristas are too cheap to buy a separate foaming device specifically for mocha production. It's all about quality control.

"Danny and I are close friends, CC. The awkward period is long past. We see each other and talk regularly."

"You shouldn't do that, you know. I don't believe it's actually possible to be friends with someone who broke up with you. I know from my experience with Shrimp. 'Just friends' does not last. You're fooling yourselves."

"I appreciate your optimism. But for your information, Danny and I are managing it just fine. You don't spend a decade of your life with someone and then all of a sudden shut them out. It doesn't work like that."

Um, yes it does—for most people. The shutting-out strategy has certainly been working for me and Shrimp—too well, in fact. But Aaron is not most people. He's an ex who brings over his custom creation chicken soup when his former love has barely a smidge of a cold. He's a guy who, along with his disarming lack of homosexual fashion sense, plays in a crap band of longtime buddies just for the chance to hang out with them whenever—and to play punk, metal, and grunge tunes, not campy karaoke ABBA anthems (which have their important place in the musical appreciation arena, but blessedly not within the pantheon of Aaron's perfectness). Hmmm . . . the empty area at the corner window of L U _ C H _ O N E _ T E could be transformed into a performance space for a band just like Aaron's—which could potentially bring in lots more customers.

"Don't worry about me and Danny," I told Aaron. "It's just an, um, blip on the radar screen." My fingers twitched with the need to call lisBETH with the Aaron report. I didn't even realize I was capable of craving her company before now. Hostile sister-bonding—yet another of Aaron's previously unknown superpowers.

Aaron said, "While I don't condone the Cold War between you and Danny, I do want you to know you're welcome to crash at my place whenever you want if things are tense and you two need a break."

"Thanks, but I stay with Max when I need a break."

Aaron shook his head. "Only you would seek out and befriend the neighborhood crank."

"Only you would seek out your insufferable ex's suffragette sister and offer her a place to crash."

Maybe Aaron had found out about my L U _ C H _ O N E _ T E job, but no way could he know I was, in fact, double-secret employed. Max hired me to clean up and organize all the years of newspapers and magazines in his apartment—and now that I've had a professional furniture cleaner come in and steam-clean Max's sofa, the sofa has proven to be a great crash-landing site on the nights when Luis is in school or I can't stand the fucking sight of my beloved brother. Of course, I call the Commandant on those nights and let him know I'm crashing on the neighbor's couch. Wouldn't want to disobey Commandant's rules.

Thinking of Max reminded me of an important question for Aaron: "Do you happen to know anything about Hot Nude Yoga?"

"Sure. I've been. It's a really strenuous yoga class for gay men. Way too strenuous for me. I just want to have a quick stretch and use that to convince myself I've earned a big slice of pie after."

Of course Hot Nude Yoga would be for hot gay guys, and of course the hot gay guy who left the Kama Sutra book behind in his old apartment would have tried it out. I wonder if the Nancy and Trixie sleuth girls feel the same letdown when their mysteries are solved. I gulped down the remainder of Aaron's mocha. The boys shouldn't have exclusive domain over *all* the good stuff. "Figures."

Aaron laughed. "You sound like lisBETH!"

I might not know Myself anymore.

Johnny Mold arrived at our table. He grunted at me, "The latte crowd has found its way inside, and they're awaiting your barista mastery."

I told him, "Gimme a few minutes. I'm talking with my friend. Anyway, why don't you learn how to use that machine yourself already, *hombre*?"

Johnny stroked his goatee with his tattooed hand that just this morning I'd given a manicure. Black nail polish is so hot on guys—especially Johnny. He sighed, "Too many knobs. Too much pressure." Then his casual voice turned over to the hostile one that typically scares customers away until I step up to the counter. He pointed his index finger at me—damn, I'd done a great job on his cuticles. "And why don't you take your own self-improvement advice and learn a new language instead of just dropping inane trying-too-hard-to-be hip foreign words?"

I answered, "Pete told me to tell you *malaka wanker gamisou.* That's 'fuck off' in Greek. And I'll be over in a sec to make the lattes, Mold. Try not to kill the customers with your charm in the meantime."

"Will do. And will you be making us a grilled cheese lunch to share together again today, or is a run to Blimpie in order?"

"Blimpie, Mold. I'll have my usual."

"Beautiful, Myself. I'll make the run after you hit the espresso crowd." Johnny turned away to return to the counter area, but over his shoulder added, "*Fok jou.* That's 'fuck you' in Afrikaans."

"You're welcome. In English. For bringing customers into this joint and making a regular clientele of them."

"Whatever," Johnny said.

This is how we get along. I believe it's the best relationship I've ever had with a boy.

"What the hell was that?" Aaron asked me after Johnny Mold stepped back over to the cash register and resumed his Game Boy–playing and customer-ignoring. "Don't tell me goth boy over there is the latest competition to Shrimp or Luis or whoever is your current love slave."

"Nah," I said. "He's like my boss or something. Kinda my friend, too."

Johnny and I get along too well to ruin our burgeoning work-friendship with crush trauma. I guess Johnny potentially could have been in competition to be my love slave, but he proclaimed himself to Myself as a straight-edge vegetarian celibate. He doesn't drink, smoke, do drugs, eat meat, or have sex. He does caffeinate, with dairy products, so I can still respect him in the morning. Of course I'm dying to know which gender Johnny would choose if he did decide to have sex, but when I asked him outright which way his straight-edginess swings, Johnny said, "Don't try to label me straight or gay. I'm celibate, simple as that. No interest in all the drama."

For real, how did Aaron end up with a Blip? I asked Aaron, "Is it serious between you and this new guy?"

Aaron said, "Don't know. How about whatever is going on between you and Luis that I'm still waiting to hear all about? And so is your brother."

"Wait a little longer." I got up from the bridge table but

decided to lay my cards down before transforming Myself back into barista goddess. "Aaron, why the hell can't you and Danny work things out and get back together? What's holding you back?"

Aaron's not without flaws. His honesty comes at the cost of his own heart and hurt. He answered, "I'm right here."

TWENTY-TWO

Luis is indeed beautiful to look at, but lately I'm distracted. I'm thinking more about the passengers he looks at in the rearview mirror of his livery car. Something could definitely be wrong with me if I could have a Hot Nude Luis lying in my bed next to me, stroking the blue side of my hair as I pressed my cheek against the soft skin of his rock hard chest, and my postlust conversation was this: "So the customer you dropped off at JFK terminal three for Aeroflot. You didn't even ask him why he was going to Omsk, Siberia?"

"No," Luis whispered.

I said, "Danny's not here. You don't have to whisper." Commandant and Aaron went to an old movie at the film museum in Queens, which left, by my approximation, a good hour and a half alone in the apartment for me and Luis. Since we'd already completed the primary purpose of Luis's visit, that left time to try to get to know Luis a little better—at least try to know him some way other than physically.

"I'm not whispering because of your brother, *niña,*" Luis whispered. "I'm whispering cuz it's, like, sexier after . . . you know."

"Oh," I stated. Loudly. If you have to proclaim moves as sexy, are they thereby rendered unsexy? "So when you finish earning your night school degree, do you think you will ever want to go to Siberia?"

"No." Too bad. Cross Luis off my future Siberia adventure passenger list. Last year when I asked him, Shrimp totally said he would go.

"Do you think you will still drive a livery car to make ends meet after you get that business degree?"

"Hopefully not. That's kinda the point of busting my ass working days and going to school nights."

"When you're dropping customers off at the airport all day long, don't you ever think of getting out of the car and hopping on a plane to some random place, just because? Doesn't the sight of all those planes, all those people of all those nationalities and all their luggage and their passports and all that, doesn't it make you wanna go somewhere?"

"I live in New York City. Why would I ever want to go anywhere else?"

Point taken.

I kissed a map of the long, narrow island of Manhattan down the length of Luis's chest. Then I rested my chin on his innie belly button and asked him, "If you had a time machine and identity theft abilities, which New York Knick past, present, or future would you want to be? And don't say Wilt Chamberlain because he had the legendary way with the ladies. That would be boring."

"Wilt Chamberlain didn't play for the Knicks, he played for Philly. Also boring. If I was gonna be a ghost of New York Knicks past, I'd probably want to be Patrick Ewing."

"Yeah?"

"Yeah. But I'd cheat a little, go pre-Knicks, back to Ewing's college hoops days. I'd get to be a scholarship student at Georgetown— no complications of having a part-time job making airport runs in a Lincoln Town Car to deal with, you hear what I'm sayin'? I'd be coached by John Thompson, I'd play March Madness against Michael Jordan, I'd be set for life. How righteous would that be?"

"Righteous for sure, so long as you don't have inferiority issues over the whole Michael Always Prevails thing. I mean, it's *your* time portal, you shouldn't have to deal with being a chronic second best, when in fact you're a superior player—just competing against the ultimate superior player ever. Okay, next question . . ."

Luis rolled over on top of me and pinned my arms above my head. "What's it gonna take to get you to shut up?"

My dark coffee eyes met the light honey of his. I smiled sugar back. "You know what it takes."

Luis kissed my wrist, en route up the length of my arm, placing kisses so alternately soft and hard and delicious that my fist wanted to punch the air in frustration when he stopped. He'd reached the obscure underside of my upper arm. He pointed to the tattoo on it. "Why do you have a tattoo of a piece of shrimp on your arm?"

"In honor of my ex, Shrimp," I sighed. "We got tattoos together when we broke up. He got a Nestlé Crunch bar tattooed on his upper arm in honor of my favorite candy bar habit, and I got a little shrimp." I almost started to tell Luis how my great admiration of Johnny Mold's full-body collection of tattoo art has inspired me to consider adding on to my Shrimp arm tattoo with new tattoos symbolic of each successive lover I have in my life—maybe I'd get a Jell-O logo in Luis's honor? But Johnny Mold has advised that while the charm arm bracelet of lover tattoos is a promising concept, it could also be considered a potential serial-killer move by future boy prospects, so I haven't acted on it yet. I didn't say anything about it to Luis.

"You're a weird girl," Luis said. He gave up on my arm. I turned over onto my stomach. Luis ran his fingernails down my bare back, not quite a massage, not quite a scratch, but altogether mmmmmm to the ahhhhhh.

rachel cohn

"Thank you," I whispered. Verdict on pillow talk whispering: medium sexy. My face pressed against my pillow, I whispered one more question, "If I hadn't gotten a morning-after pill and it turned out I got pregnant on Halloween, what would you have done?"

Luis drew his own map of kisses on my back. Felt like the Bronx, wide and dangerous, tantalizing. Then he said, "I would've said nine months after that night you'd make a great babymomma, because I don't believe in abortion, and I don't believe you or me is ready or wanting to be married."

"Oh," I stated again. Not so loud this time, and definitely not at all sexy.

TWENTY-THREE

All my investment in cleaning out Max's apartment paid off.
Yvette Mimieux has finally acknowledged me. She's evolved from
Max's phantom roommate, heard scurrying around the apartment
but not seen, to occasionally peering out at me from behind book-
cases or underneath the sofa, to teasing me with sly rubs against my
ankles as she darts from room to room, to now she's a full-on slut.

"It's about time," Max said. "Cyd Charisse, meet Yvette
Mimieux. Yvette, meet Cyd Charisse." Max's scaredy-cat laid next
to me on the couch, nestled against my thigh, purring as I rubbed
her belly.

"I'm a dog person," I told Max. "I don't understand this." Not
only am I surprised that Yvette decided I am worthy of her attention, especially after she invested weeks in hissing at me as I cleared
away piles of magazines and newspapers and closets full of junk that

144

have traditionally been her hiding places, I'm also shocked that I could enjoy the cat-petting experience at all. Cats are so hateful and useless and entitled, like heiresses with their own reality TV shows. Give me a slobbering dog with farting problems any day. Dogs are pure love, not discretionary love.

Max said, "Yvette may take a while to warm to people, but once she does, she's irresistible. As you can see."

"Why'd you name her Yvette Mimieux?" As Yvette's spotted near-tiger face of copper, black, ginger, and white fur stared up at me, she rivaled in adorableness the faces of my younger sibs Ash and Josh that used to melt my heart even when I was screaming at the squirts to stop messing with the stuff in my bedroom. It's like I would scream at them just so they wouldn't know how madly I loved them—and needed them.

"Asks the girl whose mother named her Cyd Charisse? Probably for a similar reason as your mom's. Yvette Mimieux was Tony's favorite movie star." Max lit a fresh memorial candle and placed it on the piano, next to Tony's framed picture. Max may be a crank, but he's one who could teach the Commandants of the world about true, true love. Max's partner has been gone since before I was born, yet Max keeps his memory alive every single day.

"Subtitles didn't bother him?"

"Of course they bothered him. They bother everybody. But while Yvette Mimieux had a French name, she acted in American movies. Really, Cyd Charisse, I count on you to know these things. However, Tony was a subtitle sucker for foreign movies with any guy named Jean-Paul or Marcello."

Max sat down on the piano bench and lit a cigar. I said, "Max, you promised on the days I'm visiting and it's too cold to smoke out in your garden that you would not light up at all."

Max shooed me with his hand. He repeated his adage, "My apartment. My rules."

"I don't like your rules." Yvette backed me up with a Mimieux's *miaule,* "meow" *en francais.* I patted her head in appreciation, then walked over to Max. I took the cigar out of Max's hand, walked it to the kitchen, put it out under the kitchen sink's tap water, and chucked it into the garbage. Then I told Max, "I have not invested all this time in making this apartment look like a Village palace after decades of neglect, bloody scrubbed the walls down with bleach, and had the furniture and carpets steam-cleaned to get rid of the funky smoke smell, just to watch you defy all that work with one of your cigars."

"Is that the reason, or are you worried about my health? I suspect the real reason you took on this job to begin with is you're just a cleaning fetishist at heart. My God, I've never seen such a passion for Clorox. Nor anyone as obsessed with making me the perfect dinner bowl of ramen noodles before she takes off for the night with her fella." Max got up, opened the piano bench, and plucked a fresh cigar from a box inside the bench, and then lit up once again. "These are genuine Cubans. Please don't waste them. They're the perfect way to close out that perfect bowl of ramen noodles. Only because your name is Cyd Charisse, which almost makes you a sister to Yvette Mimieux, shall I forgive your momentary indiscretion. And may I remind you—I lost not only Tony, but a whole generation of friends. The prospect of cancer doesn't scare me after what I've lived through."

Max glanced in the direction of the front hallway that led from the apartment's front door to what he calls his "Wall of Sadness." I hadn't spent weeks removing pictures from the walls so I could scrub the walls down, then dusting, polishing, and returning the pictures to the walls, to not feel intimately acquainted with the ghosts on that particular side of the apartment. The wall pictured a generation of lives shared together, from beach vacations to Fire Island with Tony, trips to Europe and South America with their friends, and summer stock performance troupes touring the U.S. of A. The Wall of Sadness looked like it could breathe eternal life, however bittersweet, for the souls of Max's loved ones who couldn't be here to go on with him.

Dismantling, refurbishing, and resurrecting the Wall of Sadness has helped diffuse the Danny situation. I still don't like Danny's rules, but he's who I have here in New York City, the person in this sphere who cares most about me. I can't imagine how it would feel to, like Max, within only a few years' time lose your true love and a majority of your friends to a disease that nobody back then even wanted to acknowledge, according to Max. When they were young, Sid-dad and Frank-dad both lost friends who'd fought in the protest war, but their friends had whole cemeteries and holidays dedicated to their memories. Max's generation got Walls of Sadness in the homes of those lucky (or unlucky) enough to be left behind. Maybe that's why Max has little pride flags, and country flags from the places where his friends were from, like Brazil and China and Alabama and Greenwich Village, affixed to the old photos of his friends—to level the field of memories.

The need to level Danny has passed, sort of like a kidney stone. It was there, it hurt like hell to hate like that, and now there's still a tender sore spot, but the resentment is dissipating. And like a true soul-mate brother, Danny sensed the Cold War thawing in my heart without my having to announce its temporal opening. He appeared at L U _ C H _ O N E _ T E and instead of calling me out on my state of employment, which I still hadn't bothered to tell him, he ordered a straight espresso shot. Danny kept his say simple. He announced, "I can only hold the part-time assistant job in my baking business open for so long. The cupcake world is expanding into lascivious cupcakes, if you know what I mean. So if you're acquainted with any culinary school dropouts who might be interested, have them contact me ASAP before I give the job away to someone else." He chugged down his shot. "Crema on top just right, my compliments to the secret agent barista bringing the long lines into this dump. Pass on the word for me, will ya?" He winked at me and left.

I'll try working for Danny now that the Max cleaning job is complete, but I'm still not telling him about what is or isn't going on between me and Luis. That's my business, just like it's Danny's business why now that Aaron and Blip appear to be getting serious, all of a sudden Danny urgently needs exclusive access to Aaron's time for help going over the accounting books for Danny's baking work; anybody who knows Aaron knows when it comes to work-related issues, he only cares about food—Aaron couldn't care less about numbers being in the black or the red, a primary reason why his and Danny's former café went under. It's Danny's business why all of a sudden he's jeté'ing to performances of Aaron's beloved New York City Ballet at Lincoln Center when Danny hates ballet, says it's only useful for catching up on nap time—a sore point of irritation for Aaron back when he and Danny were a couple. Now Danny is wide awake at those performances on the occasions Blip can't make it. Or so says lisBETH in our regular text messaging sessions analyzing Danny's business.

Can't keep Max from knowing my business. When my cell phone rang, Max waved his hands in the air and said, "It must be Luis! The fellow with the swarthy biceps who waits for his girl outside on the street rather than come inside and be subjected to the weird old queen."

"I'm not Luis's girl," I told Max. "And you're no queen. Your lavender robe has sweat stains, it's hemmed too short, and a proper tiara would surely fall off your comb-over hair, even with bobby pins to hold it in place."

"Ooooh," Max squealed. "Bobby's!"

I rolled my eyes at Max and answered Luis's call with a simple, "I'll be outside in a few."

It almost seemed a shame to take off with Luis when Yvette Mimieux and I were just getting to know each other. I went outside to where Luis's Lincoln Town Car idled, double-parked in front of Max's building. Luis rolled down the window, smiling that honey smile that truly toys with my resolve to not think of him as anything more than a friend with benefits. "You ready for the trek up to Washington Heights for the best Dominican food you'll ever have, or what?" he purred.

"What do you say about a new plan? Park the car in the garage and let's hang out with Max. You always just say a quick 'Hi' to Max and never get to know him. He's a cool guy, trust me. We'll order in and play Monopoly or something."

"How fun for me," Luis monotoned. "No, c'mon, *niña*. Let's go."

Max had a point about Luis being uncomfortable hanging out with a queen. "Why do I have a feeling you'd have no problem

rachel cohn

staying in if it was my brother we'd be hanging out with and not Max?"

Why did I suddenly have a painful stab straight through my heart that Shrimp would have no problem hanging out with Max and playing Monopoly, so long as we let Shrimp be the racer car and no player could be the thimble cuz Shrimp has a superstition about the thimble bringing on bad luck and bad waves?

Luis exercised his fundamental-boy-flaw muscle, answering too fast, too honestly. "Your brother's easier. He's a dude, not all flaming."

No. Our differences in attitude could no longer be bridged. "What are we doing here?" I said, all of a sudden into my own business. My experiment in fling: quite nice indeed, but ready to be over, done, *finito*.

Luis paused before answering, like it took him a moment to realize I was talking about more than where we'd go on a Saturday night. He did the classic head-dropping-followed-by-head-shaking guy maneuver, as if to say, *You're gonna make me have this conversation when I'm double-parked, my driver's side window down so I can look up at your serious face wanting serious answers to something I wasn't considering seriously at all a minute ago?*

He reached through the window and tugged gently on my hand. "I thought we'd already established that we didn't know what we're doing here besides having a good time together, and we were gonna be all right with that. Why does it matter now?"

"I don't really understand it myself, but because all of a sudden it just does matter." I pulled his hand to my lips and placed a light kiss on his palm. "You are a great catch—maybe now you should go on out and get caught by someone as great as you are. You hear what I'm sayin'?"

Again he waited to respond, like he was trying to decide whether to lodge a protest. Then:

"I hear you," Luis acknowledged. That smile, one last time. "Disappointed, but I hear you."

No block in this neighborhood is ever empty of people or cars passing through, no matter what time of day or night, and I wondered if the folks strolling past us with their grocery bags in hand or dogs on leashes, or the delivery truck driver honking at Luis for blocking the narrow street, knew or cared that they were watching two friends expire their benefits.

I kinda think if I can't have pure love, I'm not feeling like discretionary love anymore. I'd rather be on my own, enjoying my sphere of people.

TWENTY-FOUR

With the San Francisco side of my New York sphere of people deciding to relocate back home, I decided Autumn and I needed one last blaze of Manhattan glory to share together before she returned to the land of fog and yummy dumplings. Our choices for how to spend our last time together included:

1. Circle Line boat tour around island of Manhattan—nixed due to complete cheesiness of the idea (also, we'd be too cold);

2. An afternoon at the arcade playing DDR/Dance Dance Revolution—nixed due to my namesake Cyd Charisse's spirit intimidating my lame CC white girl fumble-dance abilities;

3. One last round of sittin' round Central Park, people-watching—nixed also due to EXCUSE ME, IT'S

COOOOOOLD in December, and we are from San
Francisco and thought we understood the concept of frigid,
but hah, we've been proven wrong about that; and so
we settled upon

4. The space show at the Museum of Natural History, in
   celebration of Autumn pulling off a B-minus miracle in her
   astronomy class and therefore not completely closing off her
   future ability to transfer to Berkeley, and because the Laser
   Zeppelin show that was our first choice was sold out (damn
   us for not realizing that good stoners have the foresight to
   order tickets in advance before arriving baked at the show).

Of course, Autumn and I talked the whole way through the space
show. Who could care about understanding the infinite nature of
the universe when our New York time together ticked to a close?

We pacted. Me: "I will not let my desire to get some get sidetracked by drunken inability to open a condom wrapper." Autumn:
"I will not let my desire to get some get sidetracked by my inability
to deal with school and money stress." We clinked Danny-baked
lunch-box cupcakes—mine a vanilla peppermint, hers a chocolate
peppermint.

From behind us: "SHHH!"

I whispered into Autumn's ear, "What do you think is happening in the Shrimp sphere of the world?"

From behind us: "No food is permitted to be eaten inside the premises."

She whispered back, "Longing for you. Of course!" Such a good friend to say what I wanted to hear, even if we both knew Shrimp could well be in love with some new Kiwi girl by now.

"SHHH!"

I sang out, "I left my heart . . ."

Autumn finished, ". . . in San Francisco." Then she added, "How do you think I am going to manage back home again?"

"Just fine," I said.

TWENTY-FIVE

Maybe I am a Cyd Charisse with more in common with an Yvette Mimieux than I expected—at least when it comes to bio-dad Frank. I don't know that I'm capable of ever feeling pure love for a guy who is like one infinitesimal sperm cell of a father figure in comparison to Sid-dad, but the discretionary love? There's possibility.

Infinitesimal. I may have no career ambition at this stage of life other than to be a barista-waitress, but that doesn't mean I can't throw down the college words. Still, Frank apparently thinks there's plenty of education I lack, and he's taken it upon himself to fill that gap.

Our routine works like this. Frank calls my cell phone to say "How are you doing?" or "Do you need anything?" or some such, but really he's waiting for me to say "How are YOU doing, Frank?" so he can tell me all about how retirement is a bore and Danny and lisBETH work too much; they're never willing to take a day off work to spend with their poor old man who's putting golf balls all alone in his Upper East Side apartment just waiting for his kids to put in some face time with him, hint-hint, sniff-sniff. I'm fresh blood, and obviously I'm a dog person, because like a puppy craving attention, I fall for Frank's pity party and I will be like "Well, what did you have in mind?" Once Frank figured out that I could be coaxed into pretty much any experience not involving a boring lunch at his boring apartment, we finally got some quality experiencing going on.

Frank's preferred venue is a fancy museum, where he drags me around and sounds very important and news-anchorman-like as he lectures to me about so-and-so artist painted this boring-piece-of-crap during the artist's raging latent transsexual stage, as a revolt against the religious persecution brought down by the insert-name-of-ye-olde-king-or-queen-no-one-cares-about. I pretend to be interested and pretend not to notice my skirt-chasing old man checking out all the pretty women going by as he baritones, enunciating extra loudly when the ladies' skirts are cut above the knee. As a reward for my pretending this never happens, Frank pretends to be interested when I drag him to a French patisserie to sample French coffee and pastry, which is much nicer and less insouciant (trump that word, college kids!) than having to go all the way to France for the real culinary education. Frank then pretends to be offended when I play the "Do you think the barista behind the counter is straight or gay" game. Franks says I am way too interested in other people's sexuality, and I tell him he's one to talk, and somehow we're laughing together and it's probably as much of a bio-father/daughter moment as we'll ever know, but there it is—a moment we own together.

It's our time, and it turns out not to be a waste of time. Familiarity may breed contempt, but it also breeds family. I no longer feel weird and lost in his presence. I just feel kinda used to him. It's a relief.

Before I knew Frank, Danny, and lisBETH, when I only knew of their existence, I used to fantasize what it would be like to be part of their family. I imagined I would enter their lives and magic-like-that, there'd be this weepy scene of true-love-family finding each other, like TV airport reunions between birth moms and the grown-up children given up to adoption when they were babies. The bio-fam and I would have tons of things in common, like birthmarks in the same weird places, and dust allergies, and whoa, you like to eat spaghetti and meatballs on Tuesday nights? Me too! CONNECTION—instantly achieved!

The reality is, as a family unit, we had a rocky start the first time I came to New York. The true love did not happen, except between me and Danny. The second time, at Easter last year with Danny, Frank, and lisBETH, it felt awkward—but easier. Now that

I'm a regular fixture here, making regular appearances in the lives of lisBETH and Frank, along with sharing an apartment with Danny, I understand that there never was going to be, or ever will be, a magic "aha" moment that declares We Are Family. It's like something you grow into without realizing it's happening, like my new cleavage.

As a family unit Frank, lisBETH, Danny, and I have grown into this: We spend holidays together. Although in true Frank-precedent fashion, we do cheat, just a little. This year we've convened to celebrate almost-Christmas, as in big family dinner at Frank's apartment on the night before the day before Christmas Eve.

The bio-fam are scattering like infinitesimal sperm cells for the actual holidays. Danny—get this—is going to Key West on a "just friends" vacation with Jerry Lewis, Blip, and Aaron (I predict disaster); Frank's going skiing in Colorado with a new "lady friend" he met on a plane trip a while ago and whose name he chooses to keep anonymous, as apparently it's not a true love situation but a mutually agreeable one (I'm way more scared by how much I'm like Frank than by how much I'm getting to be like Nancy); and major news flash—GET THIS—lisBETH is going "on holiday," as she says, with her new beau, the baldy from the nail shop.

Me, I am all about the self-actualization these days. With the Luis thing over, I am operating in a strictly crush-free zone, and it turns out to be rather nice. (Although my earlier contempt for sad-sack single females searching out the naughty toy shops may have been premature. Lesson: don't rush to judgment.) I'm digging the L U _ C H _ O N E _ T E gig, looking forward to starting work with Danny after New Year's, enjoying hanging out with Johnny Mold and Max. For the first time in a long time, not only do I have no boy situation, I'm fine with that. Life builds even without a boy—it can also be mildly satisfying. Go figure.

It's likely I'm one of those people who peaked too young with true love and therefore shall never be able to recapture the experience again in her life, which conveniently leaves more time to focus on Myself, who will be celebrating her highly actualized single state by going home to the Bay Area for Christmas. More important than the holiday vacation, I have a new sister to celebrate.

I'd like to imagine it was a holiday miracle that Nancy managed to give birth on my San Francisco family's favorite holiday, December twelfth, but it was no miracle. Nancy scheduled the C-section for that most sacred of days, the birth date of Frank Sinatra. I'm sure when she is older and as actualized as her eldest sister, Frances Alberta will thank our mother for this astrological gift. I'm also confident that when Frances Alberta grows up, she'll prove herself the smartest of us all and will be so actualized as to actually know what actualization is, and she will share that knowledge with me, sweet thang.

Note: Johnny Mold can be torn away from his Game Boy and

his latte to dance-thrash to the Ramones blasting from the stereo after telephone calls announcing the birth of Frances Alberta.

Johnny Mold is my new role model on many levels. I like his totally chill, no expectations frame of mind. And like him, I've decided it's socially acceptable to ignore the persons around me to focus on the technology in front of me. This new philosophy is how I came to be transfixed in front of Frank's TV watching a movie while lisBETH and Danny went about the work of preparing our almost-Christmas meal and Frank went about the Head of the Family business of shuffling through his newspaper, his stomach audibly grumbling in anticipation of the feast. I suspected this scattering of related persons to be the last sure sign we've evolved into a quasi-family unit—we're comfortable ignoring one another at family gatherings.

Well, I'd like to think so. I tried to watch *White Christmas,* but Frank kept talking at me like I was supposed to be paying attention to him while he sat on the couch opposite the one on which I reclined, wearing the lovely house slippers he brought me as a gift from his recent adventure trip to Japan; he's caught on that travel is an exceptional way to pass the retirement time, and that his bio-daughter who doesn't want his money will nonetheless be delighted to accept presents from the Takashimaya store in Tokyo that he personally picked out to match her green-blue toe days and her blueblack hair.

Frank said, "Have you met lisBETH's beau?"

I'm dreaming of—

Pause button.

"No."

Play button.

—a white Christmas.

Bing Crosby: no way gay.

"But you've seen him?"

Pause.

"Right. But only once and only from behind."

Play.

Just like the ones I used to . . .

Danny Kaye: Max, my friend, I'm not convinced, but I could see the possibility.

"Do you think it's serious?"

Sigh. Pause.

"How would I know, Frank? They've only been dating a month. She's yet to subject him to my interrogation."

Nancy-level sigh. Play.

"But she's been spending all her time with him! She's going to Bermuda with him for Christmas! It must mean something."

I finally gave it up to the Stop button on the remote.

"You're going skiing with your lady friend. Does it mean anything?"

"But it's different with lisBETH. She doesn't casually date; it's not her nature. She's too serious. LisBETH . . ."

"Did I hear my name?" lisBETH chirped as she stepped into the living room. She wore an apron over her executive lady business suit, holding a soup ladle in one hand, with a kitchen towel beneath it in her other hand. She passed the ladle over to Frank. "What do you think, Daddy? Does the soup need more salt?"

I'd say if people have auras, lisBETH's has faded from dark Popsicle-tongue-purple to light violet cream. Pleased. Clueless that Frank would have no idea whether a soup needed more salt.

All those years I spent wondering what lisBETH would be like had ended in terror the first time I met her—she was a nightmare (the feeling was mutual). But now that we'd grown from instant despise to somewhat tolerating each other to almost getting along, now that she looked so violet, I figured the time had finally come for the very important question I'd longed to ask her, but had never found the courage to before.

"LisBETH?"

"Yes, my dear?" she chirped again, clearly practicing her positive inflection voice for her vacation with baldy, who never did find his courage to ask her out on that first date—but was glad to oblige when lisBETH asked him.

"Did you ever think we could be sisters like the two sisters in

White Christmas? You know, all song-y and matching Christmas outfits and finishing each other's sentences—"

"No," lisBETH snapped, looking at me like I was the biggest moron she'd ever had the displeasure of being genetically linked to.

I mean, I was joking, but only sort of kind of.

Maybe lisBETH noticed my sort of kind of crushed face, because she added, "I hate that movie. It's nothing personal. Musicals just . . . What is it you say, CC? They 'bug.'" She laughed at her own joke. Then her aura changed to Nancy. "Do you think you could be troubled to detach yourself from the couch already? Danny needs help setting the dining room table."

I considered pointing out the inherent sexism in lisBETH demanding my girl touch to the table fixin's when a Frank-version Head of Family could easily have accomplished the same task. Maybe he'd put the salad forks on the wrong side, but cut the guy some slack, he'd probably never been a Girl Scout and forced to learn the art of table-setting for the sake of a gender-biased merit badge. Instead I told lisBETH, "Sure thing. And why don't you take over my place on the couch for a few. Frank wants to have a serious talk with you. He wants to know what's really going on between you and your beau, but he's too chicken to ask you to your face." I turned to Frank. "You're welcome," I said.

If I'd traveled down the college girl path, I so would have been a psych major (minor in feminazi studies).

One final girl touch called on my way to the dining room. I stopped in front of lisBETH and snapped open the top two buttons of her blouse. It's like this little skill set exchange we have going on. We don't get all song-y and whatever, but I do teach her how to make her outfits more slutty and baldy-enticing, and she does stop by L U _ C H _ O N E _ T E on occasion to run the numbers on my tips and help me figure out my living expenses budget—less the money I have to pay lisBETH back for the culinary class I ditched, unless I change my mind and reenroll, in which case, I'm back in the black with the lisBETH account. "Ask Frank about his lady friend while he's interrogating you," I whispered in her ear.

"Ask Danny about Aaron," she whispered back in my ear. "I can't get anything out of him on the topic."

"There's my Dollface," Danny said when I joined him at the dining table.

"Don't call me that; it's sexist." Actually, I think it's a nice nickname, but I want to stay on top of the subtle social cues that tell Danny I'm an adult, not some dumb kid sister who needs rules.

Danny teased, "But you look so purdy with your Morticia Addams black dress and the Jesus pin with the blinking lights that says 'Wish Me Happy Birthday!' on it. How can I not call you 'Dollface'?" He handed me a container of fancy silver forks, knives, and spoons. "Could you please set the silverware around the plates?"

"Surely," I said. "Could you please not leave your dirty socks on the bathroom floor, and if you borrow one of my CDs, could you please put it back in proper alphabetical order rather than just any old where? Also, there are like nutrition bars that can be used as breakfast sources of protein and iron instead of soft-boiled eggs. Just letting you know."

I set the silverware around the plates while Danny trailed me placing the wine- and water glasses above the plates.

Danny said, "I'm sure I could tackle those issues if you could manage to write down my messages before deleting them from the house phone voice mail, and golly, if you could unlearn how to stomp around the house wearing your combat boots so you wake me up at three in the morning, and throw in not leaving the windows wide open when you leave for work so I come home to a subzero climate apartment, that would be peachy-keen-swell."

"Done," I said. Then added, *"Commandant."*

"Appreciated," he said. "Dollface."

I thought living with Danny would be so easy and then it wasn't but maybe now it will be.

Pure warm love invites the admission of secrets, especially after a defrost. I told Danny, "Luis and I are *finito.* It was just a physical thing—and the statute of limitations ran out on my desire for anything less than true love. And the secret to why my electric toothbrush is always so much cleaner than yours is, I take it apart and clean it with a Q-tip dipped in rubbing alcohol." Danny and I are both mental about dental hygiene, which documentary film-makers should take note of for the insta-CC-Danny connection segment of the TV version of our bio-fam story.

"At last! I knew I'd break you and eventually you'd divulge the toothbrush secret. Oh, and, uh, don't know whether this news flash has penetrated through your and lisBETH's not-so-secret communiqué fortress, but Aaron's new boyfriend has let the L-word slip. Don't know how I feel about that."

"Yes, you do—or should I tell you? Or I can call your sister in here to do it along with me?"

"The denial is so much easier, Dollface. What do you say you and me go back to freezing each other out?"

"No, thanks. That would be too much work, and I am all about the slacker vibe these days. But when you're ready for me to tell you how you feel about Aaron, and congratulations by the way on finally discovering the jealousy factor, you just let me know. Don't wait till it's too late."

Danny flicked my Jesus pin. "God help me."

Danny had a point about the chill. As we shared a taxi home together after dinner later that night, I shivered like a California girl while the first flakes of winter snow teased the city. I rested my tired head on Danny's shoulder and thought about what a tease plane rides are. Whether to Omsk, Siberia, or back home to San Francisco, plane rides somehow offer the hope of a completely new, original adventure, or at the very least the hope that you could meet an amazing, cool person who will change your life, even though that only happens in movies or to serial lotharios like Frank, but what's it matter anyway because you're so very content being a single gal. In real life you get a snoring businessman with long legs who blocks your way to the bathroom (that's probably how Frank met his lady friend), you get crappy movies, but at the end you do get a destination. And I couldn't wait to leave for my destination the next morning, to meet Frances Alberta, to see my friends and family and hot dentist back home, to chill like a Johnny Mold in the San Francisco fog. Would my self-actualization be as readily apparent as my new B cup, or would I have to announce it (them) to everyone?

Except, when we stepped out of the taxi, Danny and I were greeted by a true night-before-the-day-before-Christmas-Eve miracle waiting in front of our apartment building.

Shrimp.

And no way would I be stepping onto that plane tomorrow. Not with pure love staring me in the face and asking, "Miss me?"

TWENTY-SIX

Self-actualization proves useless when confusion reigns supreme.

This shall be the first lesson imparted at Miss Cyd Charisse's Little Schoolhouse on the Prairie commune. Class, this pioneer schoolroom has been specially chartered to ease the path of your denial. In this little one-room shack of a schoolhouse with a window view out onto the wide open prairie, you can accept true love back into your life without needing to question how the hell—oops, heck—it came to find you again.

The second lesson is that if a Shrimp arrives carrying a refrigerated bag of pork pot stickers from Clement Street in San Francisco even though he's a vegetarian—that's just how compassionate he is, caring more about your need for pork than about the pig's need to not be turned into pork—well, you accept that on blind faith, and do not question the health hygiene issues involved in the cross-country transportation of meat products. Clement Street pot stickers are hard to come by on the prairie. Those dumplings are gold, the currency declaring that Shrimp knows what you want better than you know yourself.

When you ask why he is here, what happened in New Zealand, do not be annoyed with his vague responses. You can read between the mumbles. Shrimp followed his parents to New Zealand, where they were going to become organic farmers, but his parents neglected to clear the immigration and visa hurdles that would have allowed for a permanent relocation there. Kiwis are uptight about hippy parents with marijuana-trafficking legal entanglements in their pasts. Oops. Be compassionate. Be a cupcake. You've made some less than smart decisions yourself. Lots of folks have wanted to deport you. Don't judge.

Why did Shrimp find you at your schoolhouse? Why now? Who cares!

Focus on the important things. Look at his tight little surfer body, way leaner than you remember, by way of either stress or kiwi diet, you don't know, but surely you'd like to experiment on the differential of his body's equation. Stare deep inside the deep blue of his eyes on his deeply tanned face, newly hardened by antipodean sun but overcast by bad choice haze; admire his new preppy-cut dirty blond hair with a wind-whipped, sun-kissed golden patch spiking up through the middle but slanted to the side, like a

rachel cohn

Mohawk modeled on the Leaning Tower of I Love You More Than Ever. Transitioning back to that make-believe commune of making out will clearly be a bigger priority than all those damn—oops, darn—questions.

Believe the dream. Even self-actualized schoolmarms sometimes look out their open schoolhouse windows, into the nothingness, only to find somethingness floating their way. This apparition is not just possibility. It is actuality. Ghosts don't need to properly explain why they choose to appear out of nowhere. That's why they're ghosts. Demand too much of them and they will disappear again, stealing your actuality and all the possible kisses they might have brought along with them.

Class, Shrimp is lost and you can help find him. He needs you. That's the only lesson you need to know.

TWENTY-SEVEN

We interrupt the return of true love for an emergency broadcast parental freak-out.

"CYD CHARISSE, DID I HEAR YOU PROPERLY—YOU WON'T BE COMING HOME AT ALL FOR CHRISTMAS? HOW COULD YOU WAIT THIS LONG TO CALL ME WITH THIS INFORMATION? FERNANDO WAS JUST ABOUT TO LEAVE FOR THE AIRPORT TO PICK YOU UP! WHAT DO YOU *MEAN* YOU DIDN'T GET ON THE PLANE HOME TO SAN FRANCISCO THIS MORNING?"

Well, Mom, would you believe a blizzard struck Lower Manhattan around dawn this morning—planes were okay to depart from JFK and Newark, but what help's that if no cab could make it to my apartment building to take me to the airport? No kidding, the mayor declared a snow state of emergency from Wall Street up to Fourteenth Street. Totally

*freak snowstorm—if it had only diverted a few blocks north, I'd have
been fine, winging my way home this very minute. Swear.*

I braced myself, then said the word quietly, almost in a whisper: "Shrimp."

"SHRIMP!" My mother's voice was not almost a scream—it
was more like a deafening screech. "You've GOT to be kidding me.
He's there NOW?" I could totally picture Nancy clenching her
teeth and balling up her fists in frustration. The vision was almost
comforting—just like old times.

"Yeah, he showed up unexpectedly last night. He's had a hard
time, Mom. I can't leave him alone now."

In exchange for Danny's reluctant acquiescence to my request
for Shrimp to stay at the apartment while Danny was away on vacation, I promised I wouldn't lie to my parents about the reason I'd
bailed on going home for Christmas. Initially Danny said no way
could Shrimp stay, and neither could I for that matter, but rather
than throw a tantrum disputing Danny's unreasonable edict, I
stated the simple fact that I'm old enough and responsible enough
to make this decision for myself, independent of the Commandant's
rules. Danny sighed like a Nancy and said, "But if you don't go
home, your parents will be mad at me." And I corrected him: "No,
they'll be mad at *me.*" Danny shrugged his agreement. Trumped.

As he left the apartment for the airport this morning, Danny
did ask me to promise to think it through carefully before jumping

back in with Shrimp, but I could give no such pledge. True love waits on no false promises.

"I thought Shrimp was in New Zealand," Nancy said.

"He returned to San Francisco last week. But there's a new baby at his brother's house, so he felt weird about getting in the way there, even though his new niece is amazing and one day she will be number one female surf champion of the world. His parents took off to stay with friends in Humboldt County, and Shrimp didn't know where else to go. He had a free airplane ticket because he'd agreed to get bumped on the flight back from Auckland, so he came to New York on a whim. He was gonna stay with some surfer friend from Ocean Beach who now lives in Brooklyn, but he came to look for me first and he brought me pot stickers from Clement Street and—"

When I had called Autumn this morning to tell her I wouldn't be sharing the plane ride home with her after all, she'd said, "Shrimp has a friend from Ocean Beach who now lives in Brooklyn? Riiiight." Then, "Be careful," she'd advised. "Don't worry," I said, "I'm back on the pill." "I meant with your heart," she said. "For that boy to show up out of the blue means he is probably seriously lost, and looking to you to find his way for him. You work on *your* way, please?"

"I can't believe you're going down this road again," Nancy interrupted. I couldn't believe she knew without me telling her that

rachel cohn

I was in fact going down this road again—not just considering it. "After everything you two have been through. After you'd finally made the decision to move on with your lives." Epic San Andreas fault 7.0 Richter scale Nancy-sigh. "I can't believe we're back to this same place again. But you know what? I don't have the energy to argue this one. I can't tell you what to do, but I will tell you I'm very disappointed in you. I'm disappointed with Shrimp for manipulating your romantic idealism by springing up in Manhattan with no warning. Dad and Ash and Josh and Fernando and Sugar Pie will also be very disappointed not to share Christmas with you. And the baby . . ."

Frances Alberta is my new favorite sibling, because her crying in the background of my phone call with our mother distracted Nancy's epic disappointment trying to burst my Shrimp glow-bubble.

Shrimp does not manipulate. He's not capable of it. He's Shrimp. Applying any form of the word "manipulation" in relation to him is a complete oxymoron—he's the most mellow person in the world. "Manipulation" would harsh him into being an oxy-depleted moron, and he would have none of that.

Sid-dad got on the phone in Nancy's place. "Cupcake, what's this I hear about you not making it on the plane home this morning?" *"Ask her why!"* Nancy shrieked in the background as she tended to the baby. But Nancy didn't wait for me to tell my dad before spewing, *"Shrimp decided to show up in New York yesterday ON A WHIM."*

Onawhim. Would make cool band name. Would also make compelling tryst of Scrabble letters.

Sid-dad took his time before responding to the news my mother hadn't given me a chance to deliver myself. I wasn't sure whether he was directing his comment to me or to Nancy when he said, "Well, she is eighteen. What can you expect?"

Turns out I'm capable of shrieking like my mother. "That's patronizing!" I snapped.

Calmly, Sid-dad answered, "But true."

Twenty-eight

Shrimp is a liar.

I've got his passport in my hand to prove it. "Your real name is Philip! Or is this passport a fake?" I paused to suck in a deep breath, and to ponder every supposed truth I've ever known about the universe. This couldn't be right. "You told me your real name was Shrimp. You even showed me a birth certificate that definitively stated your legal name was Shrimp."

Shrimp took the passport from my hand and tossed it against my bedroom wall. "Actually, the birth certificate was the fake. My brother had it made for me as a joke birthday present one year. The birth certificate was supposed to be used as ID because I don't have a driver's license. Wallace wanted me to show the birth certificate to get the shrimp birthday special discount to go along with the gift certificate he gave me, good for dinner for two at Red Lobster."

"That's just mean."

"No kidding. Like I'd eat at Red Lobster?" (Said the boy who proposed marriage to me at Outback Steakhouse.)

"Wait a minute. Your real name is Philip, and you don't have a legal driver's license, either? But you drove your brother's car around everywhere when you lived in San Francisco."

"Yeah. So?" Shrimp nuzzled his head inside my neck from behind me, then pulled the blanket up higher over our bodies. "It's burr-ito in New York. Did you know about this?" His body spooned into mine, I felt no cold draft.

No Jell-O shots had been necessary to bring us back to the ecstasy where we'd left off. We've lost and found each other too many times to bother with the Will We or Won't We mating dance. We know we will. We did. It's, like, predetermined. We waited about as long as it took for Danny to leave the apartment this morning, for him to walk down the five flights of stairs, and for me to see him from our front window down at the street curb, hailing a taxi and being whisked away to the airport.

God, it felt holy-fantastic-great to mind-soul-body merge with Shrimp again. Like all was right with true love and our place within it. Praise Jesus for Christmas miracles!

"Why didn't you write me or call me from New Zealand?" I asked him.

"I was respecting your explicit directions. You told me not to contact you at all when I left. You said it would be too painful. Clean break. Your idea. Remember?"

I hate when guys take everything a girl says literally.

Shrimp added, "I noticed you didn't contact me either? So the clean break was an equal opportunity one, don't you agree?"

We'd both agree that we wouldn't dare the real question hovering over our clean break: "Have you been with anyone else?" Neither of us was ready for that answer. Hover elsewhere, question.

I pitched the soft serve inquiry instead. "Phil, what do you want from life now?"

Shrimp pressed tighter into me, and I almost rescinded the philosophical entreaty merely on the grounds of his left hand exploring the right territory. The new fullness of me matched the new leanness of him, like a yin/yang balance reflecting the changes in our lives as a result of what had happened in our lives since our News—York and Zealand.

Shrimp's slow hand definitely appreciated my growth spurt. As his hand surfed my curves, he talked to me, warming me further. He'd never been one for talking in the past. "For right now I want to be here with you. For later, I don't know. Maybe get my GED. Seems like the only job worth having that I can get without a high school diploma is working either for my brother or as a truck driver. Not that I really want a job or a career, but I guess eventually I'm gonna have to sell my soul to make the cash to travel again."

"What about your art?"

"I love creating art, but it's like you never know when inspiration will strike. I don't want to be obligated to it. I want the canvasses or the sculptures or whatever it is to happen when it wants to happen, and not happen because a car needs insurance or rent has to be paid. I want to live free of all that."

"That's what you want to do? Travel?"

"Seems like a decent and honorable goal to me, spiritually fulfilling and personally satisfying and whatever—the essence of what life's about, I guess? There are beaches I dream about in Vietnam and Kuala Lumpur and Norway and Cyprus, where the surfing is supposedly like—"

I turned over to look at him, to separate our bodies from their tight soul clasp. It's like I had tried to forget what his face looked like so I wouldn't hurt from missing it, and now I wanted to drown in the beauty of it. I placed my index and middle fingers on his full red lips. "Shhh," I whispered.

Seriously, he'd just told me more about himself in the last two minutes than in like the last two years of our knowing each other. It was overwhelming.

Shrimp instigated a silence of kisses, but I strangely couldn't focus on the taste of his mouth. I was reconsidering this new Phil creature whom I'd never known. My head flipped through mental images of Phil ten years in the future, long burnt out on surfing, never having bothered to get the GED even though that Cyd Charisse girl who'd been the love of his life back when he was a Shrimp had told him not to drop out of high school, had told him he'd eventually regret that decision. Years after her prophetically brilliant observation, Phil's regret finds him with a new life working as a truck driver, with a not-CC wife and kids in Modesto. Truck driver Phil makes regular pit stops at his favorite refuge along the I-5, where he'd be all, "Evenin', Polly, I'll have my usual" to the waitress. And Polly would be all perky and like, "Vegetarian quesadilla comin' right up," *giggle giggle,* because Polly couldn't wait to deliver Phil-not-Shrimp the blue plate special as his reward for steering clear of the strip clubs while on the road and choosing the side trips to Hooters instead—not like the old wife would mind. Wife came from a long line of Hooters waitresses; in fact that's where she met Phil, and he promised on their wedding day while they stood before the Elvis impersonator chaplain at the Reno Chapel of Love with her eight-and-a-half-months-pregnant belly sticking out that he would never love Hooters other than hers, and she believed him. Girls will believe anything when they're blinded by love.

"Where'd you go?" Shrimp asked me, his face pensive and no longer attached to mine.

I had no response. I no longer understood my relationship to truth.

Shrimp answered for me. He whispered, "I still love you."

I whispered his old standard back: "Ditto."

Manipulation does not spout "I love you." It's not possible. Manipulation does worry that the sentiment, however sincerely felt, might not have been truly earned.

TWENTY-NINE

My mother is evil. She drops these little comments that seem stupid or insignificant when she's sighing them, yet somehow they have the power to get under my skin. "I hope you know what you're doing letting Shrimp back into your life just when yours seemed to be getting on track. . . ." Nag, nag, nag.

Really, what does she know?

Except, sigh, I sort of see her point. Annoying, annoying, annoying.

Theoretically I assumed that if Shrimp and I were together in New York, I would be bursting out of my skin wanting to share this city with him. We'd go ice skating in Central Park, explore art galleries in Williamsburg, eat our way from Chinatown to Astoria, slam with the punks at dive clubs in Alphabet City. And of course we'd fit in the requisite time in my bedroom, hiding out from the world, lost in each other. The reality was, I loved that Shrimp came to Manhattan and found me, but I felt powerless about how that choice was made. He just showed up. I had no say in the when and the whim of how our lives once again intersected. My heart burned all these months for wanting him to share my new life, but with him suddenly here live and in the flesh, giving no indication as to whether he planned to settle in or pick up and leave for the next killer curl somewhere else in the world, I really *didn't* know what I was doing with Shrimp. Should I relax and enjoy it for the moment, or expect our reunion to evolve into a new relationship like before, only now we were grown-up and living on our own, accountable for our own choices—and mistakes?

Life seems to sort itself out for me at L U _ C H _ O N E _ T E, so I figured I'd better dip Shrimp into the well there, test him in my new environment and see how he fit in with that part of my new life. Experimenting with how a San Francisco surfer boy adapted to my Manhattan Project could yield important findings.

"What are you doing here, Myself?" Johnny Mold asked when I arrived for a Christmas Eve day shift, Shrimp in tow. "You're supposed to be in San Francisco."

The joint jumped with people, shoppers with all their cheery holiday bullshit gift bags, the yoga mommies and their infinite realms of strollers, and a hella strong gathering of Chelsea boys. Clearly Johnny needed me, regardless of whether he expected me.

"Then why am I here, Mold?" I stepped behind the counter, intending to show off my pride and joy to Shrimp. But my path to La Marzocco was blocked by a hulking figure standing at the machine, with a pitcher of foam milk in his hand, readying to pour the milk over a pull of fresh espresso. His Hunky Tallness had long, wavy black hair, a chiseled face with big green eyes and long black eyelashes under heavy black eyebrows, a roman nose, and morning why-bother stubble surrounding his mouth. He looked either like the Aramis man or the hero dude of questionable sexuality pictured on the covers of Harlequin romances, except one who wore prayer beads around his wrist and a yellow shirt picturing a happy big-belly red Buddha. All I could say to him was, "Who the fuck are you?"

"Such language!" He laugh-smiled. The Jolly Harlequin Giant looked toward Johnny Mold. "This is the barista you write to me about who bring the buzz back to this place?" He had some weird foreign accent, like maybe Italian, and in his warm eyes and wide grin I knew he was one of those genial, good karma people whom everybody instantly loves. I hate people like that.

Johnny Mold said, "Cyd Charisse, meet Dante. Dante, CC."

NO WAY. Universe is a shambles, crumbling at my feet.

"Why?" I stated, directing my comment to Johnny. *That stupid handsome legendary espresso man is the reason I spent the first six weeks of my new life stranded in a fifth-floor walk-up apartment! And why, oh why, does that espresso pull in his hand smell SO GOOD!*

Johnny said, "I hired him to fill in during your supposed vacation. I've been trying to lure Dante here from La Traviata for the last year, but he didn't agree until now. There's, like, buzz about the buzz of this place, you know? Dante's been in Corsica for the last couple months, but he wanted to spend the holidays in Manhattan, and this time he finally said yes to my invitation."

Lure. Dante. Here.

I suspected the straight-edge celibate of having a not-so-straight crush, but I knew better than to acknowledge the possibility that Johnny could be more interested in a person than, say, his Game Boy, or his band. Instead I grabbed Johnny by his Mikado/Penzance hand and dragged him to the bathroom. We had to shove aside a good half dozen people to get past the line for Dante. Word of the great espresso man's return to Manhattan must have spread quickly.

Inside the bathroom I hissed at Johnny, "I thought you were going to close this place during the holidays."

"I was. But there are like lots of Jewish and Chinese people who need food and caffeine before they go to the movies on Christmas day, and lots of business people who have to stick around for end-of-year business accounting or something like that. Why shouldn't this place be the one to serve the people who don't go away for the holidays? Half the restaurants in this neighborhood close the week between Christmas and New Year's. I figured the opportunity was ripe for us to grab some of their business then."

"You're not supposed to have ambition! I count on you for that!"

"Excuse me, but you weren't supposed to come here and know how to use the espresso machine, to fix up the furniture and arrange it like all invitingly for customers, to recruit book clubs to have meetings here, to threaten a movie night. Now I have to stay on top of employee schedules and supply orders and—"

"Dante's not replacing me, is he? You swear he'll leave after New Year's?"

"Dante's a barista-wanderer. He roams from café to café, city to city. It's like a whole philosophy and lifestyle for him. I couldn't get him to stay even if I wanted him to stay."

"Do you want him to stay?" Nudge-nudge.

"Don't be coy, Myself. I have no interest in Dante other than in continuing to build this business, because now that my grandpa Johnny the First has seen the hint of profit in the accounting books, he apparently wants to see more. Dying old man's wish, whatever. This pressure's gonna kill me, I tell ya. I haven't been to band practice in weeks."

Now it was Johnny's turn to drag me, this time leading me out of the bathroom and back toward the front counter. "Who's that guy?" Johnny asked me, pointing at Shrimp, who had joined Dante at La Marzocco and taken on junior pilot responsibilities, writing down customers' orders to help move the line more efficiently. Had I been delusional, questioning how Shrimp would adapt into this atmosphere? Shrimp's brother owns an independent coffee chain business in San Francisco—Shrimp lives and breathes java almost as much as surfing or painting. He's natural selection here.

I answered Johnny, "He's my . . ." *boyfriend*—not quite, "he's my . . ." *true love*—too much backstory required to explain, "he's my . . ." *lover*—too grown-up. "He's my Shrimp," I finally said.

Shrimp said something to Dante, causing Dante to laugh and slap Shrimp on the back. *He's my Shrimp who's so not getting any if he doesn't cool off the brewing friendship with the Dante inferno.*

Johnny patted my shoulder. "Good lure," he said. "You oughta do some shifts with Dante. You could learn a lot from him." I shoved Johnny's shoulder. Hard. "That hurt!" Johnny whined.

What truly hurt was that Shrimp possibly fit into this environment more than I do. By the close of business that day he was on a first-name basis with half the customers, and he had a pile of business cards from people who wanted to hire him for odd jobs. Even Johnny fell under Shrimp's spell. Shrimp drew a set of dragon sketches for Johnny so good that Johnny had to leave work early to deliver the sketches to the tattoo parlor needle man for immediate slayage onto the remaining open skin space at the back of his neck. Worse, the afternoon Shrimp spent assisting Dante at the machine, chatting and sipping shot after shot, had revealed that Shrimp and Dante were almost related, like barista-*sympaticos*. Conversation about their travels had unearthed the connection that Dante knew Shrimp's brother, Wallace. Dante and Wallace met when they were both backpacking around Indonesia. They shared a mutual passion for coffee and they traveled together for a while, in search of the perfect Indonesian blend. Then Wallace fell in love with a Balinese girl and Dante found the dharma, and eventually the two friends lost touch with each other, but connection is connection, man, it's deep, which must by why fate had delivered Wallace's brother to Dante's Manhattan temp job. Small world.

This was *my* world. "Go ahead!" I said, when Shrimp asked me if I'd mind if he and Dante took off for a couple hours to get dinner together, because I was so totally not threatened by their connection, I could even subdue my burning desire to sterilize La Marzocco from Dante's fingerprints the moment Dante and Shrimp walked out the door. "I'm fine to cover the evening shift here." Myself's turf.

Left alone again at La Marzocco, I pondered how even when things seem like a mess for Shrimp, they fall into place for him anyway. A week ago Shrimp was broke and alone, getting bumped off a flight from New Zealand after the parents he followed there—and for whom he gave up his true love—got bumped off the island; he had nothing and no one to go home to. Now he'd found himself at the center of the world, his old girlfriend swiftly reinstated into his life and into his pants, a jar full of tips tipping his wallet into a positive balance, and the legendary espresso man Dante buying him dinner. Merry freaking Christmas.

Myself decided to celebrate the impending holiday by giving a little gift to all the sculpted Chelsea boys and taut body alpha mommies who arrived that evening on the hunt for Dante. I replaced the Equal containers with real sugar and poured whole milk into the containers marked skim. 'Tis the season to be jolly—and fat.

I am evil and I love me.

THIRTY

Evil personally called to me on Christmas morning. Evil whispered: "True love is too good to be true. Don't believe. Let go now, before it's too late."

I hear you, Evil, I really do.

Breaking up would surely be hard to do on Christmas morning, but I would manage. I always do. Evil offered to lend a helping hand should I falter.

Just because a day's a holiday doesn't mean a break from the naturally selected order of the world. Reality had awoken me out of Evil's whisper-slumber, shouting to me that THE UNIVERSE DOES NOT INTEND FOR THIS THING WITH SHRIMP TO WORK OUT. IT HASN'T IN THE PAST, SO WHY SHOULD IT NOW? ACCEPT *THAT* TRUTH, AND MERRY FREAKING CHRISTMAS AND GOD BLESS YOU, ONE AND ALL.

Alone together for the first time in our new incarnations as independent adult-types, with no parents or school or other distractions demanding our attentions away from each other, I awoke Christmas morning knowing that the blessed time with Shrimp most likely operated on a holiday schedule. After New Year's, Danny would return to the apartment, and Shrimp's lease on staying at our apartment would terminate. Shrimp and I would be back to the same place that broke us up last time—we want each other, but beyond that, we want different lives. He yearns to travel the world. I yearn to travel the world that is the island of Manhattan. I prefer hanging out in a cool job. He prefers not to be tied down. I strive to discover the meaning of actualization. He strives to experience killer curls. Stalemate.

"Mate," I was gonna say when I located where Shrimp had gone after slipping out of bed early this morning, not knowing I would fall back asleep to Evil and awake to Reality, "this situation is stale. Let's stop fooling ourselves, for good. We've had this reunion we both longed for, but let's end this while it's still good."

The San Francisco boy did not care about New York winter chill, because Shrimp stood in my living room on Christmas morning, nekkid but for a pair of Santa-themed boxer shorts covering his lower middle, and a furry red Santa hat covering his upper head. When Shrimp-Santa saw me come into the room, he kicked the play button on the stereo. He preempted the breakup song I was about to dedicate to him by turning on "Waiting" by SF boy Chris Isaak, from a favorite album of our San Francisco days that Shrimp and I listened to back at Wallace's house at Ocean Beach, when Shrimp would come in from surfing and I'd be waiting for him, to towel him dry and then share a special San Francisco treat with him—an Its-It bar, two oatmeal cookies with vanilla ice cream sandwiched in between, dipped in chocolate.

Shrimp couldn't produce a genuine Its-It in New York, but he did a damn fine Ocean Beach replay scene. While Chris sang about here I stand with my heart in my hands and I offer love to you, Shrimp pulled me into his arms for a slow dance. Shrimp whispered into my ear along with Chris's croon, telling me about here I stand with my world gone wrong and I wonder what to do. I nestled my head onto Shrimp's shoulder as Shrimp elevated his whisper to sing along with the record, aloud, about oh how I've missed you, I wanted to kiss you, I dreamt that I held you and lost you again.

Inside our dance, over Shrimp's shoulder and under Chris's song, I saw the result of Shrimp's morning's work. The living room table had vases of fresh flowers on either side, with a Christmas breakfast display sandwiched in between: steaming scrambled eggs, fresh fruit salad, home fries, and a stack of Pop-Tarts.

Fuck off, Evil.

After breakfast, after the belches and the kisses, followed by more belches and kisses, Shrimp pulled his gift from underneath the sofa where he'd stored it, unwrapped.

"A sketchbook?" I asked, confused. Shrimp knows I have no artistic talent, nor the desire to try my hand at artistic talent that does not involve trying to make rosetta latte art with steamed milk and espresso swirls.

"Open it," Shrimp said.

I opened the sketchbook to see that it was indeed about me and my art—just not drawn by me. As I flipped the pages, I saw me after me after me, pictures Shrimp had drawn with colored pencils during his time in New Zealand, using photographs of me as models—or just memory of me to hue the lines. There I stood on the Staten Island Ferry floating by the Statue of Liberty, waving to the camera memory of Shrimp's sketch hand. Gray fog enveloped black-clad me on the sandy dunes of Ocean Beach. Café me had a cappuccino mug in one hand, a Nestlé Crunch bar in the other. Half 'n' half me pictured a face split down the middle—half my face, my formerly long hair drawn in green, and the other half the real Cyd Charisse but drawn in black, with the razor sharp bobbed flapper hairstyle of her green-dress dance from *Singin' in the Rain.*

"When I was in New Zealand and missing you, this sketch-book was how I kept you with me. I imagined you in place of being with you."

I felt bad because I had no present for him in return, had given no thought whatsoever to finding him a Christmas gift since his unexpected arrival. "I'm sorry I have nothing for you," I said. *Evil lurks within my soul. Do you understand that, Phil? I intended to send you packing this morning.*

But Shrimp said, "You give me you. That's all I want."

I wanted to shove him for saying the perfect thing after the perfect present after the perfect breakfast, but I didn't. I burst into tears instead.

Shrimp did a walkabout around the living room during my cry, which I appreciated, as a huggy-kissy follow-up moment would have wrecked the scene. He touched the various framed photographs while he walked, Danny and Aaron at their old café; Max and Yvette Mimieux in Max's garden; a close-up of Johnny Mold's Harry Potter tattoos on his lower back; me with lisBETH, Danny, and Frank grimacing at the tofurkey lisBETH prepared this past Thanksgiving during her brief flirtation with vegetarianism. "Don't cry," Shrimp said. "Just look at the life you've grown here, all these people who care for you." I sputtered, "But everything always works out so easily for you, Shrimp. I'm just a goof-off." But Shrimp was not playing with me. He said, "Things work out for you because you work hard to make them happen." He did not mumble the sentiment.

Later, comatose on my tears, his Pop-Tarts, and a Chris Isaak croon hangover, we devoted the afternoon to quality couch potato time, my head on Shrimp's lap, who sat watching football like a proper boy, but with the sound turned off at commercials. During the breaks Shrimp gave me the best present of all—he told me about Himself. He'd gotten into meditation while in the Land of the Kiwis. Meditation helped counteract the feeling Shrimp had that the world could be a pretty hateful and overwhelming place when he wasn't lost inside waves or art; it had helped center his mind, so he could see that it was time to return home and deal with the real world again. He said maybe it had been a mistake for him to follow his parents to New Zealand, but he'd wanted that time with them. He wanted to feel like he could trust them, like they could be there for him after having deposited him to live with his brother for most of his high school years while they traipsed across the world. He said he suspected before he left that it probably wouldn't work out, but he felt like he had to try—for them and for him. Now he didn't have to wonder anymore. Now he knew he was on his own.

As Christmas night broke into Boxing Day early morning, I said, "I can't remember you ever telling me so much about yourself at once."

Shrimp said, "I can't remember you ever listening so much at once."

THIRTY-ONE

Warning label: **THE SURGEON GENERAL CC HAS** DETERMINED THAT DANTE'S ESPRESSO CREATIONS SINGEING THE LIPS, CHURNING THROUGH THE MOUTH, AND GLIDING DOWN THE THROAT MAY CAUSE FULL BODY CONVULSIONS, AND NOT JUST THE CAFFEINATED JOLT KIND.

Salut!

I admit it. Dante is the supreme god of baristas. Watching Dante brew is like what I imagine it would be like to hear Pavarotti in his prime sing from *La Traviata*, or to watch Michelangelo paint the Sistine Chapel. There's a reason the guy has an international following and can pick his gigs at any café around the world. He's a master. He earns the title.

Like Frank-dad, Dante likes to lecture. Unlike Frank-dad, Dante actually seems to know what he's talking about. Lesson number one: Espresso-making is both an art and a science—and should never be treated as just a job. Lesson number two: Always remember the four fundamental *M*s necessary for a good cup: *miscela* (the blend), *macinatura* (the grind), *macchina* (the espresso machine), *mano* (the skill of the machine operator). Lesson number three: The four *M*s result in the optimal espresso pull, which should be full-bodied and almost syrupy, so rich it requires no sugar or other flavorings, and topped with a thick layer of crema.

Dante advised I should have not been surprised by the lack of good espresso to be found in New York City—it's all about the water. The water here has the necessary purity and flavor to significantly contribute to the quality of the area's outstanding bagels and pizza dough, and to make a decent espresso possible, but the water is reportedly deficient in calcium, which gives body to espresso. If I want to taste perfection, I need to go to Naples, where the volcanic soil from Mount Vesuvius provides the world's most superior water source for espresso.

Dante reeducates as well as lectures. "*Bella*, La Marzocco is not the 'Cadillac of machines.'" It's an excellent machine, agreed—though it's a Toyota Camry, always reliable and it will last forever, but art? No. The best espresso machines have long unpronounceable Italian names that sound like symphonies when articulated out of Dante's mouth. I'd have to go to Italy to see them, because they're surely not going to be found in this land of coffee philistines—and *signorina*, those machines are Lamborghinis.

I am but a mere barista novice, according to Dante. My instincts are good, but I have *molto* to learn. But he sees my *potenziale*. Dante sees Shrimp's potential too—but advises that Shrimp is like him, someone who will be a barista to support the wandering lifestyle, as opposed to Shrimp's *vero amore* (me), who will wander around only until she finds a barista lifestyle to support.

Gurus are so full of themselves with the *spiegazione*, but with espresso that tasty, what do I care? Keep bringing on that enlightenment.

My Shrimp-love-haze-fog streams so thick I don't sweat Dante's superior abilities. I'm young. I'll get better and better. I totally ace Dante's art and science of espresso-making with the pure love I dose in. And I have my own true love—reinstated, if admittedly indeterminate, but who cares? The here and now is good, good, good. What's Dante got? Caffeinated nerves of steel and a passport.

Also, I am a way better polka dancer than Dante.

"You're stepping on my feet!" I said to Dante after the record skipped from our dance-jumping. I slipped out of Dante's arms and added a penny onto the needle arm of the old portable record player borrowed from Max's apartment. The penny addition helped—the

Lawrence Welk record from Danny's one dollah LP collection mellowed to basic scratches instead of skips.

Last year on New Year's Eve, after a "just friends" period following our first breakup, Shrimp and I reunited and it felt so good. This year, after yet another breakup and reunion, we had no interest in the Times Square ball-dropping or the champagne. Instead we got drunk on caffeine with Johnny and Dante, played Parcheesi with them, and finished up the celebrating with a round of Lawrence Welk polka dancing. The glamour never stops here in Manhattan.

"I am a fantastic dancer!" Dante disputed. "Ask Johnny!"

Johnny shrugged over the sci-fi/fantasy paperback novel gripping his attention. "Dante's pretty good," he mumbled. The poor boy looked spent from our New Year's Eve celebration at L U _ C H _ O N E _ T E, but the hard-core straight-edge punk won't acknowledge he has a hard time staying awake past ten in the evening—which may offer some *spiegazione* as to why none of his bands survive.

"*Bella* just wants to save herself for Shrimp's last dance," Dante said.

Vero. Shrimp felt too far away even from a few feet away. I settled for sigh-staring at his beautiful backside standing at the front window, as Shrimp spray-painted the missing L U _ C H _ O N E _ T E letters with the missing N, E and T, graffiti-style.

The D-Man down in KW was not experiencing the same lover

bliss as his sister CC. I knew trouble had found Danny in Key West when I saw his name flash on my cell phone just as I was about to polka Shrimp home and ring in the New Year with him properly.

I answered, "Danny boy, you gave up the Village on New Year's Eve, so shouldn't you be acting like the Village People down in Key West and not calling your younger sister at one in the morning?"

"CC," Danny slobbered from his end of the call. "Help me! I'm lost!"

"Where are you? Should I call the police?"

"No, I'm in my hotel room. Perfectly safe."

"Then what's the problem?"

"The empty Veuve Clicquot bottle beside my bed might be part of the problem?"

I so wanted to lay some rules down on my drunken brother, but I decided to go the compassionate route instead. "Regret finally fucking caught up with you?" I asked him.

"YES!" he sputtered, sounding near tears. Then his lips let rip, almost like my caffeinated-polkanated state had roared through the cell phone airwaves and into his inebriated bloodstream. "Ceece, do you understand? Aaron and I got together in high school, we never dated anyone else. I was in a committed relationship from the time I was eighteen. I never got that time of dating other people and finding myself or whatever it is you're supposed to do in your twenties. And then the business went under and everything was a mess and I needed change. I needed to experience new things, new people, independent of Aaron. I let him go. But now I'm getting my shit together again and I want him back, and I don't know what to do. I royally fucked up. I don't deserve him, but I want him back anyway. It's not just that I won't ever do better than Aaron—I know I won't, knew that even when I broke up with him. It's that now I'd never want to have anyone other than Aaron again. And this other guy he's seeing is talking moving in together; he's practically ready to register them at Macy's! Aaron *hates* Macy's! Anyone who truly loves him knows that Aaron is partial to Bloomies! Stop laughing, that's not an insignificant detail. Ceece, they're making me physically sick! I can't fake this 'just friends' thing with Aaron any longer. What am I supposed to do, sage little sister?"

"Earn him back," I said. "And call me back when you're sober so I can repeat that advice so's you'll actually remember it."

If Danny could earn Aaron back, surely I could believe that my holiday vacation love haze with Shrimp had the hope for a happy ending rather than the old stalemate.

THIRTY-TWO

Yvette Mimieux has been outed as a diva. Diva fault number one: She's very ornery about sitting in one place for long periods of time to pose for Shrimp's cereal still-life paintings of her. Diva fault number two: She hates to fly on airplanes.

Max's sentence for Yvette's diva crimes: Yvette should stay home for the month of January instead of accompanying Max for his annual winter visit with his elderly mother in Sun City, Arizona. Her stay at home would be made possible by Shrimp, who should cat-sit while Max is gone, thus giving Shrimp enough time to convince Yvette to sit still long enough for Shrimp to complete a whole series of cereal paintings in her honor.

Max held Yvette on his lap, crouching over to kissy-face her as he told her, "Yvette, you minx, you'd better comply since Shrimp is sparing you the airplane trauma and sparing you a month with my mother, who hates you and kicks you when she doesn't think I'm looking. Remember Mommy Dearest, Yvette?" Max turned Yvette so she faced a framed photograph of Max's mother. Yvette *miaule*'d her displeasure and jumped off Max's lap, scurrying to her favorite hiding place underneath the piano.

Shrimp peeked out from behind his easel (belated Christmas present from me), where he sat on Max's piano bench completing the final touches on Yvette's portrait. The artwork consisted of oat and bran cereal glued onto a canvass in cat form, then painted over in Yvette's colors and face, like cerealsy brilliant impressionism as only Shrimp could bring it. Shrimp said, "I don't remember agreeing to this situation?"

Max and I both proclaimed, "Of course you agree!"

The whole situation could be like killing two birds with one Shrimp, which Yvette, who hates birds more than Max's mother hates her, could surely appreciate. The cat-sitting gig would allow Shrimp to stay in NYC longer, once Danny returned home and kept me to my promise that Shrimp would only stay at our apartment while Danny was away for the holidays, and it would give Yvette a reprieve from her annual visit with Mommy Dearest. Everybody would win.

But Shrimp wavered. "I don't know," he said.

"I'll leave you two lovebirds alone for a few minutes to discuss," Max said. He headed to his bedroom, squealing *"Chirp, chirp!"* to us before he slammed the bedroom door closed.

rachel cohn

I sat down on the piano bench next to Shrimp, cozying up to his side and resting my head on his shoulder. "Pretty please?" I pouted.

"Don't do that; it's icky," Shrimp said.

Honeymoon's over?

I dropped the pout and called it straight. "I want you to stay. Do you want you to stay?"

Last night in the dark we both whispered "yes" to the hovered "Has there been anyone else?" question that finally pushed itself out of the closet. We both answered "no" to the follow-up clean break question—"Does it really make a difference?" I don't know which mattered more—our ease of honesty with each other, or that the honest answer honestly didn't matter. Fair is fair. Trust is trust.

Instead of answering the stay or go question, Shrimp picked pieces of cereal off the canvass. He held up a Cheerio painted ginger, from a spot formerly on Yvette's portrait face. After about a minute of intense Cheerio contemplation, Shrimp announced, "I want to stay." He sealed the deal with a kiss on my neck.

Book us that honeymoon suite, Max!

"What made you decide?" I asked.

"Cereal mandalas."

"Huh?"

"I'm going to take this painting apart and do it over. Like a sand mandala."

"Huh—times two?"

Shrimp said, "I'm inspired by the sand mandala philosophy right now, want to apply it to the cereal art. Remember when I went out with Dante to the Tibetan Buddhist place near Union Square? Well, some monks had a sand mandala on exhibition there. What happens is, teams of monks use metal funnels to place grains of dyed sand into these incredibly intricate patterns that are formed into geometric designs symbolic of the universe. You have to see it; you'd be awed. Dante said the mandala represents an imaginary palace that is contemplated during meditation. The monks'll spend days creating a single mandala, and then they have like a spiritual ceremony to celebrate it, and then—you can't believe this part—*WHOOSH,* they destroy the masterwork. It's meant to be about the transient nature of existence. Dante said the destruction of the mandala serves to remind one of the impermanence of life. I imagine it's like surfing—wiping out over and over as a metaphor for the meaning of life. Heavy shit. Or sand, as the case may be."

Not bad for a high school dropout, I'd say. To Shrimp I said, "So the fact of me had nothing to do with your decision to stay?"

Shrimp laughed, kinda. "Of course it had to do with you. Everything's about you. Obviously." Says the boy who presented me the sketchbook devoted to Myself. Make up your mind, buddy! "You think I actually understood Dante's sermons on transcendental transience or whatever?"

My mind was made up. My loverboy was as smart and deep as

he is beautiful. "I totally think you do. I think you're intrigued to know more. I think that's pretty fucking cool."

"I think you know me better than me."

"That's why I'm me who loves you even though everything's obviously all about me." I pinched his side gently, kinda.

"Ow," he muttered.

"Look around this apartment, Shrimp," I said, admiring the movie star magazine photographs, the flags, the art deco furniture, the hot-pink lamps with the velvet tassels hanging down from the lamp shades. Inspiration, everywhere. "You belong here."

Shrimp pulled me closer to him. "No, *you* belong here. But I will make good use of the time here." He pulled a stack of business cards from his pants pocket. "I've got all these people who want to hire me for odd jobs. So when I'm not painting Yvette or hanging with you or going off on some meditational daze, at least I can be building up the cash situation until I figure out the next move."

Thank you, Max, thank you for the month. I know Shrimp and I will figure out the next move by then, and it will be a move in together. I believe!

Max came back into the living room. "Documents have been drawn up and printed on the computer in my bedroom. Now, Cyd Charisse, if you'll just sign here, you're agreeing to take custody of Yvette Mimieux if my plane crashes. . . ."

Assuming Danny's plane home doesn't crash, now all I had to

do was break it to the Danny diva—the one person who doesn't love Shrimp like everyone loves Dante—that Shrimp would be sticking around longer than expected. Like, maybe permanently without danger of the impermanent nature of transcendental mediation, or meditation, or something.

Bottom line, that's all about me, me, me: This diva win, win, wins!

THIRTY-THREE

Hallelujah. As predicted, Danny's vacation was a complete disaster!

What I could not have predicted was how hard-to-get Aaron would play it. Good on him. He's making Danny earn it.

Danny cannot recount the tale to me enough, but I love the story, I don't mind. At six in the morning in Danny's rented kitchen space, I barely had the energy to sit upright at the cupcake decorating preparation table, much less engage Danny in conversation myself.

Even before caffeination Danny could fire into the story full steam ahead and at the same time go about the business of massive cupcake production. "So I got off the phone with you on New Year's Eve and went down to the beach, thinking I'd have a walk or maybe just pass out on the sand. But there was Aaron and what's-his-name, strolling along the surf, hand in hand. Pass me that oven mitt, will you, Dollface? Look at this, yet another exquisite batch of red velvet. Go, us. This process goes so much more efficiently with your help here." I passed Danny the oven mitt and breathed in the aroma of the freshly baked cupcakes. Mmmmm. Waking up. "So I watch Aaron and that other creature for a while; then I panic when I see them stop their stroll. Because the boyfriend was getting down on bended knee, and all of a sudden I had a very bad feeling that was not just about the champagne in my stomach wanting to heave up!"

"Where was Jerry Lewis?" I always remember to ask.

"He has a real name, you know. But what's that matter, because I have no idea where he'd gone. He'd already gotten sick of me and my mooning over Aaron by that point in the vacation, and he went out clubbing with some people he'd met at the hotel bar."

"Good. I love the part where he permanently exits the picture. He used too much hair gel."

"I know! I never wanted to put my hands around his head when we were kissing! No, Ceece, hold the parchment paper like this, wrap a little tighter—right. You just made what's called a cornet to pipe the filling into this tray of cupcakes. Good job, my most excellent apprentice. So where was I? I know. I'm walking on the beach and I see Aaron and you-know-who . . . ,"—here Danny and I both stuck our fingers down our throats and emitted a *bleh* sound—"and what's gag-me doing but proposing to Aaron! And I'd

rachel cohn

just had enough. I marched right into that proposal and told Aaron, 'You can't marry that moron, because you belong to me!'"

My coffee kicked in. "And Aaron said he doesn't belong to anyone, he's his own person!"

"Right, and gag-me was like, 'Excuse me, Danny, why are you present every time I'm trying to have a moment with my boyfriend?' and I was like, 'Excuse me, but Aaron's not *your* true love. *I* am Aaron's true love.'"

I thumped my fist to my chest and swooned, "And Aaron was like, 'Danny, you're my true love? Still? Really?'"

"Exactly! Aaron forgot all about gag-me sitting right there on bended knee, under the moonlight and on the beach, proposing to him on New Year's Eve in full cliché mode, with a ring from Tiffany and everything! I mean, how lame is that? I don't know what circles gag-me runs in, but in mine and Aaron's, there is no such thing as a gay engagement ring."

Aaron did not forget how to take care of his true love. Once Blip left the scene, Aaron rubbed Danny's back during Danny's postdeclaration of love Veuve Clicquot heave, then held his hand as they laid on the beach for the post-spew, pre-sunset pass-out nap that Danny needed.

But we don't like to discuss the barfing part of the story in front of the cupcakes. "How expensive do you think the ring was? Seriously, how many carats?" I sampled a taste of the frosting that the chest-thumping swoon had caused me to gob on my apron. Outstanding. I've finally mastered making the praline frosting myself, without Danny's help.

Danny said, "Doesn't matter, because Aaron thought the engagement ring was ridiculous too. *And,* Aaron chose me." Danny danced a jig in front of the oven. He really ought to feel more compassion for poor Blip's loss, but apparently Blip proposes to every boyfriend he has (that ring has allegedly seen more action than Cinderella's slipper), so I hope the karma gods will look the other way for Danny dancing a jig celebrating his own joy at the expense of Blip's heartbreak.

I reminded Danny, "Well, not exactly."

"Drink more coffee, sister. Aaron *did* choose me. Only he said we had to take it slow this time. No commitments. No spending the night or other indoor sports, as Aaron's treasured Judy Blume would say—at least not as of yet. We'll go on proper dates. Get to know each other all over again. Start fresh."

"Aaron wants romance! Aaron wants you to unlearn how to take him for granted!"

Danny grinned at me. "Aaron's *getting* romance." Since they returned from vacation, Aaron's getting fresh flowers delivered to his apartment doorstep every morning, he's getting Teddy Pendergrass and Luther Vandross baby-making songs dedicated to him on the R & B satellite radio station for the whole world to hear, he's getting Danny wide awake and holding his hand at the ballet—and at the movies, on the subway, strolling through Washington Square Park. He's getting Danny-love loud and proud.

Aaron's also getting a Commandant who shouldn't be passing judgment on romance clichés, since he himself has turned into positive mush. "Shrimp's staying an extra month in Manhattan, Dollface? Hurrah! Maybe this time he'll grunt more than two words to me and actually let me get to know him."

Danny grinned so wide I knew the time was ripe for a fresh Shrimp pitch. "Shrimp is all about the romance too," I told Danny. "He's picking me up after breakfast time and taking me for a walk to his favorite place he found in Central Park. The Cali surf boy has never seen so much snow before in his life. We're going to have a picnic in the snow and then Shrimp wants to sketch me standing on the red-yellow bridge, with the white frost and iced-out pond behind me. Doesn't he look scrumptious with that tanned face wearing that harsh Siberia winter hat with the flaps over the ears?"

Danny ignored my Shrimp pitch. He passed me a cupcake decorated like Cartman from *South Park,* then sang along with the stereo, rendering a verse of "Kyle's Mom Is a Bitch" by bellowing aloud about how "She's a big, fat, fucking bitch!" When Danny finished his rousing chorus, I scolded him like I was Kyle's mom, just without the histrionics. "You're skipping the Shrimp entrée. I want you to tell me you like him."

"I like him. I don't know him. I've been back from vacation two weeks and he hasn't bothered to spend a minute of time interacting with me other than to compliment me on the cupcake artwork when he comes to pick you up for your playtime between your morning job here and your barista job later in the day. Sounds like Shrimp connected with Johnny and Dante instantly. He's even apartment-sitting for that old crank, Max. So what's wrong with me?"

I don't know what Shrimp's problem with Danny is. Alone with me, Shrimp couldn't be more attentive. But ask him to join me and Danny for our weekly special *Dynasty* viewings from the episodes we recorded from the classic soap channel, and Shrimp sits next to me, his arms crossed, not saying a word, staring straight ahead at the TV like he couldn't be more bored. He doesn't draw or join in on the nonstop cackle-chatter Danny and I share. Ask Shrimp to show Danny his Yvette paintings or his new sketchbook of the uptown places—the Cloisters, Harlem, Saint John's cathedral—that Shrimp and I have been exploring because we're on a quest to find truth in the rumor that there's life not just above Fourteenth Street but above Central Park, too, and Shrimp mumbles "Maybe later."

I had no answer for Danny's question, so I lobbed a different question his way. "Danny, are you going to teach me how to make the naughty cupcakes or not?"

"Are you kidding? I grew up in Connecticut. I might show the artistry to my kid sister, but teach her how to craft the lasciviousness? No, you'll have to figure it out yourself. The ingredients are right over there." He pointed to the naughty cupcake-decorating table, heaped with bowls of pink frosting, chocolate sprinkles, and whipped cream. "I'm just not that cool. It would be too weird."

"Then you lured me here under false pretenses. You said you'd teach me."

"You wanted to be lured." From the stand below the baking table, Danny pulled out a tray of vanilla cupcakes with erotic icing designs. He teased, "So do you want to be the person to divert delivery of this batch from the gay *Jeopardy!* tournament in Chelsea to Daddy and lisBETH instead?"

"You know what's weird?" I said, thinking about how when I moved here last summer, we were all single, but things change, we've evolved. The NY bio-fam all rung in the New Year with significant others. "We've all got somebody."

Danny teased again, "We should enjoy it now, because given our histories, and especially Daddy's, surely that will change." He sing-songed again, "Bye-bye, love." He picked up the Cartman cupcake and turned it over onto a plate, destroying the artwork. Poor misunderstood Cartman.

"I know," I said, feeling the happy mood of our morning kitchen space routine turning to knotted stomach anticipation—of what, I didn't know. "There are like mandalas all about it."

THIRTY-FOUR

Truth or dare.

"CC, when are you going to give up your scattershot jobs and give in to a proper culinary school curriculum already?"

Silence.

Still being on the outs with Truth, and never one to turn down a Dare, I had no choice but to accept lisBETH's challenge. She dared me to help her inaugurate her New Year's resolution to try a yoga class.

"I like your little man," lisBETH whispered to me as she bent over in Down Dog position. Shrimp oddly can't ignore Danny enough, yet he easily accepted lisBETH's odd-job offer. After a week in her apartment installing new blinds and repainting her living room, Shrimp's rather taken with her. He wants to paint a canvass of lisBETH and Myself standing back-to-back. He'll call it *Hostile Takeover*. That Shrimp had the very idea to create the painting is a good sign, I believe—it means he's considering staying in NYC even after Max returns. That lisBETH would never agree to pose for such a painting is a Reality not factored into the idea.

LisBETH's idea for us to take a yoga class together could have used some Hot Nude Yoga brand of inspiration. A class with hot naked guys, even if they were off limits to us, would have to be more interesting than the Upper East Side Yoga for Uptight Stressmonger Wenches that lisBETH had dragged us to. I did appreciate that even though lisBETH and I share little besides DNA, we were both total yoga spazzes. Our genetically disposed terrible balance had us fumbling and falling through half the postures, though we were outstanding successes at not suppressing our giggles.

"SHHH!" hissed the yoga mommy behind us.

I ignored the Frowning Pretzel. "Shrimp likes you, too," I whispered to lisBETH. "When am I gonna meet *your* man?" LisBETH and Frank have a romance conspiracy going on; neither will cough up details of how their vacations with their love interests went, other than to say "Fine" and then change the subject.

LisBETH whispered, "Soon enough. I'm not ready yet to introduce him to my family pathology."

If I were a thick-eyebrowed, big-haired, shoulder-padded character on an eighties soap, my suspicious mind would have me poised to start a diva catfight here, or at least tantrum-throw my yoga mat in my sister's face: *So. LisBETH.* (The BETH part spewed extra dramatically.) *Are you telling me you haven't yet told your boyfriend about the illegitimate love child–sister who unexpectedly charged into your life, because you're embarrassed by your father's long-ago indiscretion?* But I am only an eighties soap character in cupcake-baking time *Dynasty* reenactment episodes with Danny. (He plays good guy/gay guy Steven Carrington and I play Steven's spoiled princess sister Fallon, the sometimes good girl, sometimes bad girl.) The real world, real time CC wondered if she hadn't met Frank's lady friend for the same reason she hadn't met lisBETH's beau—they could accept her in private family time, but full disclosure with new significant others? Not there yet.

Or maybe my mind stretched into paranoia along with the lotus pose that brought with it dreamy visions of Carringtons and their Denver oil money, which only seemed to buy them grief and truly horrible outfits to go along with their fantastically horrible dialogue.

In lulling voice the instructor at the front of the class said, "Concentrate on the quiet. Remember your deep breathing. Focus your center."

Speak English?

Obstruction of the Quiet (yet another excellent band name)

lost the instructor her contemplative focus. "What's that beep?" she asked. She looked directly at me from the front of the room. "I *know* someone didn't bring a cell phone into this class!" Her not-so-lulling tone suggested I was a kindergartner in her class and not a fully-evolving eighteen-year-old spreading her effulgent yoga wings.

I unspread my arms and returned them to my side to pull my cell phone out of my pants pocket. A text message flashed on the screen from Shrimp, and my heart rate shot up even higher than the level my pre-yoga espresso shot had accomplished. Shrimp does not approve of the cell phone, says his one major goal in life is to be accessible to mind and body but not to technology. Luckily, he does believe in the power of the haiku, and he's not above hijacking Johnny Mold's cell to text a daily love poem to me. I hoped Shrimp's latest installment would be a haiku'd announcement of his intention to ground a stick into the Big Apple; at the very least, I hoped it would be as sigh-worthy as the previous day's haiku:

cyd charisse dances
cc espresso prances—
city does not sleep.

But the latest installment did not herald Shrimp's adoration. The haiku was a first—about Himself, instead of love for Myself.

snow falls on flap-ears
How long before the wave break?
shrimp out of water.

"That's a first," lisBETH said as we placed our shoes back on our feet in the lobby area of the yoga studio. "I didn't know it was *possible* to be kicked out of a yoga class. Thank you for hastening our departure out of that misery. Check yoga off the New Year's resolution list."

"I think I'm gonna hurl," I said, whether from the release of toxins in my body that yoga supposedly encourages (Lesson: Don't caffeinate before yoga-nating), or from anxiety about Shrimp's haiku, I didn't know.

Not true. January drew to a close and the haiku had let me know—Shrimp was ready to reopen his other habit besides art. He needed the surf. I wanted him to stay. Here we go, Reality, you jerk-off.

"Me too," lisBETH said.

Despite my hurl urge, I said, "Chocolate would help." Sometimes two negatives can equal a positive.

"Good idea."

A shared slice of chocolate cake at an Upper East Side café helped my mind avoid the message of Shrimp's haiku, and allowed lisBETH and me to finally celebrate the success of our coproduction.

"Well done on suggesting the joint vacation in Key West to Danny," I told her.

"CC, I applaud your dare campaign to Aaron of 'If-you're-really-just-Just Friends-then-why-*wouldn't*-you-go-on-vacation-with-Danny.' You may have a future in the propagation of propaganda."

"Thanks. I think?"

"Please thank Shrimp for the paint color samples he left for me to consider if I decide to repaint my bedroom. He's very talented, your Shrimp. If he ever wanted a stable job to support his art, I could see him having a future in graphic design with his talent. Does he plan to go to college?"

"Hardly. He still needs to get a GED."

"You're kidding me—Shrimp's a dropout? He seems so bright and motivated."

"One has nothing to do with the other. And he's only motivated when he's into some thing or some one. He ignored me when I asked him to design some business cards and brochures for Danny's business."

"That doesn't surprise me."

"What do you mean?"

"Shrimp's threatened by Danny. You looked so traumatized when I asked Shrimp for some help at my apartment, but you shouldn't have been startled that he and I got along so well. We have more in common than you think. Shrimp and I share a certain jealousy of you and Danny."

The cake in my mouth could not wait to be swallowed before my lips demanded, "Excuse me?" Neither yoga nor Shrimp's haiku could accomplish what lisBETH had just done—dim my appetite, and make me lose my adherence to don't-speak-with-your-mouth-full-of-chocolate manners.

LisBETH said, "Do you realize how you and Danny act with each other? You finish each other's sentences. You laugh at the same jokes, love the same old movies, watch the same campy TV shows, listen to the same music—from horrible records bought on the street! You even talk alike. And now you work together." If we ever decided to let her play *Dynasty,* lisBETH would definitely be gender-bend-cast in the role of Adam Carrington, the coarse, scheming, and very much misunderstood brother of Steven and Fallon. "When you got that ridiculous haircut, I offered to send you to the salon at Bergdorf to get it fixed; Danny went out and bought a can of blue hair spray to make his look like yours for Thanksgiving Day pictures. He's thirty!" I considered interrupting lisBETH's rant to inform her of my newest hairstyle idea—a short flapper-style bob cut that I'd get streaked in the spectrum of rainbow flag colors, inspired by Aaron's contention that I am possibly the gayest straight girl in all the West Village, but I didn't want lisBETH to have a coronary imagining if

Danny might try a similar 'do. She warbled on, "You'd think it was you who was raised alongside Danny, not me, given the way you and he get along. Watching you two has been hard enough for me to adapt to as a sibling from the outside looking in, when it seems like previously I was the one on the inside. So I can only imagine how it must feel for Shrimp, loving you, but watching you treat Danny like he's your partner, not Shrimp." LisBETH paused to take a dainty sip from her ristretto (most hard-core espresso shot you can get—respect). She swallowed, shrugged, and added, "But not to worry, I'm getting used to it. Shrimp will too."

What, did her caffeine come with a truth serum?

I shoved the cake plate away. Count on lisBETH to pull off the impossible—harsh my enjoyment of chocolate.

THIRTY-FIVE

We are gathered here today to celebrate the union of Johnny Mold and Myself.

"You're late," Johnny said upon my arrival at LUNCHEONETTE. He did not look up from the erotic comic book he read at the cash register.

"Why do you care?" I placed the apron over my head and turned on La Marzocco to get it primed for my ministrations. "My hours here are supposed to be on the Whenever, Wherever philosophy."

"Moving past the whole ridiculousness of philosophizing one's life schedule by pop song titles, I'm just saying I think people should respect the idea of punctuality. You said you'd be here at three. It's almost four."

From behind him I nestled my head into his tattooed neck. "You missed me, right?"

He swatted me off. "Kind of."

I pointed at his magazine. "No woman has knockers that big naturally, even in naughty alterna-realms. It's not physically possible."

"Doesn't mean they're not satisfying to look at."

"Does that mean you go for girls?"

"I go for you to help the people lined up for espresso shots. It's not nice to keep people waiting for caffeine."

"You mean keep *you* waiting? If you bothered to look up from your comic book, you might notice there's no line at the counter."

"You're right." All Shrimp has to do is look at me to make me go warm all over, but Johnny knows the words to get me hot. "Skim latte, please. Make it a double."

"Skim? You watching the pounds so you can prey on one of those big-knocker babes cavorting through your dream landscape?"

Johnny finally looked up from the book, turned around, and pressed his index finger to his lip-ringed mouth. "Silence is as golden as punctuality. Suggestion." His eyes returned to comic book babe.

In my fantasy comic book alternate universe, I will be Super Barista Goddess Girl. Bob Mackie or one of those equally horrific eighties fashion designers will have made a custom-designed super-hero uniform for me, maybe a gold lamé apron-dress, conveniently cut out to reveal as much hip, stomach, and leg flesh as possible. Shrimp will be the comic book artist and he will want to bump me up from my hard-won B cup to a double D, and I will object on the grounds of gratuitous oversexualization of a caffeine icon dedicated to serving the public interest of stimulating hyperactivity via coffee rather than crack. I'll be secretly pleased when the final bound artwork reveals Shrimp ignored my feminist stance. Oh, and stance, Super Barista Goddess Girl is lookin' hot with those long legs and gold lamé stiletto books. *Cracks whip.*

When I handed him his latte, Johnny said, "The punctuality thing was actually going somewhere. I gotta head upstate more regularly to see my grandpa. He's not doing so well. I need to know if I can count on you to cover this place when I have to be gone? January is a doldrums business month, and I don't like to go when this place is barely surviving, but Johnny the First comes first."

"Understood, and of course you can count on me. I can work the schedule out with my other job with Danny."

"Message for ya. Shrimp dropped by on his way to his meditation class. He said to tell you not to wait for him tonight if he's late getting to your brother's boyfriend's restaurant to meet you all for dinner. Somebody your sister works with called Shrimp about painting her apartment too, so he's going over there to check out the place and give her an estimate. And he said you know how long women can go on with paint color samples, so don't be surprised if he doesn't make it at all."

Riiight.

Johnny could easily replace Shrimp as my alterna-realm soul mate. He'd at least arrive to dinner on time.

He'd at least arrive at all.

THIRTY-SIX

Return to Dynasty: CC's Trip Down Johnny Way, brought to you by a late night TV-cable-access-dream-state-nightmare.

INT. LUNCHEONETTE—EVENING

CC

No, you don't understand, Johnny. I must have you!

JOHNNY

CC, that's your multiple personality disorder crazy-
talking. You think as Fallon that you want to kiss me,
but your true self, Myself, has a true love. I won't do it.
I won't let you revert to bad girl ways! I won't kiss you!
Shrimp is my friend!

CC/FALLON

Who's Shrimp?

CC/FALLON gropes JOHNNY at an inappropriate groin point, her hand subtly shielded by a fake plant so as not to offend Bible Belt viewers who might have inadvertently flipped the channel to her poorly lit attempt at seduction.

JOHNNY

(squirming with heavy breathing, clearly falling under her spell)

I'm a straight-edge celibate. Not only would I never let you cheat on Shrimp, I would never cheat on my own values. That's what makes me true punk instead of mere goth. Got it?

CC

(pressing closer, her mouth almost touching his)

Mold, don't *you* get it? Let me give your values an analogy. That's a fancy word for a fake but similar situation. The analogy is this: You may think you're a straight-edge celibate, but in my imagination you're a devil's food cake with mocha buttercream frosting, and I am a lactose intolerant diabetic, and it's like I can't resist you. I must have a piece! I know you don't

belong to me, I know I have no right, I know the
whole world order could collapse from one taste of
you, but you're just too delicious. I only want a little
sample, and I promise I'll send you right back to
asexual world after I've tried a piece . . .

**JOHNNY grabs her into his arms and they share a passionate kiss,
or as deep a mouth twirl as his lip rings and tongue stud will allow
before CC must separate Herself from him.**

CC

So that was okay. But, dude, stop kidding yourself.
You cloak yourself in asexuality not because you don't
want to be labeled straight or gay, but because you're
really just undecided.

JOHNNY

How do you always know me better than myself,
Myself?

CC

(now cloaked by FALLON-evil, pulling a Swiss Army knife from
her waitress uniform)

I've had it with indecision. . . . Shrimp either decides

we are in this, and by *we* I mean *he* accepts my brother
along with all the other people in my life, or I'll have
to go fishin' elsewhere.

JOHNNY
(looking toward the script supervisor on the other side of the camera)
Line? I think she went off script?

THIRTY-SEVEN

My movie star namesake sister has betrayed me. Yvette Mimieux chose her side, and that side is nestled beside Shrimp wherever he may be in Max's apartment, whether he's sitting on the piano bench painting at his easel, making coffee in the kitchen, or staring at the Wall of Sadness. I think she even follows him into the bathroom. I wonder if Yvette sneaks peeks at the sketchbook he left on the bathtub ledge and resents that Shrimp has forsaken artistic study of her in favor of the written word. His sketchbook is experiencing a spiritual conversion, now being used during his increasingly frequent visits to Tibet House and Buddhist temples in the city to jot notes more than to draw images of Yvette and me in the city. If Yvette did sneak peeks, was she pleased by Shrimp's sketchbook musings, or concerned that given his lack of spelling and punctuation skills, maybe he should save his talent for images rather than words?

The four nobel truths spoken by the puddha after his enlitenment: the fundamentl truths govern our lives in samsara and provide the means for releese.

1) In life their is suffering
2. suffering is from attachment (desire/craving).
Three —attachment can be overcomme
4) Their is a path for achieiving this; the path is the Dharma. the teachings of the puddha.

Who knew my boy shared an interest in actualization? And how could I stay mad with a true love on such a path? What kinda shrewish Super Barista Goddess Girl would that make me?

It's not like Shrimp promised to come to dinner with Danny, Aaron, and me. He'd said "Maybe." I hate technicalities like that.

I hate that neither of us will say how in this or not we are—too scared to ruin our January love nest hiatus in Max's apartment.

Yvette didn't appear concerned that Shrimp should be holding me close in the middle of the night after I'd woken up from my nightmare, petting her while she lay next to him on the living room carpet in Max's apartment. My head turned to her as I lay flat on my back, and I shot her the evil eye from my position on Shrimp's other side. Yvette spared me a hiss in return; she purred her supremacy inside Shrimp's hand instead. Diva.

Shrimp murmured, "Should I be worried that you cried out

Johnny's name in your sleep?" Hair falling to the sides of his face, blond stubble surrounding his cherry lips, he looked almost painfully beautiful in the light of the dozens of candles he'd placed around the carpet sanctuary he'd created for our night's sleep because my body hurt from the yoga class.

I answered, "Should I be worried that you're a Shrimp out of water who dodges my brother at every opportunity?"

"You answer my question first."

"You shouldn't be worried about me and Johnny Mold. He's my friend. I admit I'm curious about him, but not in a way like I want to experience him physically. More like I want to know what he wants to experience. Make sense?"

"Not at all."

The nightmare, along with the fallout from the previous day's particularly high caffeine count, not to mention my achy post-yoga-disaster back, ensured I wouldn't be falling asleep again anytime soon. Now had to be as good a time as any to dig the middle-of-the-night conversation with Shrimp deeper, to end the stalemate of our indecisions by bringing our issues to the fore—or the floor, as the case may be. "I think there's an expectation that when you're our age, you should date lots of people, and I hope Johnny will part with his Game Boy and comic books and sci-fi novels long enough to find that out. But do I want to fool around with him? Of course not. In my heart right now all I want is you." I so came close to singing Shrimp a cheesy power ballad lyric like, "You fill me up, you're all I need to get by, oh baby, you and me, into in-fin-i-ty."

"Good, because Johnny spell-checks my haikus, and I don't want to think of him as competition."

I waited, expecting Shrimp to declare his desire to stay—and to be with me, and only me.

I waited.

Send love back my way.
Winter's apartment will end.
Anytime now, Shrimp.

Nothin'.

Shrimp is a way better haiku writer than I am.

The moonlight-candlelight brightened my resolve to get to the heart of the matter. "Do you think of Danny as competition?"

Shrimp said, "There's a Buddhist saying Dante told me: 'If you meet the Buddha on the road, kill him.' Dante said this means that you must not look for Buddha outside of yourself. Make sense?"

"Not at all. You're saying you want to kill my brother?" Right now I wanted to go to Corsica, find Dante, and kill him. (Cue *The Godfather* theme song.)

"I want to work on myself and not be threatened by Danny. Or your worship of him."

"Meaning you ignore him so you won't have to think about him?"

"Something like that. Divert my karma elsewhere."

I wanted to point out that I suspected Shrimp had misinterpreted Dante's Buddhist saying, which to my mind was not about diverting karma but about looking inward for truth rather than harping on the idea of a god leading you to what you had to find within yourself. Instead I asked Shrimp, "Why does your karma need to be diverted?"

Shrimp gave Yvette a series of rubs before answering, like he was using her to buy time before deciding how to answer. But even though his hand chose Yvette instead of mine at his side, just waiting for his stroke, at least he answered the truth. "Last year when I asked you to marry me, you chose Danny. And I don't trust that you won't again."

THIRTY-EIGHT

"Whassa matta, Dollface?"

I looked up from the cupcake trays awaiting my frosting minis-trations, too tired to be irritated that now was so not the time for Danny's sorry Don Corleone impression. Danny's concerned face at least diverted my attention from visions of how Shrimp's face looked when I'd stormed out of Max's apartment early this morning after our monster fight—hateful.

Danny tried again. "Wanna talk about it? Did you get any sleep last night? You look like hell."

"No. And no. And thanks."

If I talked, I feared I would capitulate into full-scale rage, which my karma did not need—any more than Shrimp's face needed the new, uncharacteristic spectrum of anger that had colored his foggy surfer beauty into all-out darkness as dawn rose through the garden windows of Max's apartment this morning.

I rechanneled my energy into the job at hand. I visualized each iced cupcake I dipped into the bowl of chocolate sprinkle splendor as being christened with a peace and tranquility that would be passed on to its future consumer. As the Buddha taught, and as cut out from a pamphlet and glued down inside Shrimp's sketchbook: *Overcome the angry by non-anger; overcome the wicked by goodness; overcome the miser by generosity; overcome the liar by truth.*

Truth and I are no longer on the outs. We now outright despise one another.

Shrimp + Truth = these revelations:

(1) Shrimp gives—I'm right. If Shrimp chooses not to get along with Danny, it must mean he wants to leave. We don't need to make a mutual decision about what to do once Max returns to his apartment. Shrimp has decided. He wants to go home to San Francisco. New York is too cold, too much energy. Shrimp needs quiet, focus, and ocean. The Hudson feeding into the Atlantic doesn't count.

(2) Without bothering with the small detail of consulting me directly, Shrimp decided that if he had asked me to go home to San Francisco with him, make a Pacific life there with

him, he knew I would choose Manhattan. I would choose Danny. So Shrimp's not asking.

(3) Shrimp thought he chose the quest to Manhattan to find me, but now he's not sure we should be together always; my life here flourishes just fine without him. Maybe why he came to Manhattan was not for me at all, but to connect with the spiritual teachings that could lead Shrimp down a fresh path. He has questions about this new path. I could obstruct his answers.

(4) Excuse me, but the girl who loves him most in the world could obstruct him how? Buddha teaching number 251: *There is no fire like lust; there is no grip like hatred; there is no net like delusion; there is no river like craving.*

    (4)(a) Shrimp didn't misinterpret Dante's Buddhist saying about if you meet the Buddha on the road, kill him. I don't know what I'm talking about.

        (4)(a)(i)   Interpret this, CC: As any Buddhist could tell you, neither the future nor the past are real; only the moment is real.

        (4)(a)(ii)   My interpretation: This moment sucks.

    (4)(b) How dare I suggest Shrimp is using the spiritual path as an excuse not to deal with his issues—like anger at

his parents' craziness, or resentment that the life he
chose in New Zealand with them did not work out.

(4)(b)(i)   This moment also sucks.

(5)   Fair is not fair and trust is not trust. (Shrimp said this, not
the Buddha, or stupid Dante.) Shrimp lied when he said
he'd been with someone else in NZ. All Shrimp did in NZ
was surf, meditate, pine for me, and watch his parents' plans
for their new lives Down Under fall apart. And what had I
done? Jumped right into bed with Luis. Yeah, *that* bothered
the hell out of him. *I* chose the clean break—not Shrimp.

I then chose to storm out of the apartment in a rage, shouting
at Shrimp that I couldn't care less if he returned to SF, and what did
he care if I chose Danny anyway? Shrimp had chosen for both of
us—chosen not to like Danny, chosen to return home without any
concern about what that would mean for us, chosen to act like he's
okay with the past choices we'd made *together,* when in fact he
wasn't. My parting words before the BAM door slam: "YOU'RE A
FAKE, PHIL!"

So ended the middle-of-the-night-into-early-morning fight—
suckilicious to the highest power.

Danny powered on the stereo to fill the void of my morning
silence. From the speakers Freddie Mercury wanted to know if this
was the real life, or was it just fantasy?

Finally my mouth could produce words. "No Queen at seven in the morning, okay, Danny? I can't deal."

"Wow, she's not even in the mood for Queen. That's a first for you, Ceece." Danny zapped the stereo remote. "Bohemian Rhapsody" faded away, replaced by the power ballad pop song about she who was not a girl but not yet a woman. Hah-hah, brother-baker-man.

"Danny," I said. "Philosophical question. Do you think I am like one of those girl singers who is so desperate for love that she creates love where none exists?"

"You mean like a classic case study pop princess who gets married too young to a real a-hole and convinces herself it's love when in fact it's just her escaping a lifetime of people who've used her body and talent to sell off her soul?"

"Exactly."

"No, I don't think you're that."

"Do you think Shrimp and I will be like you and Aaron—able to start fresh, find hope with each other?"

"I honestly don't know Shrimp well enough to make that judgment. I mean, anyone who watches him with you could tell he's totally in love with you. But what he wants for your future together? I'd like to know as much as you."

The stereo should have been playing a gospel song of prayer, since the answer to mine was delivered when the kitchen door opened—and this was real life, this was not fantasy. Shrimp stood at the doorway wearing his flap-ears hat dusted with fresh morning snow, shivering, but with a face shining back in love—or at least with hope rather than hate.

He looked at Danny instead of at me. "Got a job for me this morning?"

I resisted the urge to run into his arms and slobber him with kisses and murmurs of "Sorry, sorry, sorry, let me warm you up." I knew Shrimp was not here to be with me. Shrimp's way of saying sorry was to show me he would invest time with a questionable suspect, not because he genuinely wanted to hang out with Danny, but to try to get used to him. It was like me with bio-dad Frank. Well, maybe Shrimp was kinda here for me.

Relief.

Danny didn't need the situation spelled out to him to understand. He said, "Take your coat off and sit down here by me. I've got a bag of Oreos needing to be crushed, and I think you're just the man for the job. I'll pour you a coffee and have breakfast delivered for you if you'll promise to get as hyped as CC does after her caffeine kicks in, and regale me with stories of your life. Feel free to make shit up."

Shrimp mumbled, "Deal. But no soft-boiled eggs for me." He glanced at me. "I like mine over easy."

THIRTY-NINE

Everyone's happy.

I'm suspicious.

Max is thrilled to be reunited with Yvette Mimieux—and to no longer be in the custody of his mother, or her retirement community in Sun City, Arizona. He's so happy to have returned to cold, grumpy New York City that he's extended the welcome on Shrimp's lease in his apartment. So since Shrimp and I still haven't figured out what we're going to do about our living situation, for the time being, Shrimp's cool to crash on Max's couch, and Max is cool to have him there. According to Max, he could tolerate anyone after a month with his mother. And as we all know, Shrimp digs anyone, with the possible exception of my brother—but even they're happy to tolerate one another lately.

Danny is happy because even though he's getting on well enough with Shrimp (in the awkward-but-not-hostile "Dude, 'sup?" guy-shoulder-nudge-followed-by-complete-indifference interaction kind of way) to have also extended an invitation for Shrimp to stay in our apartment now that Max is home, Shrimp declined. Danny's doesn't think Shrimp and I are ready for the moving-in step.

I'm happy Shrimp declined to crash with us because while we'd have the apartment pretty much to ourselves, what with Danny's double happiness at finally gaining admittance back into the land of indoor sports at Aaron's (hee!), I agree with my brother. I don't want to get into a real living arrangement with Shrimp unless we're ready to decide if we're really ready to live together. Not just *if*—but *where*.

I think I could be happy to live in New York or San Francisco, so long as Shrimp was there. Right? So should I try to convince Shrimp to stay in NY, or, fair is fair, should I consider whether my life here has been a cool diversion, but all roads lead back to San Francisco, where he prefers to be, and where Shrimp and I could start a new life together in the heart-luring city where we first started out?

For now, we've settled on being happy to have worked through the monster fight and resolved the back-end issues. We have agreed that the "clean break" might originally have been my call, but Shrimp answered it by not contacting me while he was in New

Zealand. Yet, trust really is trust—if we are in this together, and we have agreed that we are, for now, at least within the sense of the mutually agreed upon Buddhist interpretation that neither the future nor the past but only the present moment is real, I acknowledge that I'm sorry about the Luis thing. I'm not sorry that it happened, but I am sorry it hurt Shrimp. And Luis is over, done, *finito*.

As to the *if* and *where* Shrimp and I still need to resolve—we'll get there. Just not yet.

What I wanted to know now was, "How come all these Buddhist monks look so happy?"

Because I am the Best Girlfriend Ever, I finally made good on my promise to join Shrimp for a meditation class at the Buddhist temple where he's been spending a lot of his time.

If that meditation session wasn't the longest hour of my life, I don't know what.

While the class practitioners had sat on their pillows in the prayer room emptying their minds, visualizing the Buddha, and dedicating merit for the benefit of all sentient beings, I hadn't been able to keep my eyes closed. I was too mesmerized by the bald-headed, orange and red robe-attired monks at the head of the room, who had the strangest looks of giddy peace on their faces that I'd ever seen. Like they were beyond actualization and had glided into their own realms of happiness—some weird, pure kind that I reason has to be completely phony.

Shrimp answered, "I guess the monks look so happy because they've dedicated their lives to working toward an end to suffering?"

"They're happy about suffering? That's pretty effed up."

"They're not happy about suffering. They're finding peace from trying to relieve it."

Shrimp and I held hands as we wandered out of the meditation room and into the temple's main area. The peaceful room smelled of incense, and it was lined with colorful prayer flags, Buddha statues and portraits, and paintings of Buddhist monasteries in Tibet and Nepal. A few nuns and monks passed by us, and made prayer-bow gestures at their chests when they recognized Shrimp.

"You've kind of found a place here, huh?" I asked him, squeezing his hand, so proud and awed how he has the ability to make himself part of a community—whether it's a community of artists, surfers, caffeine addicts, or Buddhist—wherever he goes.

"Sort of," Shrimp said. "I mean, I know the Buddhist path is one I want to go down. And I like this temple. But I like many different Buddhist temples I've visited. What I need next is a teacher."

"I'll teach you," I teased. What a laugh. During the hour of meditation silence Shrimp and I had just experienced together, I'd personally experienced sheer torture trying not to: (1) die of hysterics watching the happy monks think about nothing; (2) visualize my baby sister Frances Alberta as a Buddha baby who miraculously could sing every lyric of "Come Fly with Me" before she was even old enough to crawl; and (3) think about me, me, me and Shrimp, Shrimp, Shrimp when I was supposed to be emptying my mind for the altruistic intent of praying for an end to everyone else's problems.

Whereas. Shrimp had sat still for the hour, eyes closed, his face etched in total concentration, his hair spiked up, my lust for him through the roof. My dharma punk, my dirty hippie, my Philip-Shrimp.

My loverman who knows his girl's limitations. "You might not be the best candidate for meditation," Shrimp acknowledged. "But I love you for trying."

This room we stood in, this togetherness we shared—I knew we were standing in a happy bubble. But make no mistake. Bubbles burst.

FORTY

Impermanence vs. Indecision.

I'll take indecision, please.

My life as a barista-waitress is over, for now. LUNCHEONETTE is shuttering its windows for good. Johnny the First is going into hospice upstate, and Johnny Mold is headed there to share the last days of his granddad's life with the old man who raised him. Once his grandpa passes, the building and the business will be put up for sale, but Johnny Mold doesn't have the energy right now to deal with operating or selling this joint that's only just now breaking even.

So, this much has been decided for me: Hello, full-time cupcake business, good-bye to my calling as a barista. That is, assuming I stay in Manhattan.

Since our apartment building's rooftop would be too cold for a February gathering, Johnny Mold invited us to use LUNCHEON-

ETTE to throw a party—and to give the place a proper send-off. With champagne, cupcakes, music, and Danny and Aaron's friends gathered, the occasion was as much an excuse to celebrate Aaron's birthday as it was an opportunity to celebrate the rebirth of Danny and Aaron's true love.

It's funny how at parties it's the odd men out who find one another. Being the only "out" heterosexual males in attendance, Shrimp and Frank-dad bonded as party buddies even faster than I'd once initially bonded with Shrimp's mom the first time I got to know her. But at that long-ago party on the rooftop of Shrimp's brother's house back in Ocean Beach, Shrimp's mom had offered up a spliff by way of breaking the ice between us. Here, Frank offered up his patented wise counsel.

I was too amused watching Shrimp get a lecture on spirituality from Frank of all people that I had no compassionate thought to rescue him. I stood at La Marzocco (bye, baby, I love you—you'll always be a Cadillac rather than a Camry to me, no matter what Dante says), pulling shots for our party guests, at a comfortable enough distance to hear Shrimp and Frank's conversation, but not so uncomfortably close as to join in.

Frank: "One of my longtime clients—we handled the
              advertising work for his bagel stores—was a
              Jewish man, a leading member of his synagogue,

very active in fundraising for Jewish causes. We
retired around the same time, and I recently had
lunch with him and found out he's become a
Buddhist. At age seventy! His daughter married a
Buddhist, and the man became intrigued by the
sangha where the ceremony was held, and he
began visiting the temple regularly. He said he
had a recognition feeling at this temple, that
basically the teachings he sat in on there
explained what he always believed but didn't
know he believed—until he found this place."

Shrimp: "That's exactly it. It's like I don't know a lot about
it, but I feel like something is there that's right,
and that's enough for me. I get this sense of
belonging when I visit a Buddhist temple. Like it's
basic instinct to be there."

Frank: "That's what my friend said. Maybe the generation
gap on religion isn't so wide."

Shrimp: "But, dude, that's the amazing part, Buddhism's
not really about religion. It's a religion that's not
really a religion at all, but like a cooler way of

thinking about existence—you know, to stop the struggle to prove your existence to the world, and focus on just like being a compassionate person who will use existence for the benefit of other beings." Shrimp pulled a crumpled piece of paper from his pants pocket and read aloud the words he'd written on it. *"Number 183—To avoid all evil, to cultivate good, and to cleanse one's mind— this is the teaching of the Buddhas."*

Frank: "Impressive study, young man. My advice is to continue to ask questions. Ask many questions." Profound!

Shrimp shot me a sly smile, but I couldn't giggle, not with the look of profound sadness on Johnny's face. He sat at the counter in front of me, sipping a latte, but with no Game Boy or paperback novel he bought for a quarter on the street clutched in his hand.

"You know I will be here to help when you get back from upstate, right?" I asked him. I reached across the counter and patted his Mikado/Penzance hand. *"Auf Wiedersehen, Fickakopf,* for now." My assurance to my friend dabbled in not-truth. I haven't decided whether I really will still be here in NYC when Johnny gets back, but for the sake of repeating back to him Johnny's favorite parting words in German to customers he didn't like—"Good-bye, fuckhead"—I hoped I could be forgiven.

"I know you will," Johnny said, sounding comforted. (I suck.) His eyes drooped. Eight at night and he could barely stay awake, or bother to foreign-word-curse me out in return. "I'm so tired and I've hardly done anything."

"Grief is very tiring," advised lisBETH, sitting next to him. "After my mother died, I could barely make it out of bed for the next month, much less to the grocery store or to work."

My grief is that I want to see it, but I don't—how Shrimp and I are going to make us work this time around. Shrimp has decided. He wants to go back to San Francisco. He could stay with his brother or his parents, save up the money to travel, find a teacher.

When I asked Shrimp if he wanted me to move back home along with him, his reply? "If that's what *you* want to do."

I am just not sure either way.

In the hypothetical land of an actual decision, I don't stick around to help Johnny deal with death and the business and all that important stuff your friends are supposed to be around for. In hypothetical land, I decide to return to the SF-land where the people whose permanence worries me reside. My choice wouldn't only be about Shrimp. I'd go because I worry about Sid-dad's life span given his retirement age and tubby belly and the fact that he doesn't pay attention to the doctor who tells him to cut his cholesterol and get some exercise. I'd go to tick out the remaining time with Sugar Pie, who was the reason I even met Shrimp in the first place (thanks again, juvenile court). She's legitimately old, even though her seventysomething self doesn't look a day over sixty-something, and she's in legitimately dangerous health; she goes to dialysis three times a week because she only has one working kidney, and that one isn't working so good. I worry most for her because last year Sugar Pie became a bride for the first time when she married her true love Fernando and just on the basis of all the late-in-life happiness, I suspect some evil irony god will decide it's legitimately time for the reality of Sugar Pie's age and health to trump the bliss of her true love.

I worry that even though it feels like I am supposed to be in Manhattan, feels like I made the right choice, I love San Francisco, too. And first and foremost, shouldn't I want to be where my true love wants to live? Shrimp and I have already broken up twice. If we repeat the last breakup and part because we want to live in separate places even though we still love each other—well, isn't the rule: Three strikes and you're out?

True love is for real but that's not to say it's decided to stay.

Fear of impermanence sucks almost as much as the fact of it.

Poor Frank, sucked into a gay-son drama to go along with his love-child trauma. The sound of the champagne glass from Danny and Aaron's friends, demanding a soul kiss between the reunited pair, directed Frank to shift his standing position next to Shrimp, a subtle move that put Frank's back to Danny and Aaron, and effectively blocked any subtle escape Shrimp might have taken from conversation with Frank. The move trapped Shrimp—and kept Frank from witnessing Danny and Aaron's kiss.

Not-So-Subtle in Your Subtlety would make a great band name.

Which reminded me. "Johnny," I said, "once you get back from upstate and when you're ready, you should talk to Aaron about joining his band. His buddies have been jamming together for years, but they broke up a while ago. They're talking about reforming and going back to their old name—My Dead Gay Son." The band's old incarnation was named in honor of Danny and Aaron's favorite movie from when they were in high school; in the movie there are two homophobic football players who get accidentally offed in a compromising position, and their dads feign support at their funeral, crying about how they love their dead gay sons. Watching Frank with his back turned to Danny and Aaron, I finally understood with my own eyes why Danny and Aaron relate to this line. Frank genuinely wants to be supportive, but he's uncomfortable with them even after all this time—particularly when they tip his support to the brink of bearing witness to their physical relationship, which his personal generation gap can't quite grasp.

I do give Frank credit. He tries. He's here.

Johnny said, "I might be into trying a new band now that Mold has gone the way of Milli Vanilli. Any idea who would be My Dead Gay Son, Part Deux's musical influences?"

"Aaron's old band was like a laid-back band of whatever. They covered the Sex Pistols, Billie Holiday, Led Zeppelin, the Carpenters, The Clash, Backstreet Boys. The usual suspects."

My cell phone chimed in with its *South Park* ringtone, flashing a Humboldt County area code. "Yo, Phil," I called out. Shrimp looked in my direction, and I tossed the phone to him.

Did Shrimp appreciate my rescuing him from Frank as much as I will appreciate being rescued from his parents if we move back home? Because at this moment I was appreciating the twenty-five hundred miles separating us from them. I don't trust Iris and Billy. Now that they're settled into their friends' guest house up in Humboldt County (translation: They're gatekeepers for the friends' marijuana harvest in exchange for a place to live), Iris and Billy are trying to lure Shrimp back to them with talk of the awesome surfing along the rugged northern California coastline, and dangling bait about a nearby Buddhist monastery where Shrimp could become a volunteer cook in exchange for housing and spiritual guidance.

I object. They want to reel him back in because it serves their best interest to have his amazingness near to them rather than serving Shrimp's best interest to do his own thing free of them; they'd surely throw him back to picking up his life again after they moved on to whatever it is they'll move on to next. The probability that they'll leave him stranded again is less than hypothetical—it's a certainty. They've been doing it to him for the duration of his existence—and his brother's, and the half sister from Iris's first marriage, whom she abandoned to take up with Billy.

Shrimp went outside to take the call, leaving Frank with nowhere to turn, in this crowd of young people made up mostly of gay boys, but to his daughters. He sat down at the counter next to lisBETH. Since I had them both trapped, I gave up the objectionable question I'd been meaning to spring their way for a while. "Frank and lisBETH, how come I haven't met your significant others?"

LisBETH answered like lisBETH—brutally honestly. "You haven't met mine because he's not turning out to be a keeper. He's a good man, but you know what? He's boring. Also, he doesn't want to be a father, and I'm ready to have a baby. I always thought I should wait for a good man to come along before having a child, and now that one's come along, I think I've decided I'd just as soon do it on my own rather than be in a relationship with someone I like a little but will never love. I haven't cut the cord with him yet, but it's coming—and I don't care for the melodrama of introducing him to my family when I have no intention of him becoming part of it. However, you ask a good question, so Daddy, I turn it over to you. Why *haven't* we met your lady friend?"

Frank stammered, "Well . . . uh . . . she's very Catholic, you know . . ."

I was primed to lay into him, but lisBETH beat me to it. "For God's sake, Daddy, you had a child outside your marriage. She's standing here right now, she's part of our lives. Be honest about your past for once in your life—at least if you want a future with this woman."

Damn, didn't expect that one! Sister, I will never BETH you again.

A few karaoke songs and the birthday song later (sung as a Gregorian chant by Danny and friends—highly entertaining), I realized as I cut Aaron's birthday cake that I hadn't seen Shrimp at the party since he went outside LUNCHEONETTE to take the call from his parents.

And all of a sudden I had a very bad feeling about impermanence, along with a recurrent need to abandon yet another of Danny's birthday parties. I also had a very bad feeling about Shrimp's mom's love for buying cheap last-minute flights on the Internet. On a whim.

I handed the cake-slicing knife over to Lisbeth, and raced down the block, back to my apartment. I knew it! On my bed, next to Gingerbread, next to my cell phone, lay a CD—*San Francisco Days*

by Chris Isaak, with a Post-it note placed on top, in Shrimp's handwriting.

Gone surfing—left koast. I'll be waiting for v. I luv v.

Budding Buddhist be damned. Shrimp's gonna make me rescue
him after all.

Decided.

rachel cohn

FORTY-ONE

Trust my dad to have answers to the important questions.

According to Sid-dad, the big bang theory is the dominant scientific theory regarding the origin of the universe. This theory holds that the universe was created billions of years ago from some cosmic explosion that randomly hurled matter in all directions. Sid-dad says the big bang theory not only clarifies the original source of existence, it also explains the dynamic I bring to my San Francisco family's home.

I am not only Sid-dad's Cupcake. I am also his Chaos.

Chaos and her father enjoyed watching Ash and Josh jump on my parents' bed at two a.m. on a school night as the hyper-munchkin-sibs performed an outstanding sing-dance-shout number called "CYD CHARISSE'S PIECES IS HOME! CYD CHARISSE'S PIECES IS HOME!" My mother, however, holding a crying baby Frances

Alberta, failed to find the artistic merit. Nancy sat in her rocking chair with the baby on her shoulder, her classic lemon-sucking face fixated on me—her real problem child. Nancy's tired expression and her tired Ritz-Carlton stolen hotel robe failed to subdue her blonde-model classic good looks, or her figure, which no thirty-eight-year-old mother of four should manage to maintain. As I stood over her shoulder cooing at Frances, I struggled to distinguish whether Nancy's face managed to display not just annoyance over my surprise visit, but maybe some semblance of pleasure at seeing me live and in the flesh too. Even if I hadn't called ahead to announce my homecoming.

I stole a move from the Shrimp playbook. I just showed up. Logic: If I didn't give Nancy a heads-up that I was coming home in pursuit of Shrimp, she couldn't try to talk me out of it. See how nicely we've evolved into getting along?

Sid-dad didn't mind the sneak attack. When I barged into his study early this evening, he looked up from reading his newspaper and said, "Ah, the Cupcake finally bakes a visit home." He put down his newspaper like he'd been waiting for me all along, then got up to grab me into a suffocating bear hug. My mother, on the other hand, followed the trail of Ash's and Josh's squeals at my unexpected arrival into Dad's study, looked taken aback when she first saw me, but did not run over to touch me. Instead her eyes appraised me up and down, then her mouth announced, "You've gained weight. And *what* have you done to your hair? If you're going to get blue streaks and a hairstyle of lopsided angles, at least touch up the roots and keep the ends trimmed."

I was too intoxicated from the San Francisco air, foggy and moody and brisk, to be anything less than mellow in response. "Nice to see you, too, Mom." I had asked the airport taxi driver to take me home the long way, up Great Highway. And the long way's views of the Golden Gate Bridge and the mighty Pacific, with the shivering city of skyscrapers and Victorian houses perched over it, had me delirious with excitement to be home and to see my family—although not so much looking forward to dealing with my mother on the Shrimp issue.

My mother had been too preoccupied with the baby and putting Ash and Josh to bed (the first time), and with hunting me down in my bedroom, demanding to know whether I knew anything about the mysterious disappearances of her Italian thigh-high boots and her pink Chanel suit with the matching Chanel handbag, for us to have alone time to discuss the reason for my visit. And when I'd finally appeared to my parents' summons for a talk in their bedroom after all the chaos I'd brought to the house allegedly died down, chaos returned in the form of Ash and Josh busting out of their own bedrooms and bursting into performance on our parents' bed, and waking Frances out of her sleep.

As Chaos, as in my careers as a barista-waitress and as a cupcake-baker, my work ethic never fails to amaze. Thank you, thank you very much.

A pillow hurdled into the air and nearly collided with an antique lamp, causing my mother to finally snap. "STOP IT, ASHLEY AND JOSHUA! WE GET IT, YOUR SISTER IS HOME!" Sid-dad took the baby from her and into his arms for soothing, not as oblivious as Nancy that her shouting only agitated Frances more. For a woman who gave birth four times, I swear my mother knows nothing about children. If she did, she'd know Ash and Josh were wide awake in the middle of the night from the sugar infusion Double Rainbow (SF's real treat) ice cream sundaes I took them out for after dinner, not from the frozen yogurts we told Nancy we got, or from the simple excitement over my return home.

The kids dropped down onto the bed after our mother's screech, but their silence only lasted seconds, broken with cries of "PHONE!" and "AWWWW, CYD CHARISSE'S PIECES CELL RINGS FUCKING CURSE WORDS, MOM!" My mother looked at me and pointed in the direction of the door leading to the hallway. "OUT!" she yelled. To me, not the kids.

Ash attached her hand to mine as I stepped outside my parents' bedroom to take the call flashing the name "Maxim." "You have boobies," she whispered to me.

"Aren't they cool?" I whispered back. I sat down against the hallway wall. Ash plopped herself into my lap, but a third grader in the ninetieth percentile weight range was too much for my tired legs so I shoved her off. She snuggled into my side instead. She smelled like the Pixy Stix she hides under her bed.

I answered my phone. "I know, I'm sorry, Max. I should have come to say good-bye before I left Manhattan this morning, but it was all pretty last-minute."

"Yvette is not pleased with you," Max sniffed. "She was looking forward to having you over to watch a movie with us tonight."

"Max, it's five in the morning New York time. What's really on your mind?"

"Nothing . . . just . . . good luck. With Shrimp. I'll light a candle for you."

"Thanks, Max." *Shrimp and I are not dead yet.*

Clearly any serious thought I harbored about transplanting myself in San Francisco with Shrimp needed to take Max into serious account. Max may have survived the last twenty years without much human companionship in his NY apartment, but he's like used to me now. Max will not last without me there. I may be Chaos, but I am also indispensable.

Josh ventured into the hallway and plopped himself down at my other side. He smelled like a boy who said he'd taken a shower before bed but lied. "I told Mom I'd only go back to sleep if you'll read to me from Harry Potter first." The sixth grader never out-grows wanting to read any grades of Harry.

"And what did Mom say?" I asked.

"That she doesn't negotiate with terrorists."

Shrimp is my true love, but Josh was my first little man. I only dissolve at the sight of his princely face. "Get back into bed, pick a spooky Azkaban chapter, and I'll be in your room in five minutes." I turned to Ash. "What's it gonna take to get *you* into bed, terrorist?"

"Promise to play Hack the Barbies with me tomorrow."

Grim-faced, I said, "Terms accepted." Fun!

I listened to a voice mail from Danny before hyperkid bed-turndown time. *"Hey, Dollface, Aaron and I want to thank you and Lisbeth for the Valentine's Day present. I'm sure we'll put that gift certificate for Hot Nude Yoga to good use. I'll even wager you that Aaron and I will be able to make it through the whole class without getting asked to leave, unlike some conspiring sisters we know. And just so you know, I'm giving you a week's unpaid vacation from cupcake bondage. You are not relieved of your job and you are commanded to return home. Which would be here in Manhattan. Love from the commandant."* Beep.

But, Commandant, I thought, *my home is as much my old San Francisco family and friends as it is my new New York family and friends. Somehow the twain must meet, and if it's Shrimp who splits that difference—then shouldn't I choose that home where he wants to be, earn my place beside him like you earned yours back with Aaron?*

When I returned to my parents' bedroom from Ash and Josh servitude, Nancy sat in her rocking chair nursing Frances. I sat down on the bed next to Sid-dad, who had finally found a moment to finish reading his newspaper. I plucked it from his hand.

"Do you love having me home or what?" I asked them.

Sid-dad said, "Somehow I have a feeling your visit isn't about an altruistic, long overdue visit with your family."

Nancy muttered, "Somehow I have a feeling *That Boy* is involved here?"

Uh-oh, back to "*That Boy.*" Situation in need of damage control. Idea delivered to me in the form of Frances Alberta, who looked like a total Buddha baby, happy and calm and chubby. "Shrimp's becoming a Buddhist," I told Sid and Nancy. What parent wouldn't approve of a Buddhist?

"Super," Nancy said. My looks may come from Frank's side, but I definitely get the sarcasm from her genes.

"Is he back in San Francisco seeking enlightenment?" Sid-dad asked, but without my mother's cynical tone.

"If he was, and I decided to stay here with him to do that—what would you say?"

Nancy sighed instead of said. Sid-dad answered for them. "We'd say we think you're too young to make that choice. You know we'd love you living back home, but not at the cost of leading your own life. Where's that independent spirit we know and love?"

"It's true love," I said.

Nancy barged in with, "It's truly a mistake to follow a boy who is struggling to find his way and will only leave again." I wondered if her assessment wasn't just about her long-running mission to sabotage my life, but was based on the chaos Frank delivered to her own life when she'd been close to my age.

Ash's loud cry from her bedroom brought Sid-dad to his feet. "Ashley's not adapting so well to not being the baby in the family anymore. We get the crying bed routine every night since Frances was born." He stared down at me, all short and adorable and bald, like Frances. "I'll assume this potential move of yours is an ongoing dialogue, not a done deal, and open for more discussion later?" He kissed the top of my head and left the room to tend to Ash.

I asked my mother, "If Shrimp's struggling, shouldn't I be there to struggle alongside with him? Grow with him?"

"Are you actually asking for my approval to follow Shrimp wherever he may go?"

I wasn't sure what I'd meant, but I said, "Guess so." Did I really just ask for my mother's approval?

"Then the honest answer is, No, I don't approve. But I know you will do what you want to do regardless of what I say, and regardless of whether it's the right thing to do. I also know that somehow you'll still be fine." Two years ago her comment would have immediately sparked a yelling fight between us; now I could understand it as less of an ornery statement and maybe more an acknowledgment of trust or something. Of course, Nancy followed it up by sighing the Nancy Classic, yet she almost seemed content, too, rocking in her chair while she stroked Frances's head. "I'm too tired to debate the Shrimp issue right now. Talk to me about something else while Frances feeds—this can take awhile. Tell me about your life in Manhattan, something about those periods of time when you're not hanging up on your mother's phone calls. What have you learned?"

Well, Mom, it's like this. The morning-after pill has to be taken within seventy-two hours of unprotected intercourse in order to be effective. Art installations can be found on Walls of Sadness as well as at the Met. If you're headed uptown from the Village, the C train is less crowded than the 1 train, but you have to wait for fucking ever for it to come.

I said, "For one thing, that I'm more like Frank than I think I'd like to be. Why couldn't I have turned out like Dad?" I held up a framed photograph of Sid-dad holding my hand in front of this beautiful Pacific Heights house, taken when I was five, the day Nancy and I arrived here to become his family. Frank would never choose a home on the basis of true love. Maybe he'd never have that opportunity either. Whereas Sid-dad made that opportunity for himself, made a home for Nancy to choose.

It only took her ten hours since my arrival home, but at last Nancy threw a genuine smile my way. "You are like Dad."

"How do you figure?"

"You have his heart."

FORTY-TWO

Sleep? Who needed sleep with friends to see, boys to retrieve, and dumplings to eat?

I felt like I'd barely fallen asleep when the ring of my cell phone woke me up at seven in the morning. "Hello" hadn't been uttered by my lips before Helen's voice barked, "Princess, if you want to see me and Autumn, your ass better be at our old dim sum place on Clement Street in an hour. I have Lamaze class and Autumn has Econ at City College at ten."

During the tail end of our senior slump last year, we three used to spend hours hanging out at the dim sum place, eating dumplings and drinking bubble teas, laughing and talking. Now we were all about time management. At least we could still keep up the tradition of enjoying the real San Francisco treat together—

major consumption of pork products first thing in the morning.

Forget about ol' loverboy Phil. I could move back to San Francisco solely on the basis of the food on Clement Street, my favorite SF street of Asian restaurants and Irish pubs, and more important, a street on which you can find almost any Hello Kitty product imaginable (except for the pornographic ones—you have to go to Castro Street for those). Breathing in the cold SF air while fog literally sliced through my body as I stumbled the City's streets awoke me even better than the fresh Peet's coffee in my hand. There is no fog-eucalyptus-ocean-coffee-dumpling air as luscious as San Francisco's, anywhere. Period. The heavy fog helped evaporate my fear that this City, as it likes to capitalize itself, feels too small to contain me now.

Helen greeted me in front of our former hangout on Clement Street. "Your messed-up angles of blue-black hair look even scarier in person than on a camera phone." This from the girl who had copper dye in the shape of a hand on top of her shaved crew-cut head when I first met her.

"Your belly looks like it's about to pop, which is just as scary," I responded. Helen was a little chunky before, but that was her doughnut addiction talkin'. Her massive belly and radiant face now promised a new being that looked like it was ready to drop into the world any minute.

Autumn said, "Where's the hostile love for me, who didn't

get knocked up or sprung from Manhattan out of the blue?" She appeared the same, all multi-ethnic fabulous, but with a new, relaxed vibe to go along with her old dazzling smile.

Group hug and shit. My girls.

We ordered at the counter and brought our feast to our old table in the back, cornered against the wall where we could watch the never-ending line of mostly Chinese customers (which was how you knew the place's food quality was ace), who shouted their orders in Mandarin and Cantonese to the counter ladies while enormous circular trays of steaming fresh dumplings and chicken and pork buns were brought out from the kitchen at regular intervals. At our favorite perch in our favorite ambience-less dim sum joint, our trays heaped with pot stickers (pan-fried pork dumplings), *har gow* (shrimp bonnets), *fun kor* (steamed rice-paper-wrapped dumplings filled with pork, water chestnuts, and peanuts), and—Phil, so sad you're a vegetarian and missing out on your namesake dumplings—tender, sweet, chive-flavored shrimps wrapped inside a delicate rice noodle. *Hsieh hsieh ni, Clement Street de hsiao long bao, duo bao zhong!* Thank you, Clement Street dumplings, and blessings upon you!

fog city with friends
succulent dumpling goodness—
I would stay for shrimp

I asked Helen, "So your mom's recovered from that breakdown she nearly had when you told her she was going to be a grandma?" Since my mother doesn't hide her displeasure at the prospect of becoming a mother-in-law figure, I wanted to know how Helen's mom—whose sweet and sour disposition could give my mother a run for her Prozac—was dealing with the transition in her daughter's life.

Helen said, "Recovered and then some. She's all into baby projects now. She just finished clearing out the family room and turning it into a baby room. She's setting up the crib this morning, her faithful Eamon puppy at her side. She was so massively pissed when I got pregnant, yet she was the one who marched me and Eamon down to city hall to get married. She hardly said a word to him for like the first month he lived with us, except to come into our bedroom and yell at him for blasting music too loud—even though it was me controlling the volume. Then two of her waiters at the restaurant came down with the flu on the same day, and she trudged upstairs to ask my help, and I was like 'I've got morning sickness, Mama, ask Eamon' and she was like 'No, YOU ask Eamon' but Eamon himself was already downstairs helping out. Do you know Eamon is the most popular waiter in the restaurant now? Aside from being the most capable and charming person there who also sings Irish ditties to customers as he serves them noodles, the just plain oddity of my fair, red-haired Irish soccer boy working in a Chinese family restaurant in the Richmond seems to rake in tips for him. I LOVE IT!" Helen rubbed her belly. "It's kicking. Wanna feel?"

Autumn and I both reached over to touch Helen's moving belly. Kick, kick. Cool, cool! Weird, weird!

HELEN'S GOING TO BE A MOM! HOW THE *FUCK* DID THAT HAPPEN? I mean, I know how it happened, but that doesn't mean seeing the late-third-trimester prospect stretched out before me wasn't shocking anyway. Her stomach reminded me how last year at Shrimp's brother's wedding Wallace had been all groom nervous and happy, teasing me that soon it could be me and Shrimp sharing such a union. And I'd thought—*No way. Marriage and baby-making, that's for old people.*

Helen is the same age as me and Autumn.

Autumn said, "Helen, promise us you won't become one of those new mothers who can only talk about when the baby makes a poo? Those mommies hang out during the day at my coffeehouse job, and that's all they talk about."

"I promise," Helen said, nodding solemnly.

"Don't promise," I told Helen. "Cuz I guarantee it will happen to you. I've been working the East Coast café version of Autumn's job, and trust me, it's not just a West Coast phenomenon. It's a universal mommy thing. Obsession with poo, and sleeping patterns, and . . ."

"Ohmygod, enough talk about babies," Autumn interrupted. "Let's talk about a real babe." She whipped out her camera phone and flashed us a photo of a surfer chick with short spiky strawberry blond hair, kinda butch build, in her wet suit, and one massive Autumn-size smile on her freckled face. "That's April, my new lady," Autumn announced. She looked directly at me. "I am walking the walk. I am in school, working, and in the first throes of new love. So glad I came home."

"April and Autumn? Has to be true love, it's too cute not to be. Good for you," I said. Then I slipped in: "Think I should move home to be with Shrimp?"

"NO!" My girls answered.

Little known fact: Superheroes on rescue missions are often the loneliest people in the world.

"Why?" I said.

Autumn chimed in, "If Shrimp wants to live in San Francisco, then it's because he doesn't know where else he wants to be. He wants the safe and familiar. He wants the old waves, the old life."

Helen backed her up. "You know we love Shrimp, and we would love to have you close by again, but you should only move back to San Francisco if this is really where you want to be. Otherwise, it won't last. You must already know that."

I love how my friends give me credit for being smarter than I actually am.

Autumn said, "There may have been some Shrimp surveillance."

"Excuse me?" I asked.

Autumn continued, "My lady hangs out with the Ocean Beach surfer crowd. She told us about Shrimp coming back. Helen and I may have gone over there to hunt him down and check out the situation."

"May have or did?" I asked.

"Did," Helen said, nodding.

"And?" I asked.

Autumn said, "We went purely on a fact-finding mission on your behalf. Wanted to find out why he left New York so suddenly, what he planned to do now. We got nothing out of him, other than a flyer for some meditation retreat up north he said he wanted to try. He is deep into thinking mode, not talking mode."

Helen handed me the flyer, advertising an upcoming Buddhist weekend retreat in Humboldt County, where his parents are living. "Turn it over," she said.

I turned over the flyer and saw a new Shrimp masterwork drawing, etched in crayons. It pictured him and me, sitting on a backyard deck patio with prayer flags hanging from an overhead line. Strips of fog wisped through the Golden Gate Bridge in the background. In the foreground I stood at a patio table wearing an apron, and Shrimp stood at the grill wearing a wet suit. Two children sat in high chairs: perfect hybrid-babies with my dark hair (Mohawked) and his cherry lips (pursed). What was most notable about the picture was that, unlike the pages and pages of sketchbook art he's devoted to rendering me in since we first got together, he hadn't drawn me this time in movie star or comic book fantasy projection. He looked like a regular Ocean Beach surfer dad, minus the golden boy beauty halo I would have drawn over him, and I looked like a regular Ocean Beach bohemian mom chick, with long hair in a solid black color. In Shrimp's back-of-a-flyer snapshot drawing of our potential future life together, we just looked like us. But older. And chill. In love. A family. No more, no less.

What have I been agonizing over? This choice should be so easy. I want that picture. Shrimp wants that picture. We should do it—wherever and whatever it takes.

Watching Helen and Autumn watch their watches, I knew my gift from my girls was the proof of the flyer, but not the luxury of time to analyze the art in a girlfriend forum. Helen stood up and took a business card out of her purse, handing it to me. "The artwork's yours to figure out how you want to answer it. You know we support you no matter what you choose. Just choose carefully, 'kay? And for chrissakes go see my auntie at the salon on this card. She's just down the street. Tell her I sent you and she'll give you a good price to get your hair fixed."

Autumn stood up and pointed at Helen. "What she said." They both kissed me on the cheek and left.

WHAT HAPPENED TO US? We were once rebels! Proudly

insolent teenagers! Helen used to draw a comic book series about an action hero called Ball Hunter who chased golf balls along with other *cough* misadventures, and she used these alluring comics as bait to lure over-twenty-one boys into buying her beers when her underage self was hanging out in local pubs. (She's now married to one of those conquests!) Autumn used to get high with other girls' surfer boyfriends and then use these boys (and some of the girls, too) for sexual experimentation while she came to terms with her own sexuality. I got kicked out of boarding school after the boy there who got me pregnant was busted for selling E out of his dorm room, and when I returned home to finish out high school, it wasn't long before my parents had me on lockdown in Alcatraz due to my exemplary bad attitude problem and the matter of an unauthorized sleepover at Shrimp's.

Now Helen is happily pregnant and married, Autumn is competently juggling school and job and girlfriend, and I, who was once banished to Alcatraz, am considering a permanent, peaceful move back into its realm. I don't know whether to be scared or pleased.

FORTY-THREE

A fertility potion must be woven into the San Francisco fog, what with all the procreation running rampant here lately.

All this procreation, and all I can think about is death.

"Promise me you won't die," I demanded of Sugar Pie.

"Anyone ever tell you that you need a restraint device for your mouth?" Fernando asked me from the driver's seat of my father's Mercedes.

From the back seat I grimaced at the big broody Nicaraguan through his rearview mirror observation of me. I answered, "Yes. You. On practically every drive you ever gave me to or from school or work or the beach or whatever while I was growing up. But listen up, señor. I've known your wife longer than you have— need I remind you I introduced you to her? And I know she appreciates the demand as an expression of my devotion to her rather than as a death wish for her."

Seated next to Fernando, in the front passenger seat, Sugar Pie allowed, "The young lady is right." She turned to face me. "As for promises, we all know I can't promise I'm not going anywhere anytime soon." This young lady has always admired Sugar's use of double negatives. "I'm"—(*cough, indistinguishable number, cough*)—"years old with one remaining kidney that's failing. I plan to enjoy every day that comes to me as I get it, and the good Lord willing, I'll pass on in my sleep with Fernando at my side, but beyond that, I have no wish or expectation for when or how it will happen. Could be tomorrow, could be next year, could be on the dialysis chair, could be sitting in a car with you like right now." To let her husband know she bore no ill will about my death comment, Sugar Pie opened a box of See's candy. "Now baby, I'm going to offer you to take a piece, but as you can see, there aren't many left, so I'm hoping you'll be a polite young lady and say no. I know you wouldn't want to take an old lady's last piece of chocolate." She held out the box to me. "Cyd Charisse, would you like a piece of candy?"

I shook my head. "No, thank you, Sugar." Must be true love between us for me to turn down a chocolate. Hypothetically I never imagined a universe in which this scenario could play out, so now seemed like the appropriate time to play out another hypothetical with Sugar Pie. "It seems a shame that you finally moved out of the old folks' home and in with Fernando at the apartment at the side of our house, and then I'm not around to hang out with you more. Do you think I should move back home?" I didn't add the "with Shrimp" part, for the sake of blind judgment and all.

"Follow your heart." Sugar Pie has always been a mind reader.

"What if my heart's in conflict with my mind?"

"Mind!" Fernando shook his index finger at me from the rearview mirror. "Use your mind more, already. What's that I heard about you never bothering with culinary school?"

Sugar Pie added, "You've told me about all these gentlemen in your life in New York—but what about friends your own age, girls, like Helen and Autumn?"

I told them, "First, I did try a culinary class. School is not for me. And, I did make one friend, this girl who works at a nail shop in the neighborhood. But then I guess I came on too strong or something, must be cuz I don't have that restraint lock placed on my mouth yet, since what seemed like it started out as a cool friendship just went nowhere."

At the same time Fernando and Sugar Pie both said, "Did you try again?"

Their evolution into coupledom sync-talk is truly off-the-charts impressive. I liked that when I looked at them through the car mirrors, the reflection of contentedness on their faces was not a false mirage. They're another year older, and they looked it—but another year happier, and they looked that also.

As the car approached our destination in Ocean Beach, Sugar Pie told me, "The cards have confidence you could make a successful go of it wherever you chose to live."

"But what do *you* think, Sugar?" I asked.

"I *am* the cards," Sugar Pie intoned as Fernando stopped the car to drop me off. "How have *you* not figured that out yet?"

FORTY-FOUR

Maybe I should have caffeinated more heavily before showing up at Java the Hut, the coffeehouse owned by Shrimp's brother, Wallace, aka Java. Along with looking forward to dosing up, I'd been looking forward to revisiting the sight of my first barista gig, where Shrimp and I used to work together, but instead the sight of a Dumpster in front of the café, and the sounds of work-men with saws and drills working inside, greeted me. The old café was in total disarray—that is, if total disarray meant totally closed for coffee business.

As I peered through the window, Wallace stepped outside, next to the surfboard rack, to light a cigarette. It wasn't the first time I'd ever seen Wallace smoke, but it was for sure the first time I'd ever seen that surf rack with no boards parked inside the metal grates. Java the Hut's hard-core urban surfer paradise at the end of the continental U.S., where the Pacific roared away just across Great Highway, had turned into surfer ghost town. Stupid impermanence denying me yummy visions of hot-bodied boys wearing wet suits and chugging lattes.

Wallace grinned when he noticed me. "I had a feeling you'd be dropping by here soon." Ohmygod, why did he have to smile at me like that, with those full red lips and seductive white teeth that should be way darker, given the amount of coffee he drinks? Java's getting older, true—and more gorgeous, if that's possible. Gone was his long brown hair, replaced by a buzz cut that only highlighted the sharp angles of his jaw and cheekbones on his smooth rosy-tan face, and his deep-set sea eyes that look just like what's-his-name's—yeah, Phil's,—"CC, are you listening? You tranced out?"

"Huh?"

My body tensed in anticipation of Java moving in for the California surfer dude hug-shoulder nudge thing with me. Any touch from him would be too temptingly close. So like the loyal girlfriend I am to his errant brother, I fake-sneezed as Wallace approached me, successfully warding off any attempt at hugging. Wallace backed off a couple inches and said, "I was saying I knew once Shrimp appeared home with no warning, spouting all kinds of spiritual dogma, then left almost as quickly to return to the embrace of Iris and Billy, that you'd probably follow behind not much later.

There's one boy just begging to be found." Wallace glanced down at his waterproof surfer watch. "And here you are, right on schedule. You look good—New York agrees with you. Wanna come inside and see some pictures of Kelea? Please excuse the mess while we remodel."

I had plenty of time for inspection of the latest round of procreation, since Fernando had to drop Sugar Pie off at the dialysis center before returning to pick me up, so I stepped inside, despite the danger I felt at wanting to pull Java into a supply closet and do with him in there like I used to do with his brother. But Java's a solid family man, and I am long over my jailbait stage. It was just a hypothetical wanton desire. I have 'em all the time.

Java's like this perfect reflection of who I imagine Shrimp will be several years down the road—devoted partner, devoted to his business and to his community, a real man who still looks really good in a wet suit. *Keep imagining, CC. It's such a happy place.* Shrimp will be devoted to me all right, devoted of body, soul, and art—so long as that devotion allows him the freedom to not have possessions or be bound to any one place.

Wallace said, "Delia's at home with the baby right now. She'll be sorry she missed you. Looks like Kelea got mommy's red hair. She's beautiful, yes? Not like I'm biased or anything." I thumbed through a photo album of Wallace and Delia with their new baby, named after the Maui surf chiefess in Hawaiian mythology.

This baby could be my baby's cousin . . . someday, I thought. I decided that when Shrimp and I reached the stage of cousin-making for Kelea, Helen and Autumn would be aunties, and Fernando and Sugar Pie would be godparents, and my mother would make up some name our kids should call her like "LaLa," because she'd die before answering to "Nana." Come to think of it, Shrimp drew our family right, our babies probably would have my hair and his lips, and whoa, hopefully that would be long after I got more livin' on my own accomplished.

I turned to a picture of Iris and Billy with their baby grand-daughter. "Kelea's as gorgeous as her name. Are Iris and Billy enjoying being grandparents?"

Wallace smirked. He built the Java the Hut business with no help from them—they'd pretty much flung him out in the world on his own by the time he was sixteen. "Let's just say if the new grand-parents were not offered a place to live in our new house with our new baby when they returned from New Zealand, there's a reason. They're Iris and Billy, you know? They're into the cute, cuddly moments, but when the real business of baby-tending comes into play, they've got a joint to light up, a nature hike to explore, a global political demonstration to attend."

"Any idea how long Shrimp intends to stay with them up in Humboldt?"

"Well, since Iris and Billy have chosen to live in a caretaker's house with no phone—tell me the logic there—and Shrimp refuses to carry a cell phone, the answer to that would be no. I asked him to stay. I could use his help with the remodel, and he's welcome to live with us as long as he wants, even if Iris and Billy's living privileges with me and Dee have expired. But Shrimp mumbled something about big questions he needs time and ocean to figure out, and then he headed up north. He gave me no idea how long he's intending to stay up there, but I can tell you where to find him."

"Yes, please."

Wallace drew a map on a paper napkin. "I'm writing down directions to Iris and Billy's, but if you want to dodge a visit with them, try this beach first. If I know my brah, he'll be hitting the waves there around noontime any day he can. I'm writing down a message for Shrimp on the back of this napkin. Something that might help him with those big questions. Read it on your way up and see what you think." The map Wallace sketched, zigzag lines of barren coastal highway leading to unmarked parking spots leading down to an isolated beach nook, looked like a treasure hunt mission to find our lost surfer boy. "And, Cyd Charisse?"

"Yes?"

"You know you can't save him, right? Shrimp has to find himself."

I thought I didn't believe in aha moments anymore, but just like that, I was snapped out of the Land of Indecision.

I am Chaos. I am a hellion. I am not a cupcake.

I am sick of everyone looking out for my and Shrimp's supposed best interests. That's our job. Aha, and so there!

Shrimp and I will not go back to the old stalemate that broke us apart last year. If I have to move home to lock him into a future—whether it's finding a Buddhist teacher or getting his GED and finding some direction in life—I will, so long as he wants me by his side. Why shouldn't we get in on the procreation action too? I'm not saying I plan to find Shrimp and propose babies and marriage, but can I propose we create a life together here? Hella yeah.

Life is too short not to compromise on something as easy as a city, if I want my true love served up to me on a permanent basis.

FORTY-FIVE

Buddha teaching number 208: *Therefore, follow the Noble One, who is steadfast, wise, learned, dutiful, and devout. One should follow only such a man, who is truly good and discerning, even as the moon follows the path of the stars.*

The noble man to seek out, according to Wallace's treasure map, ran the general store in an off-the-beaten-trail little town in Humboldt County. All I wanted from this man was fresh caffeination and the day's secret surf code, which seemed my due after the five-hour drive north from San Francisco, but the ZZ Top doppelganger man hedged.

ZZ handed me a cup of coffee so strong I almost lost my balance from the heavy smell. He said, "Whatcha so curious for? Folks passing through here know not to ask questions." This one store on this stretch of one-lane highway had more than one person inside to nod agreement to ZZ's statement. For a ramshackle shack in the middle of northern California nowhere, it felt possible that every town resident—all ten of them, all looking like refugees off the FBI's Ten Most Wanted Stoner Outlaw list—was in attendance to back up ZZ and make sure CC did not find her man.

You'd think I'd asked for da Vinci's fucking code rather than made a simple request for how to find the hallowed surf spot. According to Wallace's directions, morning surfers set out a daily beacon each day on top of the unmarked hill above the obscure beach to let the afternoon surfers know the wave quality. The beacon—some days it might be a Harley flag dug onto the hill, some days it might be a STOP sign nailed into a tree—also served to tip off would-be adventurers as to whether the fuzz happens to be bored that day and might be found harassing the lone surfers on the renegade beach that was officially closed to the public by the state because of safety concerns.

Through the open door to the bathroom behind ZZ's stand at the shack's cash register, I eyeballed the premium toothbrush resting on the sink counter and sensed my in. I whispered, "If you tell me where to find the beacon, I'll tell you the secret for getting your electric toothbrush perfectly clean. I also know stuff about the big bang theory, in case you're interested."

On the down low, ZZ muttered, "Meet me at the back behind the '58 Chevy truck. Make sure no one sees you."

And so the noble ZZ man learned the CC on the DL, and revealed the path to reach the Shrimp.

I parked the car in a ditch behind a forest of trees off the highway, under the redwood tree with the Bazooka gum box dangling from a branch (good waves, no cop interest), and set out on my trek down the steep cliff. I think I've decided I am a New Yorker at heart, but it was impossible not to be awed by the sight of the mighty Pacific, surrounded by forest and mountain, as I stumbled down the cliff scattered with mist and fern. The secret path offered no simple jaunt for a city girl—it was more like a path for serious hikers who carried all those complicated rock-climbing gizmos that often go along with the cool clothing at mountaineer gear stores.

A city girl on a quest for her man would not be dissuaded by the fact of her inability to rappel such a terrain. I reached the bottom promptly at noon, surprised to find myself still alive—but delighted to find myself alone at a slice of California ocean paradise of spray, sand, and surf. Make that almost alone. In the distance, near to a beach cove, I glimpsed Shrimp.

Simple and soulful in his solitude, he sat on the sand, wearing a wet suit and waxing his board. Love sigh.

I wanted to run to him, fling myself into his arms, but I also wanted to savor watching him in his element.

His element. Not mine.

Shrimp finished waxing his board and stood up, walking toward

rachel cohn

the sea, but still I paused. Now was my opportunity to approach him, before he immersed himself in the water, but his movement at, not inside, the ocean, stopped the motion of my feet in his direction. He placed his board on the sand and stood tall against the sea, reverent, his beautiful blond hair spiked high, glimmering in the sun. He reached his arms up from his sides, almost like a victory pose, then brought them down as he leaned over, as if he were taking a bow.

I may have been kicked out of yoga class, but I've been a surfer's girlfriend long enough to recognize the sun salutation yoga pose that an actualizing surfer offers up to the sea before communing with her.

The Pacific goddess owns him like I never will.

A slight gasp, maybe it was a wince, I don't know, alerted Shrimp to my presence. He turned around from his sea stance and caught me standing several yards behind him, at the base of the cliff.

"Hey," he said, like he'd been expecting me all along.

"Hey," I said.

He picked up his board and walked over to me. He kissed me soft and sweet, first on my cheek, then on my lips. But his hands, holding on to his board, with prayer beads now wrapped around his wrists, made no movement to touch my body. Up close, I saw new words painted on the tip of the board, on the reverse side of where he'd painted a skull years earlier. *Happy indeed we live, we who possess nothing. Feeders on joy we shall be, like the Radiant Gods.*

Stalemate while I paused to rethink my moment of truth with my true love.

I had our reunion moment all planned out. I intended to say: "Shrimp, love of my life, if you need to be by the sea, I will stay in San Francisco with you, even if New York seems more suited to me. It was rather lame of you to take off without any notice and make me come find you, but I needed the adventure. You always give me what I need. You are all I could ever want in a soul mate. And if you feel like you want to move home to San Francisco, then my answer is clear: I choose you. Wherever you are is where I want to be." Shrimp would then pull me into his arms for a deep kiss, there'd be a non-lame Beach Boys soundtrack song playing from a nearby boom box, and we'd fall to the ground in the passion of our embrace as waves broke over us in this total cinematic moment of true love, The End, forever and ever, baby baby baby.

The actual words I said were: "Shrimp, Phil, whoever you are— I love you. But I don't belong here. I belong in New York. If you want to be there with me, I will be waiting for you." Betrayed by my own lips.

Sun salutation, you and I are no longer friends.

A Nancy sigh escaped my lips as I reached into my pocket and handed Shrimp the napkin with Wallace's message scrawled to Shrimp—a napkin I hadn't been sure I would have the courage to deliver until I saw the sun salutation that kissed my fate with Shrimp.

I'd crayoned my own haiku at the side of Wallace's message, and that was what Shrimp read first:

Kathmandu café
Everest climbing season
Dante will school shrimp

"Say wha?" Shrimp wanted to know.

Doing the right thing is completely overrated, and yet the concept seduced me. "Dante contacted Wallace, trying to track you down. Dante's got some gig at a café in Kathmandu. It's the season for tourists who travel there en route to Mount Everest, and Dante of course is the stupid barista man of choice for climbing season in Nepal. Dante says he wants to show you the Buddhist monasteries, introduce you to the monks who are his friends there. Nepal is the epicenter of the spiritual action you seek, apparently, and Dante wants you to join him there. You're, like, looking for a teacher, but I think you already found him. And I think someone as cool and talented as you should have that, pursue it, see where it leads. If you read through Wallace's message, he says he's got plenty of work for you the next couple weeks to earn your fare to Kathmandu, if you want to go."

I am a New York hypergrrl for sure, but the California free love free spirit in me will not be denied.

No one's more surprised than me.

The sunstruck smile on Shrimp's face let me know his answer. "There it is," he said. "The dharma path."

I arrived here determined not to let Shrimp go like last time, but now I realized I'd made the right decision the first time, when he proposed marriage and I said no because I wanted us both to be free to pursue our dreams.

Maybe I am smarter than I think.

I want Shrimp to follow a path he's running to, not away from. I expected to cling to him, to fight for us not to repeat the old stalemate, but now I genuinely *wanted* him to go to Nepal. I won't be the girl to obstruct his answers.

I have my path, and he should have his. If our paths are meant to intertwine, they will. The permanent intersection just hasn't happened—yet. If we force it, we lose it forever.

I always thought at the end of the road, I would find him. Now I know—Shrimp will find me.

I'm already who and where I want to be. Myself.

FORTY-SIX

For old times' sake we said good-bye in the backseat of Shrimp's brother's hand-me-down Pinto parked near the top hill near the hallowed surf spot. Our lovemaking encompassed the soul-kissing-touching-talking-until-the-sun-set-over-the-Pacific variety. The midafternoon nap inside his arms, with the sun cascading through the window as we lay enveloped in ocean breeze and in each other, more than compensated for the nakedness our bodies did not share, what with the Pacific cold and the sand all over my little man's little car.

"So how's it gonna be this time?" he asked me before I left. We stood against the ancient Geo Metro car I'd driven up north that used to be mine and that my parents still hadn't given away. Shrimp pressed against me, and I held him tight, rocking, kissing his neck and running my fingers through his hair. I didn't want to stop touching him. Ever. I momentarily considered pitching Shrimp on the idea that we get a reverse Siamese twin operation that could join us together forever, instead of separate us back into two independent beings.

"No clean break," I whispered in his ear.

"Then what break?" he whispered back.

Last time, we made the right choice, but executed it the wrong way. This time around, we couldn't make that same mistake. I said, "No break at all. Cuz there is like technology around now that makes it possible for us to see and talk to each other every day even if we're on opposite sides of the world. We're gonna make that technology our bitch."

"Bitchin'," Shrimp murmured. Then, in response to the fog setting in overhead and chilling the air, sending goose bumps across our arms, he added, "Burr-ito."

"Enchilada and tamale," I answered.

"Tostada and guacamole."

"Me amo Shrimp."

"My name's *'Camarón' en español.*"

"My name's still Cyd Charisse in other languages, I believe."

"Just promise not to call me Phil ever again?"

"Promise. I still *amo Camarón.*"

"Ditto."

I could only break my body apart from his after we shared a vow that we were not breaking up at all, but rather diverting to a temporary holding pattern, spiritually together but geographically apart. We promised a proper airport good-bye a few days later when I returned to Manhattan, complete with longing kisses and tears, and plans to reunite in New York after Shrimp's time in Nepal.

Promises had other plans in mind.

My attempt to extract a Don't Die promise from Sugar Pie was requested of the wrong person. When I returned to San Francisco from seeing Shrimp, a message waited for me from Danny. I needed to return home to New York immediately.

Max had moved on to the big commune in the sky. He died of a heart attack the night after I arrived in San Francisco. A lifestyle of junk food, smoking, and not visiting the doctor regularly since his partner's death, had finally caught up with him.

Sid-dad didn't want me to be alone after I'd lost a friend—the first friend I've ever lost to death. He offered to accompany me back to New York. I told Sid-dad, "I'll be okay, you don't have to come, I have Danny." He said, "You need your father." I said, "You're right. Thank you."

As our plane traveled back east, Sid-dad snoozed next to me and I rested my head against his arm. I didn't know whether to laugh or cry because maybe Max's timing was his sick way of giving me a last gift: grief for him distracted the heartache I otherwise would have felt for finding myself on an eastbound plane, again, after having let Shrimp go, again. Our young friendship—the one

I shared with Max—had been cut too short. Max and I had never gotten around to watching his Ann Miller movie collection together, he'd never seen my barista mastery skills, owing to his desire to never leave his apartment unless absolutely necessary, and I'd yet to see Max in action when he crank-called his upstairs neighbors and played obscene noises from his laptop.

Even if Max was a grouch, I decided that he'd see it as no dishonor to his memory if I celebrated the bright side of his passing. Max lived twenty years essentially alone in his apartment after his partner died, and he was eager to ride out eternity with his true love. So when I think of Max, I will picture him up in heaven, reunited with Tony and their friends, building new walls of not-sadness. They're having garden parties with Ava Gardner and Lana Turner, drinking proper British tea, eating beets from a can, ramen noodles, and lots and lots of cupcakes. They're learning the real answers to the universe's crucial mysteries: Who was driving the car that killed Grace Kelly—Princess Grace or Princess Stephanie? How did Marilyn Monroe really die—and why? Did Sid Vicious off Nancy Spungen at the Chelsea Hotel—or did the drug dealer who visited them that night really do it? Liberace . . . *WHY*?

Yvette Mimieux greeted me when Sid-dad and I arrived home at Max's to retrieve her. She *miaule*'d, *So maybe you've lost a friend and your true love has flown the coop once again, but you've gained a movie star namesake sister. You promised.*

rachel cohn

FORTY-SEVEN

A cappuccino bought me my life.

The espresso pull tasted too watery, and the newbie barista still can't get a good head of foam on milk—skim *or* whole—so I didn't bother actually paying for the drink. Instead I stuffed a dollar tip down the barista's shirt, for effort. He's here, he's trying. He's Johnny Mold, our first employee, who hopefully won't consider my dollar-down-the-shirt tip as grounds for a future sexual harassment lawsuit.

Johnny said, *"Toon vor es,"* to my tippage.

Myself may also be called Cupcake, Chaos, Little Hellion, CC, Ceece, Dollface, etc. (but I'm not yet called "Etc."—to my knowledge), but even in Armenian I didn't think I cared to be called an ass. Lisbeth beat me to my own defense. *"Toon esh es,"* she responded to Johnny. She then handed him her Armenian phrase

299

book to go along with her piece of advice. "Maybe you could learn some words that don't involve offending someone?" At the rate their friendship has ignited since Aaron's birthday party, Johnny the Armenian jackass, and not Frank, will be accompanying Lisbeth to Armenia to adopt a baby next month.

Lisbeth's going to be a mom! More important, I'm going to be an aunt!

Johnny Mold may have lost his grandpa, but like Lisbeth, he's gained a family. He said, "So that's the new plan—you two ganging up on me?"

Lisbeth sang out, "Sisters."

Our brother Danny stood up on the platform in the corner window area of the establishment, clinking a fork against a champagne glass to get the group's attention. "People," he said. "Let the voting on a new name begin. I'll start the bidding by suggesting 'Dollface.'" He looked in my direction. "If we name the place after Ceece, perhaps she'll have less inclination to bolt every time we hold a party here?"

I had no intention of abandoning this particular celebration. The venue hosting our party, the Village establishment formerly known as LUNCHEONETTE, is now an unnamed café that, as of today, officially and permanently will host Danny's cupcake business. Make that, *our* cupcake business.

While it may be a joint business of which I am co-owner, Danny's nickname for me shouldn't bear the brunt of becoming our business name. Too cute and obvious. Nixed. "'Pastabilities,'" I chimed in. "That's what I think we should call the place."

Aaron asked, "But isn't the plan for this business to indulge the sugar more than the pasta side of the carb food chain?"

True loves be damned, I smelled a voting bloc. I said, "Is that distinction really so important? Who wouldn't want to eat in a cupcake place called 'Pastabilities'?"

"I wouldn't," Johnny Be Damned said.

"I wouldn't either," Lisbeth seconded. "But I'd be glad to have my management consulting team research and develop an appropriate corporate brand name—"

The Danny and CC voting bloc: "NO!"

Johnny mused, "As hard as it is to operate a successful food business in Manhattan, it's even harder to come up with an original name for it. So I'm throwing 'Geldof' into the suggestion pile, after Sir Bob Geldof—"

I interrupted, "Who's not actually a proper 'Sir,' since he's not a British citizen, even though he gets called 'Sir'—"

Only to be interrupted back by Johnny, "And Danny could formulate special brand cupcakes named after Sir Bob's biological and adopted daughters."

"I like it," Danny said. "The black-and-white cupcake becomes the Fifi Trixibelle, the spring fever cupcake becomes the Peaches Honeyblossom . . ."

Aaron grabbed Danny's hand, inspired. ". . . And the flower frosting cupcake becomes the Pixie Frou-Frou! The peanut butter cupcake becomes the Heavenly Hiraani Tigerlily! I can already see the marketing campaign: *Come to Geldof—cupcakes catered to your every groupie craving.*"

Danny laughed. "There's our niche! I foresee customer lines out the door and down the block."

Sid-dad shook his head. "What's the matter with simply calling the place 'Cupcake'?"

Sid-dad is biased. Frank-dad is not. "How about just sticking with the name LUNCHEONETTE, until inspiration strikes?" he said.

We all more or less grumbled, "Okay." If it ain't broke, don't fix it.

I always imagined it would be too weird to see my two families merge, but watching Frank and Sid-dad step aside to inspect the preliminary remodel plans at the counter together, I realized it was in fact too overdue. The two dads, former college roommates and former best friends, their friendship long lost to the Nancy riff that produced me, converged in New York for a talk after Max's funeral service. A talk about me. They emerged from that talk to pronounce that while I may call myself a slacker, I'm in fact anything but.

Despite my refusal to go to college or to culinary school, they decided that with the right backing, Myself was fully capable of learning how to run a business. They were equally bullish on Danny's prospects. And so Our Two Dads (being that Sid-dad is also Danny's godfather) teamed together to formulate a Plan. Trust funds were cashed out, offers made, papers signed. Danny and I, along with our families as investors, now own LUNCHEONETTE.

Hmmm: Our Two Dads. Potential band name . . . or potential café business name?

The sound of a champagne cork popping open announced our celebration was ready to get lively. A glass of sparkly arrived in my hand courtesy of the honored guest who'd brought the bottle to help us christen the New-Old establishment. "I see your doll still travels with you," said Miss Loretta, the NY bio-fam's longtime friend and former housekeeper, acknowledging Gingerbread perched on top of the blueprints lying on the counter. When I first came to New York to meet the bio-fam, Miss Loretta had extended an offer to my sixteen-year-old girl self to park Gingerbread on a shelf at her restaurant uptown if Gingerbread and I were ever ready to part ways. I'm allegedly a woman now, one with a hella remodel debt piling on, and I *still* wasn't ready to part with my childhood doll.

I pointed in the direction of La Marzocco, eternally reliable and therefore saved from the discarded appliances list included in the remodel's upgrade plans. I told Miss Loretta, "Naw, Gingerbread doesn't travel with me so much as hang out in my important places. And she's fixing for a permanent retirement. The remodel plans will provide a custom-built shelf designed for Gingerbread to sit over La Marzocco."

"Good spot for her," Miss Loretta allowed. "From there Gingerbread can lord over and grace your community of customers, family, and friends. Amen." She lifted her glass to me. "Cyd Charisse, I wish you much luck and happiness with this business, and I promise not to hold a grudge at you for breaking my nephew Luis's heart."

I informed her, "We were 'just friends.'"

She patted my back. "You just let yourself go on believing that, honey."

I hadn't let myself believe that Chucky would show up after I sent the invitation to her at the nail shop, yet here she was, holding a glass of champagne in her foxy rhinestone-studded manicured hand. Though I hadn't expected her to come, I'd prepared for her just in case. I had *mucho* to hablar with her. "Chucky," I said, *"Encantada de verte. Me han dicho que no me esforcé lo suficiente para darle una buena oportunidad a nuestro primer intento de amistad. Así es que cogí un curso de español de inmersión intensivo durante un fin de semana en caso de que tuviera la oportunidad de hablar en español contigo hoy. ¡Así es! ¡Asistí a una escuela actual y me quedé el tiempo completo! Me ayudó que el profesor del curso era muy guapo, (y soltero, si tienes algunas amigas que están buscando salir con un recién graduado de NYU que estudió español como asignatura principal). Él escribió lo que estoy diciendo ahora para poder memorizármelo. Pues, ¿piensas que podemos tratar de nuevo a ser amigos?"*[1]

Chucky laughed. "Si. Cuz your pronunciation sounds like shit. You're gonna need a lot of my help, I can already tell. And congratulations on your new business. I hope to be following in your footsteps a couple years down the road, and I might be needing your help."

"I'm there for you," I said.

"Classy party for a not-yet-opened business," Chucky said, pointing in the direction of the band.

Aaron and his bandmates had set up at the corner window, conferring over selection of their first song. Now that the band is back in business, they've changed names too, also after extensive name negotiation, the result of which is that My Dead Gay Son

---

[1] I'm glad to see you. I've been told I didn't give our first try at friendship a good enough chance. So I took an intensive Spanish immersion weekend course just in case I might have the chance to talk to you today, in Spanish. That's right, I went to an actual school and stayed the whole time! It helped that the instructor at the language class was very cute (and available if you have any friends looking for a date with a recently graduated Spanish major from NYU). He wrote down what I am saying now for me to memorize. So do you think we can try again at being friends?

has morphed from No Way Gay to Yes Way Gay, Okay? Per the family business agreement, Aaron's involvement with this business shall be restricted to band performances at our café. He and Danny have chosen to play it safe this time. Despite his outstanding chef skills, Aaron will not be joining us in a professional capacity. Living and working together was what did him and Danny in last time. They won't make that same mistake.

Neither will Danny and I. Aaron is moving back into their apartment, and I am moving out.

Accordingly, Sid-dad waved a set of legal agreements in my direction, beckoning me over to the counter area. Apparently what adulthood really means is endless papers to sign, to seal your fate—for what, you have no idea. Sid-dad tried not to look at me all proud (or maybe his look was jet-lagged haze from all the SF–NY travel time he's logged between Max's funeral and tonight's christening), but with that bald head and pudge face, he wore satisfaction like a merit badge. *There's my daughter the Little Hellion—didn't think any of us would survive her teenage years, and now just look at her! Grown up, on her own, and with a proper haircut at last.* "I think that's the first time since you were in kindergarten that I've seen you wear a dress that wasn't black," Sid-dad said. "Green becomes you."

To go along with my new haircut—razor-sharp bob angled from my neck down to my chin, with blunt bangs and a single process old-school original black color—I wore a party dress simi-

lar to the green flapper one the real Cyd Charisse wore for her spectacular dance in *Singin' in the Rain*. But so we shall never forget
which Cyd Charisse is which, I've called upon Lisbeth's corporate
branding. Next to my old tattoo of a shrimp on the obscure flappy
underside of my arm, I've got a new tattoo—a simple brown coffee
bean. In honor of Myself.

Sid-dad pointed to the bottom line on the last piece of paper. I
signed and sighed. Sid-dad said, "You sound like your mother.
And that's that. Max's apartment lease is officially in your name."
In Manhattan scoring a great apartment has nothing to do with
combing real estate ads and inspecting different pads before
deciding on your perfect home. Here it's all about being in the right
place at the right time—and having the cash (and your dad) available to meet with the building super and make it all happen. Also,
being willed a cat.

I'm like Max: New York—I love it!

I told my father, "Please tell Mom we're not going to protest
her threatened inspection next month, but she can fuggedabout her
redecoration intentions for my apartment. Yvette Mimieux won't
have it." Yvette and I will allow a visit, we might even find it in our
hearts to look forward to it, but we'd never allow my mother to
ruin our apartment's CC-merged-with-Max décor with her impeccable taste.

Yvette and I have decided to work through our Max sadness by reconstructing the Wall of Sadness. We've left Max's pictures on the wall, but added new flags—red and yellow prayer flags, sent to us from Shrimp in Nepal. We've also installed new pictures, of our San Francisco and New York families, and a drawing Shrimp sent along with the prayer flags that pictures Max standing on his piano bench, broomstick in hand, banging on the ceiling to Heaven and yelling up at the neighbors, "Keep that racket down!"

The latest haiku from Shrimp (spell-checked by Dante), via text message from Kathmandu:

> Charisse owns Mimieux
> Three more months till shrimp visits
> Name café for me?

Our party at the café-not-to-be-named-"Shrimp" (I'd vote for it, but Danny would nix) was enlightened by the arrival of a lady I didn't know. Frank greeted her, then introduced her to Lisbeth and Danny before making his way over to me. "I've got someone I'd like you to meet," Frank said. "Mary, this is my other daughter I've been telling you about. CC, this is my friend Mary."

He didn't say "lady friend" or "girlfriend," and they didn't hold hands, which was nice, considering how ancient they are (i.e., not in an acceptably cool old people hand-holding way like Fernando and Sugar Pie), but Mary must have been Frank's "special" friend.

Even more creepy than the shock that she appeared to be an age-appropriate companion and not some Barbie type twenty years his junior—minus the BOTOX I'd clock Mary as being in her late fifties—was that Mary's fashionable blond prettiness could have passed her for a near-senior-citizen-age version of . . . my mother.

My head didn't even know how to deal with that thought so I just said, "Nice to meet you, Mary." I turned to Frank. "How come you didn't tell us you were bringing a friend? We'd have sent her an invitation."

Frank said, "I believe in randomness over regularity."

Saucy like Yvette! Who knew?!?

Danny tapped my shoulder. "Didja save the first dance for me?"

Of course I did. I am the cup to his cake.

The instruments tuned and fired up, Yes Way Gay, Okay? settled into their first song—a slow-tempo, tender version of "My Favorite Things." For a gay Jewish chef who can't dress for shit, Aaron could really sing him some soul.

Steven and Fallon Carrington shared the first cotillion dance, naturally. "*Salut*, Commandant," I said, my face pressed against his ear. "*Salut*, Dollface," he answered. "And don't think I didn't see you flirting with the UPS man earlier today." He mimicked, "'Gosh you're strong to carry an industrial machine like that! Want a cappuccino to ease that burden?'"

Damn all-seeing, all-knowing brother.

I said, "I was just trying to reel in a brew customer. The first one's always free. Isn't that the saying?"

"I think the saying is, 'Home is where the heart is.'"

"'There's too many fish in the sea.'"

"'Absence makes the heart grow fonder.'"

"Or some such crap."

"Exactly."

Three months till Shrimp visits this summer! The UPS man with the muscles nicely contouring his uniform shall be purely aesthetic distraction to make it through until then—a hypothetical wanton desire. Easy come, easy go, is what I will tell Danny next time he teases me about the Man in Brown.

Shrimp need not worry. I'll be waiting for him.

I'm right here.

Don't miss Rachel Cohn's latest book:

YOU KNOW WHERE TO FIND ME

Here's a peek!

WE HAVE NO BODY TO VIEW, NO PROCESSIONAL TRIP TO A cemetery. Laura always planned things through, and that didn't change with her death. She asked for cremation and no burial. She who had everything was at heart a minimalist.

Instead, we have cookies after the service. The dining room is set up with a large buffet of catered food—light salads, polite sandwiches with the bread crusts cut off and cucumbers inside, the *edamame* Laura loved to nibble, set out in the beautiful bowls she brought back from Japan. No one appears to be eating much besides the sweets. Perhaps when an elderly person dies the mourners can reflect on that person's life with a celebration of food and memories, but that is not the case here. I don't hear anyone talking about Laura, no exchange of smiles and laughter—*Remember that time when she . . . ?* I hear chatter, but it's soft, humble. Or maybe I'm too high to properly distinguish the mourners' conversations over their tea and coffee cups. The spread of food is mostly a waste, but the caffeinated drinks appear to be a hit. I'm not the only person here who wants to jolt away the numb.

And who doesn't love cookies—tray after tray of delicate Italian butter cookies; *ghraybeh*, the Lebanese sugar cookies that were Laura's favorites; and an impressive assortment of homemade sweets contributed by the guests. I sample each variety. All these fancy cookies, but the universal truth remains the same: There is no substitute for the wholesome goodness that is chocolate chip cookies. I can picture the Georgetown society ladies arriving with their Saran-wrapped plates: *Jim. Darling. I'm so sorry about your beloved daughter killing herself. Here are some chocolate chip cookies our cook made. The secret ingredient is cardamom. Delicious, no?*

We stand at opposite corners of the dining room, Jim and me, the two pillars of Laura's life. I feel like I should go over to him, touch him, talk to him, tell him I'm sorry, but I can't. I don't. The food rises high between us, buffering all these people, the fillers of Laura's life. The gathered surround Jim, offering solace, but I remain alone, observing. If Jim notices me at all, I'm sure it's to think, *That weirdo. Maybe now I can finally let her go. There's no more reason for her to stay.*

My feet are lodged to the floor in the remote corner of this expansive room. My head is dizzy and my body wants to sway. I yearn to take a very long nap. I place one hand against the wall to prop me up. I need something or someone to hold me steady. But all I have are cookies.

Professor Jesuit approaches me, looking old and kindly, which I hate. I look down, concentrate on the plate in my hand and the Oxy tingle-buzz coursing through my fingers. I have nothing to say to God's handyman. Although if I did, I might inform him that I've given the matter substantial thought, and I've resigned myself to the possibility that I am doomed to an afterlife of eternal hellfire, and I'm okay with it, really I am. It's not like I even believe in God, but still, I imagine Him and me in a powwow on Judgment Day. Saint Peter or whomever has the day off so God himself is going down the checklist for my entrance to Heaven. He goes: *Well, Miles, you smoked like a chimney and indulged in way too many trans-fatty foods, and for Christ's sake, you were high at your own cousin's funeral, but otherwise, you did all right in life. Didn't hurt anybody but yourself. Paid your taxes. Recycled. Helped little old ladies cross the street. (Didn't you?) But I don't know . . . those snarky comments, that vile cynicism during times of crisis. I'm not so sure I like it.* I will then have to set Him straight. *Hey, Big Guy, get some perspective. Who gave us a world of Holocaust, AIDS, global terrorism, famine, ecological disaster, bigotry, genocide, warfare—shall I keep going down the list? Maybe it's*

ME who should be judging YOU, and not the other way around. So step aside from those pearly gates to Heaven or Hell, whichever the case may be, bucko. Let me through to Laura. We're not scared of You.

Professor Jesuit passes me by. Minion.

The cookie plate in my hand mesmerizes me with swirls of color and texture, rainbow sprinkles and cinnamon rays and powdered sugar dust, and I must look up again because the cookies are dizzying me. I raise my eyes from their plate reverie, but my view of the mourners has clouded over, gone mute. My eyes lock with Jim's across the room, and in that flash instant, no one exists in this room besides the two of us. In that brief moment, our eyes remember a shared lifetime of Laura, and I see his chest suddenly heave, trying to contain a sob—he who has remained stoic and gracious throughout the afternoon, comforting all those who are trying to comfort him. It's like electricity passes between us, because I feel the heave in my chest as well, and tears well in my eyes. The plate trembles in my weak fingers and I must look back down again, return to my cookie-plate trance, steady my hand. To hold the moment any longer would mean neither of us could remain in this room, finish this gathering of mourning.

Jim's probably more of a weirdo even than me, in my opinion, but God can take note. I am not without empathy. I know what it is like to be Miles right now, a freak high on sugar and so much more, but I do wonder how it must feel to be Jim in this moment, too. He's a seventy-two-year-old man who marched for civil rights, women's rights, gay rights, but chose to focus the latter part of his life on raising a child. What will the latter-latter part of his life now be? A philanthropist born into extreme privilege because his great-grandfather invented an appliance still used in most First World households, Jim parlayed his wealth and privilege for relatively modest selfish purpose—a grand house, grand trips—while choosing to funnel the bulk of his time and money into activism, into his hometown. And now to have his lifetime of giving come down to this one day. His cherished daughter, his one best accomplishment, took away the fundamental gift he had created for her. Life.

My cookie trance breaks when I am mauled in an embrace by the last person here from whom I would have expected—or wanted—comfort. "It's like it doesn't feel real or something, you know?" Bex, Laura's high school best friend, says to me. Her talents reside on the field hockey field, grunting and running and hitting, so I imagine she can be forgiven her lack of articulation skills. Bex is the person who named me "8 Mile," thinking I didn't know. She didn't even go to the same school as me. Yet the name traveled.

I'll never figure out how a girl like her managed to be invited to five proms this year alone; nor do I understand why at the moment of mutual acknowledgment of our shared person's suicide, this is the thought that occurs to me in relation to Bex. But it's true—she's not even that pretty, yet somehow her shiny white smile on pink dimple cheeks always wins out, despite her plain brown hair and eyes, her curveless, boylike, field hockey body. Bex is a girl who would never understand what it's like to have an 8 Mile butt, because she doesn't even have a butt.

I step out of her arms. I don't want that stick touching me, even if she did love Laura. She's the reason I lost the last few years of Laura—Bex, and he who trails behind her, Jason, Laura's ex-boyfriend. At least he will not try to touch me. Handsome soccer-star boys who just finished their first Ivy League year won't bother trying to comfort a girl like me, heavyweight to his featherweight class.

"Hey," he says to us. He's so blond and handsome, it would almost be intoxicating, if not for his predictable, casual acceptance of it, as if those looks and that privilege were the natural right of any white boy from Woodley Park whose parents are both telegenic political media commentators.

What's there to say back? *Hey? Bummer about that suicide and all, right, dude?*

Laura took us by surprise when she broke up with Jason after New Year's. Now I get it. Laura wanted Jason to understand his freedom to move on. After.

Has Jason ever noticed how much Laura and I look alike? Shave me down a dozen sizes, straighten and dye my hair back to its natural color, take off the goth makeup and give me a fresh-faced cover-girl glow, and I could be Laura. I could be the one to console him. I could envelop him.

But it's Bex who jumps into Jason's arms, pressing her face against his lean chest. What would it be like to be her, open to touch, expecting that anyone would want it from her? She holds on to Jason tightly. In their embrace, I see that soon, their grief could potentially turn to something deeper. Laura wouldn't mind. I do.

I am not without my own knight in shining armor. Jamal has found me again. Not only is he my best friend, he's my psychic; I don't realize I am parched until I see him standing before me, bearing a tall glass of water. "Thought you could use this," he says. He hands me the water and I gulp it right down. He asks Bex, "Weren't you the girl who tutored my sister Niecy in math this year? Seems like I've almost met you about a dozen times." Niecy goes to the same school that Bex and Laura just graduated from. Jamal's a mama's boy; he had no problem going to the charter high school where his mother is the principal, but Niecy, she wanted her own path, the one with the fancy girls.

Bex loosens herself from Jason's arms and turns to Jamal, appraises him. What's not to admire about the black suit and baby-blue silk tie (for Laura), his caramel eyes and smooth cocoa skin, or the Afro hair he's disciplined into ten braids running the length of his scalp, knotted at the nape of his neck? Jamal must meet Bex's standards. She smiles, momentarily distracted from her grief. "Don't tell me. You're the brother who blasted all the D.C. go-go music from the speakers in his attic room so we had to go to the library to get any studying done in peace? I mean, I like old Chuck Brown and Rare Essence just as much as anybody who grew up here, but Niecy was trying to raise her PSAT score, and you weren't helping."

"You're Rebecca, right? *Seven-up!*" Jamal responds. Bex couldn't know Jamal's way of acknowledging a person he likes is to speak to them in snippets of songs, preferably by Parliament, his favorite funk band from back in the day.

"Everybody calls me Bex. *Ho!*" she sings back. I would not have expected a girl like her to speak in Parliament.

Jamal doesn't date white girls. Why should he, he says, when he lives in Chocolate City, surrounded on every block by the finest-looking flavors of nonvanilla?

I can no longer deny the Oxy, deny the sway gripping my body, throwing me off balance, hurtling me either toward passing out on the floor, or to a good long nap. Jamal sees it, catches me before I fall. His palm presses against the heavy folds of my arm, warming me.

"Go home and sleep it off." He leans over to whisper in my ear, and my body tingles all over again in anticipation of our private exchange, free of Bex's ears. "This is so not cool today, Miles."

Who's he to judge?

I expect Jamal to take my hand and walk me home to the carriage house, which he would do if we'd whiled away an afternoon down by the canal, sharing a joint. Instead, his hand that's holding me up gently pushes me away, to regain my own balance. His attention turns to Bex, nonnegotiable, nonreturnable.

Teenagers. So fickle.

I am still high, but crashing down.

FIND YOUR EDGE WITH THESE STARTLING AND
STRIKING BOOKS—ALL FROM FIRST-TIME NOVELISTS.

JASON MYERS

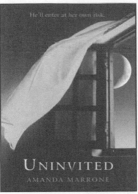

AMANDA MARRONE

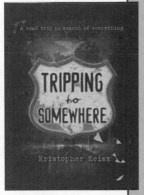

KRISTOPHER REISZ

Gritty. Electrifying. Real.

ALLISON VAN DIEPEN

LISA SCHROEDER

FROM SIMON PULSE
PUBLISHED BY
SIMON & SCHUSTER

Looking for something quirky and fun?

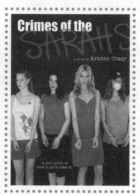

~~~ Kristen Tracy ~~~

Praise for *Lost It*:

★ "Readers will fall in love with this offbeat story."
—*Publisher's Weekly*, starred review

"Full of hilarious dialogue...." —*VOYA*

~~~ From Simon Pulse | Published by Simon & Schuster ~~~

Girls searching for answers . . .
and finding themselves.

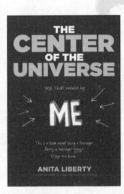

Lauren Baratz-Logsted   Anita Liberty   Cheryl Diamond

Teri Brown   Blake Nelson

From Simon Pulse | Published by Simon & Schuster

PULSE it

Did you **love** this book?

Want to get the
hottest books **free**?

Log on to
www.SimonSaysTEEN.com
to find out how you can get
free books from **Simon Pulse**
and become part of our **IT Board**,
where you can tell **US**, what **you** think!

SIMON
PULSE